"A wonderful series . . . Joanne Pence once more delivers a winner! *Cooks Overboard* is a funny, thrilling and dangerous novel to relish."

—*Romantic Times*

"Outstanding. . . . A delightfully tasty trip . . . compelling mystery . . . [that] gets more involved, twisted, complex, with every page—and it is a page turner, a humorous page-turner complete with action, lots of action."

—*Under the Covers*

Cook's Night Out

"Fans have much to celebrate in this latest installment."

—*Mystery News*

"Lucille Ball meets *The Streets of San Francisco* in this comedic farce within a first-rate police procedural. This one is definitely a centerpiece of this series!"

—*Tales from a Red Herring*

"Tasty and tempting reading."

—*Romantic Times*

"A feast for the reader's senses. . . . The author has a wicked flair for light humor. . . . A delightful reading concoction."

—*Gothic Journal*

Cooking Most Deadly

"Charmingly detailed. . . . Pence's tongue-in-cheek humor keeps us grinning."

—*San Francisco Chronicle*

"Another delightful adventure. . . . Joanne Pence provides laughter, love, and cold chills."

—Carolyn Hart

"This series just keeps getting better and better."

—*Literary Times*

"Action-packed plots touched with an engaging sense of humor are hallmarks of the magnetic Ms. Pence's work."

—*Romantic Times*

Cooking Up Trouble

"A tasty treat for all mystery and suspense lovers who like food for thought, murder, and a stab at romance. This is Pence's best mystery yet. So settle yourself on a nice comfortable chair, put your feet up, enjoy a dinner without calories, and a terrific read."

—*Armchair Detective*

"Soybeans have never been so dangerous, or so funny, as in Joanne Pence's *Cooking Up Trouble*. A deliciously wicked read. Don't miss one tasty bite."

—Jacqueline Girder

"Once again Joanne Pence serves up a feast of mystery, humor, and nicely observed human relationships. Sinfully funny writing and plot twists make this a flavorful dish!"

—*Mystery Scene*

Too Many Cooks

"Joanne Pence again proves that she is a major talent on the rise with her continuing fast-paced, humorous, and sexy suspense stories."

—*Romantic Times*

"Superbly written. . . . The dialogue sparkles like a Fourth of July fireworks display. . . . The suspense builds to a stunning, double-barreled climax. Readers should simply hold on to their figurative hats as the roller coaster swoops down on Angie and her brash actions."

—*Gothic Journal*

"Fast-paced, cleverly written. . . . I look forward to the next installment in this series."

—*Rendezvous*

Something's Cooking

"A generous dash of outstanding characters. . . . Fast-paced and clever."

—*Affair de Coeur*

"This light-hearted spoof is a delight!"

—*Rendezvous*

"Readers who have ever dabbled in the rarefied realm of gourmet cooking may well cackle with perverse pleasure. . . . An enjoyable flight into romantic fantasy."

—*Gothic Journal*

"A fast-paced and witty suspense tale."

—*Rave Reviews*

Angie Amalfi Mysteries by
Joanne Pence

Something's Cooking
Too Many Cooks
Cooking Up Trouble
Cooking Most Deadly
Cook's Night Out
Cooks Overboard
A Cook in Time
To Catch a Cook
Bell, Cook, and Candle
If Cooks Could Kill

A Cook in Time

An Angie Amalfi Mystery

Joanne Pence

AVON BOOKS

An Imprint of HarperCollinsPublishers

AVON BOOKS
An Imprint of HarperCollins*Publishers*
10 East 53rd Street
New York, New York 10022-5299

Copyright © 1999 by Joanne Pence
Cover illustration by Tom Hallman
ISBN: 0-06-104454-7
www.avonbooks.com

First Avon Books paperback printing: October 2000
First HarperPaperbacks printing: October 1999

Avon Trademark Reg. U.S. Pat. Off. and in Other Countries, Marca Registrada, Hecho en U.S.A.
HarperCollins® is a trademark of HarperCollins Publishers Inc.

Printed in the U.S.A.

10 9 8 7 6 5 4 3

To my wonderful aunts and uncles: Marie Lopez Ugarte, John Addiego, Gloria Craig Addiego, and Melvin Addiego—with love

Acknowledgments

The UFO and Roswell themes of this book have their roots in the talks and writings of Col. Philip J. Corso. I would never have heard of Col. Corso and others in this field but for hours of entertainment and fascination with tales from Art Bell's Kingdom of Nye.

The best lack all conviction, while the worst
Are full of passionate intensity.
Surely some revelation is at hand . . .

—W. B. Yeats, "The Second Coming"

The truth is out there.

—Fox Mulder, *The X-Files*

1

Patrol cars blocked the main entrance to Sigmund Stern Grove, their red and blue flashing lights harsh and garish against the gray December sky. The nearly ceaseless rains that caused the residents of San Francisco to believe they'd been transported eight hundred miles north to Seattle had stopped for the moment, but several police and park inspectors still wore yellow rain slickers, giving them the appearance of marching street lamps leading the way to the early morning crime scene.

Two men followed a narrow path through stands of eucalyptus and pine. Since the rains had washed away the gravel, their oxfords sank deep into the drenched mud, creating suction they had to fight against, as if the earth itself wanted to hold them back. Heavy, damp air filled their lungs, and a subtle tension grew with each deliberate step. Neither spoke.

Slightly in the lead was a tall, husky Japanese American in his late thirties with short-cropped black hair and a thick, muscular neck. His clothes were casual—light wool Eddie Bauer overcoat, plaid shirt, brown Dockers, and brown tie. The man behind and to his left was an inch or so taller with a lean, narrow-hipped build. He was conservatively dressed in a gray Nordstrom sports coat and black slacks, a striped gray tie, and a plain white shirt. His hair was dark brown, and his angular face was as unreadable as his icy blue eyes.

Under the broad umbrellalike expanse of a weeping willow hovered a small crowd of morning joggers and dog walkers. Their expressions were hollow and fearful, different from the curious, excited looks usually worn by crime scene witnesses. Just off the path, a police officer bent low over the bushes. One hand was jammed against a tree trunk, and a harsh gagging sound erupted from his throat.

Up ahead, yellow crime scene tape stretched from tree to tree in a fifteen-foot radius manned by uniformed officers. The two men showed their badges and signed the crime scene attendance log. A police sergeant strode toward them and lifted the tape. He looked shaken, not like a veteran who had seen a multitude of horrors during years of police work. "The coroner hasn't arrived yet," the sergeant said, breathing deeply. "Neither has the CSU."

They proceeded to the center of the closed-off area. A patrolman stood guard over the body, which was covered by a thin plastic tarp. The wet ground around the body was a mire of running-shoe patterns and dog footprints. There was no blood, no flattened or torn grass or bushes, no sign that a death struggle had taken place there.

At the sergeant's nod, the patrolman reached down and gripped the edges of the tarp. His jaw tightened as, slowly and carefully, he drew away the covering. The two men stared down at the corpse.

"Good Christ," Homicide Inspector Toshiro Yoshiwara whispered under his breath. He turned his head.

His partner, Homicide Inspector Paavo Smith, impassive and efficient, pulled a pair of latex gloves from his pocket and slipped them on, then stepped closer to study the victim.

The nude body was that of a male Caucasian, early forties or so, about 5'10", 160 pounds. The skin was an opaque white. Lips, nose, and ears had been removed, and the entire area from approximately the pubis to the sigmoid colon had been cored out, leaving a clean, bloodless cavity. No postmortem lividity appeared on the part of the body pressed against the ground. The whole thing had a tidy, almost surreal appearance. No blood spattered the area. No blood was anywhere; apparently, not even in the victim. A gutted, empty shell.

The man's hair was neatly razor-cut; his hands

were free of calluses or stains, the skin soft, the nails manicured; his toenails were short and square-cut, and his feet without bunions or other effects of ill-fitting shoes. In short, all signs of a comfortable life. Until now.

A wide band of skin in the shape of the number 7 had been removed from the pasty chest. Around the neck was a long black nylon strap attached to a bulky device that appeared to be a combination of binoculars and goggles. Made of black metal, the apparatus was as thick as a Nikon 35 mm camera, with something that looked like binoculars attached to one end and, on the other, a harness to hold them in place against the eyes.

Smith glanced over at Yoshiwara.

Yoshiwara's eyes betrayed no emotion. He shifted them to the sergeant. "Make sure your men get names and addresses from the crowd. Don't let anyone leave until we give the okay."

Smith stepped over to his partner. "Have you ever seen goggles like those?"

Yoshiwara studied them a moment before answering. "Never. The metal looks tarnished and old—like something out of World War Two, maybe."

"They were left as a message," Smith said.

Yoshiwara's gaze traveled over the mutilated corpse. "A message from a madman."

On a cliff facing the Pacific Ocean, nestled between the Presidio to the east and Lincoln Park on the west, lay one of San Francisco's most exclusive enclaves. Angelina Amalfi parked her white Ferrari Testarossa in front of a stately gray mansion at 50 Sea Cliff Avenue, on the oceanfront side of the street. After checking the address again, she gazed at the house, then smiled.

Whistling "We're in the Money" under her breath, she walked to the white double entry doors and rang the bell. Christmas wreaths with holly, pinecones, and large red bows hung on the doors. After waiting, checking her silk-wrapped raspberry-ice manicure, smoothing her gray and raspberry Anne Klein suit, and waiting a little more, she rang again.

Finally, an older woman with perfectly coifed dyed blond hair opened the door. She was short and plump, and wore billowing slacks of blue silk, a matching overblouse, and several rows of gold chains in a variety of weaves and sizes. Heavy gold rings with diamonds and pearls graced nearly every finger.

With one such bejeweled finger she fluffed her bangs as her mascara-ringed eyes surveyed Angie from head to toe. "Yeah?"

"Hello," Angie said cheerfully. "I'm Angelina Amalfi. Fantasy Dinners." At the confused expression on the woman's face, Angie added, "We have an appointment. That is, if you're Triana Crisswell." She held her breath, praying her first Fantasy Dinners assignment hadn't been a hoax. From the time she'd received Triana Crisswell's phone call, she'd felt a bit uneasy about it. That was why she hadn't told the man in her life, Paavo Smith, about this appointment. She also hadn't told her friend Connie or her four older sisters. Not even her parents. As much as she would have loved to boast about her new business to them, she decided not to until she was sure she had something to gloat over. She'd had so many failures in the business world that she was feeling a teensy bit gun-shy. To put it mildly.

"Hey, you're right, sweetie," Triana Crisswell said after a moment. "God, am I forgetful or what? Don't just stand there, come on in." She pulled the door open wide and waited for Angie to enter. "So you're the gal with the cute little dinner business," she said as she guided Angie across the entry hall to the living room. "When I saw your ad in the *Chronicle*, it sounded like such fun. I'm so glad you had the time to see me. I know you've got to be real busy, what with running a business like that and all."

"I certainly am busy," Angie said. Maybe not with her new business, exactly, but in general she was a busy person. "But simply talking to you on the phone told me that you were a person I would like to do business with. I made it a point to find room in my schedule to see you." Especially since the schedule was empty.

"I appreciate it, sweetie," Mrs. Crisswell said. "So, come on, sit down. I'll get us some coffee. You like coffee? I could make tea if you don't. Or maybe white wine?"

"Coffee would be fine," Angie replied.

As Mrs. Crisswell disappeared down the hallway, Angie settled back into a silk-upholstered chair. Although the front of the house, facing the street, had a traditional look to it, the back wall of the living room had been removed and replaced with floor-to-ceiling windows overlooking the ocean. The breathtaking view of the Pacific stretched from the Golden Gate Bridge to the Farallon Islands. Beyond the islands, dark storm clouds loomed.

The decor included the lavish standards usually found in multimillion-dollar homes: Napoléon III chairs, Louis IV mirrors, and English divans. In contrast, in the corner she saw a modern Mies van der Rohe Barcelona chair and an Eileen Gray tubular table. In the place of honor in front of the windows stood an enormous white Christmas tree solidly packed with gold-painted glass ornaments. Judging from the house, if she could convince Mrs. Crisswell to commission her to put on a fantasy dinner party, she shouldn't be stiffed for her fee.

Mrs. Crisswell came back into the living room carrying a tray with a Spode coffeepot, creamer, sugar bowl, and cups. She put them on the table, poured the coffee, then sat back with her cup and saucer in hand and loudly slurped some coffee. "God! Be careful. It's so hot I burned my tongue." She waved her hand as if to fan herself. "You're probably wondering what I'm doing in this big house without a servant.

What would I do here all day with one? Someone comes in to clean, someone else to cook
dinners—my husband is such a fussbudget
about his food—but other than that, I hate
strangers underfoot all day, telling my husband
what I do, who my friends are, you know?"

Angie nodded uncomfortably. This sudden
heart-to-heart made her wonder just how lone-
some Triana Crisswell might be.

"Well, anyway," Mrs. Crisswell continued, "tell
me about your dinners."

Angie poured some cream into her coffee,
then sat up primly, her hands neatly folded in her
lap, legs crossed at the ankles. "Well, as I mentioned on the phone, the idea behind Fantasy
Dinners is to create a dinner party around a
theme—whatever you would like it to be. We take
care of all the details, including hiring caterers to
prepare the meal and serve it, helping guests with
costumes if your party requires them, and generally creating the perfect setting for you. You tell
me what your theme is, and your budget, and
we'll build a fantasy to fulfill it."

"Build me a fantasy—my, my, doesn't that
sound great! I tell you, my fantasies were hot
and heavy when I was young, sweetie." Mrs.
Crisswell chuckled.

Angie decided she needed to come up with a
slightly different way to describe her business.
Ignoring the suggestive remark, she placed her
hand on the leather binder at her side. "In here
are many ideas for dinners. For example, if

you're interested in using ancient Rome as your theme, I can put on a dinner featuring food for the gods—nectar and ambrosia, as well as some modern Roman dishes such as manicotti or something fancier, like medallions of veal stuffed with crabmeat, fontina, and asparagus. Or whatever you'd like me to serve. We could drape fabric on the walls, and ask all guests to wear togas. Plus, as a special feature, I have a number of mystery plays that your guests could participate in. They are all variations on some basic mysteries. The Roman one, for example, is called 'Who Killed Nero?'"

"I don't know about all that." Mrs. Crisswell chewed her thumbnail. "People at my party might not care about it."

"Nero is just an example. It could be anyone you want."

"I mean, they might not care about who killed anybody. They look to the future. After all, most of us have to live in the future."

"The future?" *What in the world is a future fantasy?* "Ah, the future!" Angie cried. "Of course. I love dinners that have to do with the future. They're my favorite fantasies!" *Whatever they are.*

Mrs. Crisswell's eyes widened. "Really? You've done them before?"

"I've cooked lots of dinners, Mrs. Crisswell," Angie said. She wasn't lying, either. She had cooked many dinners. Not a single fantasy dinner yet, but she was careful not to say she had. Anyway, she had to start somewhere.

"Call me Triana, sweetie." Mrs. Crisswell smiled. Her thick lipstick was beginning to smear over her teeth.

"Thank you. Please call me Angie. Now, why don't you tell me what our futuristic dinner is all about so I can begin planning a fabulous event for you?"

"It's for a group I belong to. The Prometheus Group. Prometheus was the one who carried the world—no, that was Charles Atlas. Prometheus was the fire-and-liver guy. Anyway, these people are so smart, I can't tell you. I admire them so much." Triana stopped speaking and a dreamy-eyed look came over her. "The leader of the group, he's so handsome, like to die. Wait until you meet him! You'll want to pinch yourself to be sure you're awake.

"He's called Algernon. That's it, just one name. Anyway, he's written a book. So I want to have a party and invite important people from the media and bookstore owners and people who will buy this book from him. We'll feed them so well that they'll buy it and write good reviews, right? Don't you think that'll be a good thing?"

"I think that'll be a very good thing," Angie said, her head already filled with thoughts of an elegant meal to serve the literati of the Bay Area. This was the kind of exciting party she'd imagined when she came up with the idea for Fantasy Dinners. Running daily ads in the *San*

Francisco Chronicle for three weeks, along with an Internet site, both without a single legitimate nibble, had been discouraging, but this dinner—her first catch—was a big one. This could launch her career, along with Algernon's book.

"The book's coming out next month," Triana said. "I'd like the party soon after New Year's. Is that enough time?"

Angie saw her big launch beached before it even set sail. Four weeks, discounting all the days lost due to the holidays, was not much time. Maybe the dinner wouldn't be quite as elegant as she'd imagined. It might well be difficult to get the very best caterers in the city with such short notice. Somehow, though, she'd make do. "It's no problem at all. When Fantasy Dinners takes charge, we handle everything on time, every time. Remember: Our business is your fantasy, not your nightmare." She'd come up with that motto. But it didn't have quite the right ring to it yet.

"The dinner will be held right here," Triana said. "I think I'll invite around fifty people. This house is large enough to accommodate them. I'll give you more details as we go along."

"That will be fine," Angie said, nearly bursting with joy.

"Would you like a retainer?"

The question caught Angie off guard. How much should she ask for? She had no idea.

"No need," she said with a smile. "We can settle after dinner, so to speak. Now tell me, what is your fantasy about the future? Do you have a particular theme in mind, or should I develop one?"

"I want the dinner to bring Algernon's book to life. I want us to live what he's writing about."

"Oh, how interesting. What is his book?"

"It's called *Life Beyond Mars—The Search for Extraterrestrial Life in Our Galaxy*. And you know what?"

Extraterrestrials? Angie's heart sank. How was she supposed to create a fantasy dinner about space aliens? To begin with, no one knew what they ate. She glanced at Triana and realized the woman was waiting for her to respond.

"No, what?" she murmured.

"Algernon's proved it. Not only is there extraterrestrial life, but—you won't believe this—they're here."

"Beware the new millennium!" the speaker bellowed to the afternoon passers-by in front of the Moscone Convention Center. He stood behind a small folding table filled with brochures about UFOs. "Join us as we seek the safety of a new world. Learn what the government isn't telling you: That the end of mankind is near!"

A man, unwashed and smelly, dressed in several layers of clothes so soiled they practically stood up on their own, walked up to the table. He pointed to the cardboard sign in front of the speaker.

NEW MEMBERS! FREE DRAWINGS!
$100 TO THE LUCKY WINNER! JOIN TODAY!

"What do I have to do to join?" he asked.

The speaker frowned at the man's appearance. "Fill out a card."

"Got a pen?"

The speaker handed him a cheap Bic.

With painstaking slowness, the man filled out the card, then handed it back and walked away. The speaker glanced at the address—a Salvation Army kitchen. Homeless. It figured. Then at the name—Felix Rolfe.

Felix Rolfe!

"Hey there," the speaker shouted. "Wait a minute!"

2

Paavo stayed near the gutted corpse while the coroner's technicians performed their preliminary tests. Morinaga, one of the techs, made a one-inch-long incision just above the left hip, then attached a thermometer to a probe and inserted it, twisting it toward the liver to record body temperature. "Hey, the liver's gone, too!" he shouted. At Paavo's stunned expression, he burst into laughter. *Everyone's a comedian,* Paavo thought, even when faced with as vicious a crime as he'd ever seen in the city.

Later, after the assistant coroner's examination, as the photographer snapped rolls of film and the crime scene investigators took samples and combed the area, the technicians lifted the body into a black zippered bag made of heavy plastic, loaded it onto a stretcher, and carried it to their van. Paavo turned away from the scene to interview those potential witnesses the patrolmen had gathered together. He'd go back to the most promising of them at a later time. Every so often they got lucky and picked up among the spectators a murderer so fascinated by what he'd done and so arrogant about having covered his tracks that he would hang around a bit too long.

Paavo talked with the patrolman who had called in the death, and then with Stern Grove's administrative employees, gardeners, and security team. Following that, he moved from the park to the street and homes facing it, where he did a house-to-house, knocking on doors to ask if anyone had seen or heard anything that morning. He came up with a great big zero.

As he left the sixth house that had answered his knock, he saw Yoshiwara approaching. Rain was falling again, and Yosh, who had been canvassing on the next block, was struggling to open his umbrella. "I'm ready to head back to the bureau," he said when he reached Paavo. "I'm striking out here."

"Me too." Paavo scanned the quiet street.

"Hey, we might get lucky," Yosh said, holding the umbrella high enough to shelter Paavo as well as they headed for the car. "Missing Persons might have a story on this guy, plus twenty relatives ready to give us all the details."

"Sure," Paavo said without conviction. "They'll also tell us his uncle Harry is an ax murderer with a dislike for his nephew."

"Could happen," Yosh said. "It's about time

we got a break in a case. My wife claims she's forgotten what I look like. You got to make sure
Angie doesn't forget you. You don't want to lose
her, pal. She's a winner. Money and looks."

Paavo nodded. His feelings about Angie were
too complicated to put into words. She was
interested in marriage. So was he, in theory.
Maybe more than theory. But something held
him back. Innate caution told him to wait, to be
sure he wasn't letting his heart overrule his
head—which was an accusation no one had yet
leveled against him. He glanced at his watch. It
was already two in the afternoon. He faced long
hours trying to give this John Doe an identity,
along with figuring out who had killed him. So
much for his plans to see Angie that evening.

They reached the car. "Anything else while
we're here?" Yosh asked.

"Nothing," Paavo said. He couldn't let himself think about Angie just then. Despite Yosh's
hopes, they both knew it was going to be a long
night.

"No. Never. No way. Forget it. Is that clear
enough?" Connie Rogers jabbed her spoon into
her tiramisu, scooped up some of the layered
mascarpone, chocolate, and espresso-soaked
ladyfingers, and stuffed it into her mouth.

Angie knew better than to respond immediately. She had shown up at Connie's gift shop,
Everyone's Fancy, bearing tiramisu, eclairs, and
raspberry mousse, not to argue but to cajole.

Without comment she took a bite of an eclair and waited for Connie's inevitable guilt to begin. Despite their outward differences—Connie was a blond, blue-eyed, slightly overweight, divorced owner of her own business, while Angie was a slim, brown-eyed brunette, often unemployed and dating a man she was seriously interested in—the two were close friends. "It could really be a lot of fun," Angie said with softly voiced encouragement.

Angie had arrived at the holiday-decorated gift shop during the midafternoon doldrums—the hours between the lunchtime window shoppers and the after-work rush. She sat at one side of Connie's desk in the shop's small back office. The door was left open so they could see and hear if anyone entered the store. No one did. First Connie sipped the Starbucks nonfat lattè that Angie had brought her to wash down the desserts, then she took another bite of tiramisu and chewed slowly, giving Angie glances that said she knew exactly what Angie was up to. Without another word, Angie spooned the mousse into two cups and gave one to Connie.

"Remember what happened the last time you came up with one of your great ideas?" Connie asked. She didn't wait for an answer. "We ended up as bag ladies. And that was the good part!"

Charitably, Angie ignored the slur on their last adventure together, which had been for a very good cause, just like now. Besides, what could go wrong with planning a catered dinner?

"You know," she said, "this UFO stuff is all the rage now. Very new-millennium. Not only have I fallen into something new and exciting, but I'm willing to share it with you."

"You've fallen, all right. Headfirst. It's insane."

"It's a job," Angie cried. She sat back, realizing she sounded a little desperate. But she wanted success with her new business. This assignment was just the start she needed.

After she'd finished the tiramisu, Connie said, "If you want my advice, you'll start your business with something you understand. What do you know about this Prometheus Group? They might be a bunch of crackpots." She pushed the cup of mousse back toward Angie's napkin, as if to show she wasn't one to be bought by sweets. She peered out the door to see if any customers had managed to sneak in without causing the entry bell to bong. The store remained empty.

"It's precisely because I don't know that much about them or their beliefs," Angie reasoned, "that I need your help. All I have to do is to create a dinner party for them, not join them. I want it to be a very special dinner. After all, I didn't name my new business Fantasy Dinners for nothing."

Connie fiddled with some envelopes on the desk. They looked like bills. "What did you say your motto was? 'Your fantasy is my nightmare.' Was that it?"

Angie frowned. "I have no idea why you're

taking this attitude." She tasted the mousse. It might have been made from hair gel for all the enjoyment it gave her. She shoved it aside.

"And who's this Algernon guy?" Connie reached again for the cup of mousse Angie had spooned out for her. "What kind of a name is that? It might not be so bad if it was his last name. Maybe not if it was his first name. But his only name?"

"It's artistic license. He's supposed to be very good-looking."

"Anyone pretentious enough to use just one name had better be," Connie said.

Angie watched her taste the mousse, watched her eyes roll blissfully. Time to try again. "Seriously, Connie, I wish you'd help me. Now that I've accepted the job, I've got to make something of it. I need to find out about aliens or extraterrestrials or ETs or whatever they're called. Have you ever heard what they eat?"

Connie did a double take. "What aliens eat?"

"That's right."

"No."

"Me neither." Angie thought a moment. "Step one has to be to find out about aliens. Specifically, to find out what they supposedly eat and then serve it—or some edible version of it. Whatever it is. I think that would make a fun fantasy dinner, don't you?"

"That depends on what food you come up with," Connie said, polishing off the mousse.

"I have no idea." Angie sighed. "All I know

about space and food is that the moon's made out of green cheese."

"Green cheese?" Connie cried, reaching for an eclair. "Here I'd always thought moon pies were the real thing."

"You know, you may be on to something," Angie said thoughtfully. "For instance, there are Rocket Popsicles."

"I don't remember those," Connie said. "But I remember Mars candy bars!"

"And Milky Ways," Angie cried excitedly. She was getting into it now. "For those who can't eat chocolate, there are always Starbursts."

"Plus, we could drive there in a Saturn." Connie beamed, more and more pleased with each contribution.

"While singing a duet of 'Fly Me to the Moon,'" Angie added.

They began to laugh, but then their eyes met and the laughter turned to groans. It really wasn't such a hot idea, Angie decided. Her gaze fell over the tiny office: the gray steel file cabinet in the corner; the microwave, half-size refrigerator, and four-cup Mr. Coffee; boxes of gift supplies in all sizes and shapes stacked in six-foot-high piles. She turned her head, looking beyond the office to the shop as she pondered her situation. Maybe Connie was right. Maybe she had bitten off more than she could chew, so to speak—and she didn't even know if aliens have teeth. Maybe—

She noticed a man standing out on the sidewalk, peering into the store. He wore dark glasses, yet the way his head was cocked, the direction of his face, he might have been staring straight at her. Something about him gave her the distinct, unnerving feeling he'd been watching her for some time.

The man was a study in black. Thin, with short black hair, a black suit, white shirt, and black tie—even his sunglasses were black. Sunglasses in the rain? His skin was a sickly white.

"What is it?" Connie asked.

Startled, Angie faced her friend again. "The man in black at the window."

"Really?" Connie got up and walked to the office door to get a better view of her shop and the window. "I don't see anyone."

"It was probably nothing."

"Probably," Connie said dejectedly. "That's the story of my life with men these days."

Angie knew Connie was feeling lonely. Since her divorce she hadn't found a man she hit it off with. Angie imagined it was especially hard on her during this time of year, with the holidays fast approaching. All the more reason to involve Connie in something fun and exciting—like a fantasy dinner.

"I was probably just imagining someone was there." Angie cast a woeful look in Connie's direction. "I guess I'm so worried about my new business that I'm seeing things. Don't feel guilty, though, it's not your problem. I understand. I'll figure something out. Alone." She gave a long, loud sigh.

"Here's to your business success." Connie cheerfully ignored her and held up her paper lattè cup in a salute. "You'll be able to handle it on your own just fine."

"Thanks," Angie murmured. She slid a dish of tiramisu in front of her and picked up her spoon. Her plan to involve Connie had failed miserably. Time to eat. It tasted like crow.

Paavo Smith wearily dragged himself up the front steps of his small house in San Francisco's Richmond district, unlocked the door, and stepped inside.

Two days' worth of mail lay piled on the floor. As he scooped it up, Hercules came over to greet him. "Hey, boy, good to see you." The big yellow tabby rubbed against his legs, demanding to be petted. Paavo ran his hand a few times over the cat's thick coat, relieved to be home at last.

Stiffly he straightened up and flipped through the bills and advertisements that made up his mail. Tossing it all onto a lamp table near the door, he walked over to the sofa that sat in the center of the room facing the stone fire-place, took off his sports jacket, and laid it over the back. Without missing a beat, he continued toward the small central hallway. There he unbuckled his nylon shoulder holster and put it and his 9 mm Smith & Wesson on the top shelf of the linen closet.

The light on the answering machine was blinking. He hit the play button and increased the volume. From the hall he turned into the kitchen, Hercules running between his feet as he went. The whole process was a ritual. Paavo would be forgiven for his long absences if Herc got a can of 9-Lives to make up for the dry Meow Mix he'd put up with in the interim.

Paavo took the cat food from the cupboard and a can opener from the drawer.

The first call had been recorded about one that afternoon and was from Angie, wondering where he was. He half listened as she prattled on about wanting him to try to find time to go with her and a couple of her nieces and a nephew to the *Nutcracker* on Sunday. He had scarcely remembered that Christmas was fast approaching. What in the world could he give Angie? The woman who had everything.

He needed to call her. He hadn't expected to be on duty nearly thirty-six hours without a decent break.

This latest round of investigations had begun the previous morning, when Homicide received a call. A cab driver had been killed the night before, the body dumped in a back alley. The break in the case came because the killer stupidly decided to use the taxi as his getaway car. That night an outraged citizen called the Yellow Cab company to complain about a taxi sitting in front of a house and not taking any fares. In a matter of hours, Paavo and Yosh made an arrest. The idiot perp had even been surprised. Go figure.

Paavo had been finishing up his report on that murder, thinking about going home and getting some sleep, when the call came in that sent him out to Stern Grove.

He still had no identity on the victim. No missing-person report had been filed. A thorough search of the park hadn't turned up any clothes or identification. Fingerprint searches were being made of the SFPD, National Crime Index, California DOJ, and INS files. It could take weeks for a reading to come in unless the victim had gotten a driver's license recently or had an arrest record.

Paavo had read over the crime scene unit's preliminary report twice. Not only had the body been drained of blood, but it had been washed clean. Dried soap residue had been found on the hair and in the ear canals—since the fleshy parts of the ears themselves had been removed. The assumption was that the victim had been bathed, then wrapped in plastic sheeting of some kind and transported to the park. Not a single stray fiber or hair had been left behind. Paavo had never dealt with a Mr. Clean or Molly Maid as killer before.

The autopsy would be held at one o'clock the next afternoon. Normally, it would take a couple of days, or longer, before the coroner's office found time to do an autopsy for some John Doe. But it had taken no work at all to convince the assistant coroner to move the case up on the schedule after she saw the victim. A determination as to the cause of death would help give some idea of the type of killer they were dealing with. Since no defensive wounds were observed on the body, it was fairly certain the killer hadn't stepped up to the victim and started carving. The victim had to have been subdued, maybe even dead, before the mutilations began. The question, therefore, remained: How was he killed?

So far, the only clues Paavo had to work with were the bizarre style of mutilation, the number 7 on the man's chest, and the mysterious goggles. He'd commissioned a couple of uniforms to get military gear catalogues and manuals for him to go through. If they didn't give him answers about the goggles, he'd get the techies in the crime lab to see what they could come up with. Morinaga owed him one after that sick joke about the vic's liver being gone.

The second message was also from Angie, sounding a little anxious. He'd spent so many years without anyone caring where he was, it was still hard for him to realize that Angie not only cared but worried about him. The novelty of knowing her—loving her—still hadn't worn off. It was a good feeling.

He definitely needed to give her a call. Looking at the kitchen clock, he was astonished to see that it was nearly two in the morning. He dumped the whole can of food into Herc's bowl and broke it up with a fork.

His message machine was still clicking and whirring. Two hang-ups followed Angie's calls. Probably just people trying to sell him something. He didn't have time for any long-winded messages, anyway. He had come home to shower, catch a few hours of sleep, and change clothes. Then back to work. He knew the hours right after a murder occurred were the most likely to result in the crime's being solved.

But something more than his usual need to find the killer was at play in this case. He centered his thoughts on the steady hand needed for the pristine cuts of the mutilation, the ability to wash off a body after inflicting such devastation on it, the pure absence of emotion in a murderer of that sort.

He rubbed his eyes, impatient with the fatigue that had forced him and Yosh to leave the bureau to get some sleep. The callousness of the murder preyed upon him. Some of his past cases had involved deaths from rage or passion against the victim. This one had an almost ritualistic tinge to it. And rituals had a way of repeating themselves, over and over.

He put the cat's bowl on the floor just as the next message began.

It was nothing but static. Loud, ugly static. Hercules went over to his food and began to eat.

The static abruptly stopped and a few quick tones sounded over the recorder, then a loud, high-pitched squeal. Hercules stopped eating, arched his back, and emitted a low growl before he ran across the kitchen, through his cat door, and out into the night.

It was probably another automatic dialer or fax machine running amok—the year 2000 computer bug struck again.

3

The next morning, Angie was no closer to an idea for an out-of-this-world dinner party than she had been the night before. She sat on the sofa in her living room, her coffee on an end table, the morning's *Chronicle* on her lap. From her apartment high atop Russian Hill, she could see the northern part of the city. Rain was falling again, casting a gray gloom over the sky.

She wished Paavo was with her. Listening to the patter of rain was always nicer with someone. Alone, the sound had a bleakness that was almost sad.

When he'd called the night before, she had been so sleepy she could hardly speak, and what she did say must have been muddled, because she thought she'd heard a hint of a chuckle in his voice. All she could remember was that he'd said he was involved in a strange case that was going to take a while, and she shouldn't worry.

Just hearing his deep voice had set her mind at ease. He had told her he loved her, and that set her heart at ease. If he'd been beside her in bed to set her body at ease, she might have slept better than ever.

But she couldn't allow herself to reflect on Paavo just then. Her fantasy dinner needed a design, a structure on which to build the extraterrestrial theme Triana Crisswell had asked for.

She toyed with the idea of an astrological design but nixed it. These people, she was sure, considered themselves scientific. It might be pseudoscience to some, but to themselves, they were serious students of technology, not dilettantes of the paranormal.

She stood, folding her arms within the long kimono sleeves of her pink silk robe, and began to pace. She needed a theme that was both exceptional and unique. Something, perhaps, that the general public didn't know about.

Who did?

A shave-and-a-haircut knock sounded on her door. She knew that knock—and knew it was not bringing the answer to her question.

Angie opened the door to greet her neighbor, Stanfield Bonnette, a tall, blond, youthful-looking fellow. He should have been at work, not standing there casually dressed in off-white linen slacks and a forest green Joseph Abboud shirt. As much as he thought of himself as an up-and-coming bank executive, from what

Angie saw of his work ethic, down-and-going was a more apt description.

"I didn't know this was a bank holiday," she said, stepping back so he could enter.

"I had a migraine this morning." He did his best to feign suffering. "It's gone now. I was wondering if you wanted to go to a movie. The Castro's showing *Plan 9 from Outer Space*. With all this millennium talk in the news, I thought it would be fun."

"Considering the time of year, wouldn't *Santa Claus Conquers the Martians* be more appropriate?" she asked.

He walked into the kitchen. "If your cop friend is chasing dead bodies instead of yours—I mean, instead of taking you out—why not come with me no matter what's playing?"

"I've got work to do. I'm trying to start up a new business, but I don't want to say more about it yet." She followed him. "*Plan 9*, you said? Actually, for the business I should learn something about extraterrestrials, and maybe even UFOs."

"UFOs? What kind of business could you get involved with that has UFOs? Space cookies?" He lightly patted her coffeepot. "Ah! Your coffee is still hot."

"Have a cup. As I said, I don't want to talk about the business, except to say I need new-millennium high tech, not old B movies using pie pans for flying saucers. I need help sorting through all the UFO and alien stuff that's out there—someone to guide me to what's popular and cool."

"I guess I'm just an old-fashioned kind of guy," he said. "Oh, looky there! Chocolate-covered macaroons. My favorite. Homemade?"

"Yes. Help yourself."

He was already reaching into the jar and took two. "What does your hotshot cop friend think about this business of yours?" He bit into the cookie. "Mmm. Fabulous."

"I haven't had a chance to tell him." Nor, she might have added, would she until she was sure about this job. She was tired of making big pronouncements about her grand career plans and then having them blow up in her face. Sometimes literally. She was tired of the piteous glances Paavo and her family gave her whenever that happened. So this would be her little secret until the business was declared to be as fabulous as her macaroons.

"With all your acquaintances, I should think quite a few of them would know about UFOs and such. They're so in," Stan said.

She pondered that a moment. "You may be ri . . . yes! You *are* right!" She smacked the heel of her hand to her forehead. "How could I have forgotten?"

She dashed down the hall to the den. Stan grabbed another cookie and followed, watching as she pulled a desk drawer way out and reached into the back of it. "What are you doing?" he asked.

"I just remembered an old boyfriend, an astrophysicist. He can tell me about UFOs."

"An astrophysicist?" He gawked at the handful of old Rolodex cards she held. "Are those all old boyfriends?"

"Of course not!" She took off the rubber band and began flipping through the cards. "Only half or so. Ah, here he is—Derrick Holton."

She sat down on the white iron daybed across from her desk and stared at the name on the card. Derrick Holton.

She remembered how thrilled she had been to have attracted the attention of such a handsome astrophysicist. A rising star at NASA, no less. Her parents had been ecstatic. She and Derrick had dated for four months, but the relationship was far more serious on his part than hers.

Stan sat on the daybed beside her. "Well, if he's an astrophysicist, I can see why you dropped him. He was probably old, stodgy, and boring."

She smoothed the ragged edges of the card. "Actually, he was young and good-looking. But he wanted to get married. I was more interested in going to Paris for a few months. Which I did. He took the hint, and that was that."

Stan's eyebrows lifted. "He wanted to marry you? You were that close to him?"

"We were close, yes." She gathered the rest of the cards once more, tapped them against the desk into a smooth packet, rubber-banded them, and tossed them back into the drawer.

Stan stared at the drawer a moment too long. "I think you did the right thing," he said firmly. "You wouldn't have been happy with a guy like that: serious, possessive, with his head in the clouds. You need someone down-to-earth and fun."

"Like Paavo," she said, turning back to face him.

"Oh, now there's a barrel of laughs." Stan tightened his lips into a pout. "Someday, Angie, you'll open your eyes and discover the jewel right under your very nose."

"Forget it, Stan." She headed back to the living room, Stan following like a puppy.

"You're breaking my heart," he said.

"Have another macaroon." She flicked her thumb toward the kitchen.

"I will. Anyway, I don't think it's a good idea to call an old boyfriend. He might get the wrong impression. It could be awkward for you both."

"I'll have to make my purpose clear." She dropped onto the sofa. "That's all there is to it."

Stan called out from the kitchen over the rattle of the cookie jar's lid. "Still, to call a NASA scientist and ask him about UFOs could be taken as an insult."

"Derrick's not that way. And if he doesn't know about them, I'm sure he'd point me in the right direction."

"Well, I think you're just asking for trouble."

Balancing a stack of four cookies in the palm of one hand, Stan opened the front door to leave. He glanced back at Angie. "If you won't listen to me about this, talk to the cop."

She couldn't imagine any reason to tell Paavo about Derrick, and even less reason to tell him she planned to get in touch with an old boyfriend again. Not that Paavo was jealous—he wasn't—but he was unsure where she was concerned. "I can handle this on my own, Stan. Paavo's much too busy to deal with UFOs."

"Christ!" Henry Fisher's face blanched. "You told me it was bad, but I never expected . . ." He lifted a horrified gaze from the sheet-covered corpse on the metal slab in front of him and stared at the blank wall, his Adam's apple fluttering from hard gulps. The morgue was on the ground floor of the Hall of Justice, which made it easy to wheel in gurneys from the parking lot. It also made it accessible to the public without them having to go through the security checkpoints at other entrances.

"Are you all right?" Paavo asked. That morning the DMV computers had spit out a name and address based on the mutilated victim's fingerprints: Bertram Lambert, thirty-nine years old, 5'9", 160 pounds, brown hair, hazel eyes. The address—1551 O'Farrell Street, apartment 8—proved to be an old one. Lambert's former landlady had insisted she knew nothing about him except that he worked in the data processing center at the Bank of America. Paavo contacted the bank and was put in touch with Lambert's supervisor, Henry Fisher. The supervisor knew of no close friends or relatives nearby. On his employment forms Lambert's address was still shown as the incorrect earlier one, and the only next of kin was a sister who lived in Iowa. Paavo had tried to reach her, but there was no answer at her home. Despite Lambert's driver's license, no car registration was found.

Since no one else was available, Fisher agreed to identify the body. He'd been warned about the mutilation done to Lambert's face, and that any identification would have to be made on the basis of hair, eyes, and bone structure. He'd been warned, but obviously not strongly enough. Or perhaps no amount of warning would have sufficed in this case.

"I—I'll be all right," he said.

"Cover the face from the eyes down," Paavo told the assistant who held the sheet. The man did so.

Fisher drew in a deep breath and forced himself to peer once more at the corpse. "I would say that's Lambert's hair. His forehead . . . his eyes." He turned away again, gasping.

"Thanks," Paavo said to the assistant, who then pushed the slab back into the wall as Paavo and Fisher left the morgue.

"I can't believe he's dead," Fisher said, subdued and visibly shaken. "He was so quiet. No one could possibly want to hurt him."

"Do you know anything about his personal life? Who his friends were? If he had any friends at work?"

Fisher shook his head. "I don't think he kept friends. He was . . . I don't know, too needy. He came on too strong, overwhelming people with attention until they felt smothered and backed off. He was always looking for friends, though. Looking for clubs and groups to belong to."

They stepped out into the parking lot, and Fisher put a cigarette in his mouth. He had trouble lighting it because of the way his hand was shaking. Finally, he drew in several deep puffs, as if to rid his nose and lungs of the stagnant air of the morgue. He glanced at Paavo. "I always saw Bert as a prime candidate for some wacko cult. You know, like that Heaven's Gate group where they all killed themselves to fly up to some comet."

"Do you know if he found any groups like that to join?"

"Not that I noticed. I'll ask around at work, but the guy was—hell, I suppose I shouldn't say it now that he's gone—but the guy was boring. He led a dull life and told people all about it until they just stopped listening. At least, I stopped."

"I'd appreciate whatever you could find out," Paavo said.

"Sure. It's funny, though, after trying so hard . . . "

"Funny?" Paavo prodded.

Fisher's gaze was dull. "Considering the way he died, I guess he finally found somebody who took an interest in him."

"Hello."

The warm timbre of Derrick Holton's voice over the telephone line was exactly as Angie remembered it, and it hurled her back to the time when they had first met. He had possessed a ready smile and used to act on her every whim, remember her every word, dote on her like a man possessed. He had always been there when she needed him, not off somewhere dealing with dead bodies and murderers.

Why had she dropped him?

"Hi, Derrick. This is Angie Amalfi."

Silence. Had he forgotten her that quickly? Her hand tightened on the telephone, and she sat down on the yellow Hepplewhite chair in her living room. "Remember me?" she asked.

"Of . . . of course! Angelina, is it really you? I'm breathless."

Breathless. She smiled. That was a very Derrick-like, elegant word. The sort of word Paavo wouldn't have used if a gun were put to his head. "It's really me," she said with a laugh. "I'm sorry to bother you after all this time, but I was hoping you might spare a few minutes to help me with a project."

"I still can't believe it's you, Angelina. Are you back in San Francisco?"

She noticed he hadn't answered her ques-

tion. Was this a once-bitten-twice-shy situation?
"I'm here. I don't need much of your time, Derrick. If it wouldn't be a problem for you, that is."

"A problem? No . . . no, not at all. As a matter of fact, if you're free this evening, we could meet for an early dinner. I have to go to a lecture at eight-thirty. Before that, I'd love to meet and talk with you."

"Dinner?" She wasn't sure about that. There were certain implications about having dinner with an old boyfriend. It smacked of a date. "I only need to ask you a few questions. It won't take long. Coffee somewhere would be fine. I don't want to waste your time."

There was a lengthy pause. "It's no waste of time." His voice was low and, for the first time since he'd picked up the phone, sounded truly sincere, like the Derrick she'd once known—and tried to convince herself she loved, without success. "I'd like to see you again," he said. "To hear about your family. About you. Don't worry, I quite understand this phone call wasn't because you decided you were wrong about us. I'm not that foolish. Dinner together would be for friendship's sake only. If we met at six o'clock, that would give us a couple of hours before my lecture. We could even go Dutch, if that would make dining together more acceptable to you."

Six o'clock. She could leave her apartment a little after five-thirty and be home a little after eight. That should work. Paavo would most likely come over late that night after putting in a long day at work. This way she wouldn't miss him.

"In that case . . ." The best spot for them to meet would be a restaurant that was basic, without any of the ambiance that might give him the wrong impression or tinge their meeting with any hint of nostalgia. "I know just the place," she said.

At five-forty-five Paavo rode the elevator up to Angie's twelfth-floor apartment. He'd walked so many circles around his desk that Yosh had finally told him to get away for a while, to take a break. He'd been frustrated by the complete lack of evidence at the crime scene, along with not being able to reach Bertram Lambert's sister. They'd interviewed the victim's co-workers, but they knew nothing about his personal life.

Lambert hadn't dropped out of the sky dead. There was a reason he'd been murdered and carved like a Thanksgiving turkey ready for stuffing, and someone had to know what it was.

Paavo had spent the afternoon dressed in a paper gown, mask, and booties at Lambert's autopsy. Despite the industrial-strength disinfectant, the stench from the body permeated the room.

"I see some of my work's already been done for me," Dr. Evelyn Ramirez had said as she studied the body. The assistant coroner normally didn't hesitate before making the first slightly rounded incision from shoulder to shoulder, and the next straight down to the groin. Except this time there was no groin.

Ramirez shook her head and drew the scalpel downward from the breastbone until she ran out of flesh. The organs were those of a non-smoker in good health. No ruptures or puncture marks. Not until the coroner cut around the back of Lambert's head and peeled the skin away did they find cracks in the skull and, after the cranium was removed, a broken brain stem. The trauma and shatter pattern on the skull indicated that a powerful blow to the head—with what kind of implement, she couldn't yet say—was the likely cause of death.

The results of tests on what little blood they could find would come later, along with Ramirez's conclusions as to the type of instrument used to make the precise cuts on the body. The wounds, she noted, had been cauterized. Paavo had left the autopsy with more questions than when he entered it.

Now he knocked on Angie's door. After waiting a few minutes, he knocked again. All he wanted to do was to see her and remember that there was more to life than the stench of horrid death and autopsies. Angie brought a joy to life he had forgotten existed—or perhaps he had just never known.

Stanfield Bonnette opened the apartment door across the hall. "She's not home."

Paavo had never cared for Angie's nosy neighbor. Angie thought it was jealousy, but it was simple dislike. The man relished being the bearer of bad, or at least irritating, news. "Did she give you any idea when she might return?" Paavo asked.

"Oh, it'll be late." Stan folded his skinny arms. "Quite late, I'd imagine," he added with measured insouciance.

Paavo waited, one eyebrow slightly arched. It was obvious Bonnette was dying to tell everything he knew.

"She's gone out with an old boyfriend," Bonnette said, scarcely able to prevent a smile from forming on his lips. "A very close old boyfriend. My suggestion is—" He delicately coughed. "Don't wait up for her."

4

Wings of an Angel was a small North Beach restaurant. The owners, Vinnie Freiman, Butch Pagozzi, and Earl White, had been life-long friends and partners. Partners in crime, to be precise, and because of that, cellmates. Now in their sixties, after their last caper was derailed by Paavo Smith, they had decided to go straight. With Angie's help, they'd learned to run a restaurant and had made it a favorite among people who lived in the city and wanted tasty, inexpensive Italian food.

"'Ey, Miss Angie, good ta see ya." Earl, who had the build of a fire hydrant, greeted her warmly in his role as maître d', waiter, and bus-boy. Butch cooked, and no one knew what Vin-nie did—except that he handled the money and kept Butch and Earl in line.

"Hi, Earl," Angie said, searching the small restaurant. Despite telling herself that this meet-

ing was strictly business, she'd taken great care
with her outfit, settling on a pale blue Donna
Karan suit and sapphire earrings. To her surprise, she found that she had butterflies in her
stomach. "I'm going to be eating with a fr—" There
he was. She stopped speaking. He waved, smiling
broadly. Just like in the old days. He was still the
good-looking man she remembered. His hair
was light brown and wiry, with streaks of gray,
though he was only in his early thirties. His com-
plexion was slightly ruddy, his eyes hazel, his lips
wide; his front teeth had a boyish space between
them that gave a devil-may-care look to the serious astrophysicist that he was. She smiled back.

"Do you know dat guy, Miss Angie?" Earl
asked suspiciously. "Or am I gonna hafta teach
him some manners?"

"He's the old friend I'm here to meet." She
walked toward Derrick, who stood up as she
neared. Earl grabbed a couple of menus and
hurried after her.

"Angelina." Derrick reached for her outstretched hand. Instead of shaking it, as she'd
intended, he pulled her close and kissed her
cheek, then smiled at her. He wasn't tall—under
six feet—and had a sinewy build. "Even more
beautiful than I remember."

"Hello, Derrick," she replied. The familiar
scent of his cologne, Ralph Lauren's Polo,
brought back memories of nightclubs and
dances they'd gone to, and the way he'd held
her close. He was dressed in the casual style she

remembered him favoring: a white oxford shirt, unbuttoned at the top, no tie, a brown tweed sports coat, dark brown slacks, and brown tasseled loafers.

"Miss Angie," Earl said at her elbow, "do you wanna sit down?"

"Oh." She turned to see him holding the chair out. "Thanks." Pulling her hands from Derrick's grasp, she sat.

Derrick was about to scoot his chair closer to hers when Earl quickly stepped between them, forcing Derrick to stay where he was. "We got some specials today."

Angie gawked up at him.

"We got spaghetti an' meatballs, polenta an' sausage, an' meatball sangwitches."

Considering that those were the usual offerings, she gave Earl a cold stare.

"You're the culinary expert, Angelina," Derrick said with enthusiasm. "I defer to your judgment."

Earl's eyebrows shot up high as his head swiveled toward Derrick.

Angie sat a little taller. "The spaghetti and meatballs for Mr. Holton, Earl, and the polenta for me."

"Got it. Wine?"

"House red is fine."

"Anyt'ing else?"

"That's it," she said giving him a nod that clearly said, *Get lost.*

Glancing from her to Derrick, he frowned, then said, "I'll be back."

The minute Earl left, Derrick moved closer. "How have you been?"

"Fine. Quite fine, in fact." Small talk wasn't what she was there for. She folded her hands and leaned toward him. "The reason I called was to talk to you about UFOs." She quickly told him about her business and apologized for asking a serious scientist about such a subject.

"Your own business!" Derrick beamed at her. "How very impressive! Well, I can tell you a bit about UFOs, Angelina. There's much to tell, much that's happening now." Their eyes met and he stopped talking. Her discomfort grew as his gaze seemed to take in her every feature, her earrings, her dark brown hair (which now sported streaks of light auburn instead of her usual blond highlights—red hair was in these days), and then settled on her lips. "I'm sorry, Angelina." He placed his hand over her folded ones. "I know I promised not to think about the past, but seeing you again—"

"'Scuze me," Earl said gruffly, stepping between them once more despite the fact that the table was round and there was far more room on the opposite side. "'Ere's your wine. You want I should pour it, Miss Angie?" While Earl spoke, he stared hard at Derrick until he let go of Angie's hands and leaned back in his chair to wait until Earl finished his task.

Earl poured them each a glass from a carafe, then, with another deadly glance at Derrick, put the carafe down on the table with a thud and left.

Derrick bent toward Angie. "I get the feeling he disapproves of me for some reason."

"Don't worry," she said. "He's that way with everyone. So, what can you tell me about UFOs?"

Before replying, Derrick gave a nervous glance toward the swinging doors to the kitchen where Earl had gone. "It's funny you should ask, because that's what I'm going to hear about this evening. The times—with the change in millennium and all—are quite exciting. I want to learn all I can about the most extraordinary age our world has ever known. To think it's happening right now. Right here—"

"Sorry." Earl put their salads in front of them, plus a basket of French bread and butter.

"Thank you," Derrick said through clenched teeth.

"Yeah." Earl left.

Derrick looked at her. "Angelina, I don't want to talk about me. I'm interested in you. You haven't married, I take it. Are you engaged?"

"I haven't married, and I'm not officially engaged, although I'm seeing someone I'm quite serious about."

"There's still some hope for me, then." He smiled as broadly and easily as ever.

"I don't—"

"Don't answer! Give me time." He winked mischievously, his eyes sparkling. Yes, he was definitely still handsome. But still not her type. Was it possible for a man to be too fawning? Too smiley? She wouldn't have thought so, but what else could she have objected to about him? Paavo didn't have a fawning bone in his entire six-foot-two-inch body.

On the other hand, Connie could use someone who would fawn over her. Particularly with Christmas coming, and New Year's—and New Year's Eve parties! The more she thought about it, the more she liked the idea.

Derrick would be good for Connie. Most definitely.

"Talk to me about UFOs," she said with a lilt in her voice. Taking a bite of her salad, ostensibly waiting for him to speak, she let her mind spin ways to bring Derrick and Connie together.

"I promised, didn't I?" He gave a soft laugh and reached out, clearly planning to take hold of her left hand, since she was holding a salad fork in her right one.

"I know Miss Angie likes ta eat her salad wit' her dinner," Earl said, balancing a tray that was tottering dangerously close to Derrick's left ear. "So I brung it out ta you fast. I done good, right, Miss Angie?"

Derrick pulled back his hand and leaned away from Earl's tray.

Angie smoothed the napkin over her lap. "You did good, Earl."

He placed the food in front of them. "Anyt'ing else?"

"We're fine," Derrick said, a little too forcefully. Earl frowned and walked away.

"As you were saying about the UFOs," Angie coaxed.

"Oh . . . yes." Derrick sipped some wine, then took a taste of his spaghetti and meatballs and nodded appreciatively. "The help might not be the best, but this tastes great."

Angie just smiled.

"Anyway," Derrick began, "ufologists believe that from the beginning of recorded time, man has known he's not alone in the universe. In fact, they say, there's good evidence we came here from somewhere else. That's the real reason there's no scientific proof that Darwin was right, no missing link to prove that man evolved from other animals. It's not because God created man, but because man came from another planet!"

"That's wild," she said.

"Ufologists point to very convincing evidence. They believe humans look to the stars because we're searching for our home. And that someday, soon, our ancestors will come back to Earth for us. All the ancient prophets talk of it, the most famous being Nostradamus."

The origin of mankind and ancient prophecies were not at all what she was expecting to hear. She wanted tales of little green men and flying saucers. "Interesting," she said weakly. "So tell me . . . do these aliens look like us? Do they eat the way we do?"

He frowned, then shrugged as if he didn't know and didn't particularly care. "They don't seem to eat much of anything, I guess. I've never heard any talk about them eating. We've evolved differently from them. They're thinner, smaller, with huge black eyes and gray skin. We're far more interesting-looking—and acting. They're quite curious about our sexuality, you know."

"No, I didn't." She had the uneasy sense that although Derrick had begun by stating what ufologists believed, he had slid into his own belief system. Maybe he wouldn't be as right for Connie as she'd imagined. She had to be mistaken—after all, she'd dated him, brought him home to meet her family. He was a good and brilliant scientist, not a UFO nut.

He leaned closer. "The primary reason that EBEs—extraterrestrial biological entities, to be precise—come to Earth and abduct humans is to study our reproductive organs and—"

"Derrick!" Angie tried to laugh. "Give me a break. The people who go on TV or write books about being abducted are making up stories to get money. It's all a hoax."

"I wouldn't be too sure of that if I were you," he said with a knowing glance. "It could well be true. Science now shows that there's life beyond Mars."

"Life beyond Mars? Isn't that the name of a book by Algernon?"

Derrick stopped twirling spaghetti onto his fork in midtwirl. "Algernon! You're joking, right? You can't be saying that guy's name seriously!"

Angie leaned back in her chair, trying to ignore the way the other diners turned and stared at them. Even Earl stuck his head out of the kitchen and frowned.

Derrick's voice dropped. He leaned closer. "Algernon doesn't have any idea what he's talking about. The man's a fraud."

"A fraud?" Eyes wide, she thought of Triana Crisswell, rich and overly impressionable. Might she be the victim of some con artist? "How do you know?"

"The people I read and the lectures I go to have proved it. This evening I'm going to hear a speaker who knows all about EBEs." He began eating again.

A most interesting thought sprang to mind. She knew Connie wasn't doing anything that night. She could pick Connie up and take her to the lecture to meet Derrick. A wealthy NASA scientist might be just the thing to bring Connie some Christmas cheer. "Maybe I should go to his talk tonight, too," she mused. "It might help me with my business."

"Great! I'll take you. You'll enjoy meeting my friends. We'll make you forget all about that charlatan Algernon."

"Speaking of friends, I'm supposed to meet one—"

"The one you're nearly engaged to?" he asked.

She smiled. "No. A woman. A girlfriend."

He smiled back. "In that case, the more the merrier. We meet in Tardis Hall."

"I've never heard of it."

"It's a converted warehouse at the foot of Brannan. They'll be destroying it soon—part of the rebuilding of the waterfront area. So we get it free, while it lasts."

Earl walked up to them and slapped the bill on the table. "You finished? I guess you gotta get goin'. You gonna see him tonight, Miss Angie?"

"Not very soon, I'm afraid," Angie said.

"Is he woikin'?"

"As usual." She wished he were the one with her at that moment.

Earl looked at his watch. "Maybe he'll get off woik sooner den you t'ought?"

"No. He never does," she said with dejection.

Derrick picked up the bill and began to look it over.

Earl snatched it out of Derrick's hand. "In dat case, why don' you two guys stay and have some dessert? You two don' wanna go off alone nowhere, not jus' da two a you. We got some good pie alla—uh, you know, wit' ice cream on it. Stay. Kick back. Take your shoes off."

Derrick glanced at his watch. "I'm afraid it's time for us to leave," he said, lifting the bill from Earl's fingers.

"No need. It's oily." He grabbed the bill again.

"Oily?" Derrick glanced from the bill to his fingers.

"Early," Angie translated.

Derrick lunged for the bill.

Earl swung his arm behind his back and jumped out of the way. "How 'bout some coffee? But no more wine, t'ough." With his free hand he yanked the carafe off the table and retreated another step. "I don' wan' Miss Angie ta lose her good sense. Wha' little of it she's got left."

"Just the bill, Earl," Angie said sternly.

"Da bill. You sure you know wha' you're doin'?"

She nodded.

"Don' say I didn' warn you."

"My brother never married," Janice Hazan said with a slight sniffle into the phone shortly after Paavo broke the news that Bertram Lambert had been found murdered. "He spent most of his first thirty-five years here in Ottumwa. He traveled a little, but kept coming back home to me. Until two years ago. That was when he moved to San Francisco. It was the happiest thing he ever did, or so he said. Every single day since then, I knew it would end up this way. I felt it in my bones. I warned him, over and over. Would he listen to me? Not one bit. But that was Bertram for you."

"Where else did he live?" Paavo asked. He switched the phone to his right hand as he checked his wristwatch. It was getting late. He wondered if Angie had returned home yet.

"Oh, he tried Phoenix, Albuquerque, even

Las Vegas. He liked the Southwest, but it didn't like him. He kept coming home to Iowa."

"I see." Paavo switched the phone back again and wrote down the information.

"Do you know why he moved to San Francisco?" While he'd gone to see Angie, only to be greeted by her lying weasel of a neighbor, Yosh had contacted the post office for the address that they'd used to forward Lambert's mail. Paavo and Yosh were about to check it out when Lambert's sister returned their phone calls.

"I never understood it. My brother used his inheritance to buy himself a little house," Hazan said. "Paid way too much for it, if you ask me. He lived alone. The address was fifty-one Seventh Avenue. I understand it was a nice enough place. Not that he ever invited me. Oh well, too late for regrets now, isn't it?"

Paavo checked the address the post office had given Yosh with the one Janice Hazan just mentioned. They matched. "I'm sorry, Mrs. Hazan, to have to ask you these questions at a time like this," Paavo said. The woman hardly sounded broken up, though. "As you're his next of kin, if we could have your permission to enter the home—"

"Of course," she said brusquely. "I know you'll get in there one way or the other, so why not speed things up? Just don't mess it up too much, that's all I ask. I guess I'll have to come see it, since it'll be mine now. Right?"

"I imagine so. No one here seems to know of

any friends or close acquaintances of your brother's. Do you know of any?"

"Bertram wasn't the sort to make friends. That was why he kept coming back to Ottumwa. He said he went to San Francisco to join the city's swinging singles scene, but I knew it wouldn't work for him. He wasn't the easiest man to like. A bit on the dull side, I'm afraid. And that's speaking as the sister who loved him. Oh well. What can I say?"

"We couldn't find a car registered to him. Do you know if he had one?"

"I think he sold it a year or two ago. Said there was nowhere to park in the city, so he was better off without it. He said he used a bicycle to get around. Or the bus. Or cabs."

Paavo nodded. He was trying to fight the urge to hurry through these routine questions and call Angie again. Whom could she have gone out with? "Can you tell me about his interests? Any special lady friends? Or men friends?"

"I don't know any of his friends. Plays and ballet were all he ever mentioned, and them not often. I don't go for all that froufrou stuff myself. Plain people like us have no business putting on airs. I told him he should come home. He wouldn't listen, but, as I said, that was Bertram for you."

Paavo bit his tongue. "Did he ever mention anyone threatening him? Or that he was worried about anything or anyone?"

"Never."

"The last time you spoke with him, did he seem the same? Different? Anything at all strike you about him?"

"He was the same as ever. He never had much to say that was worth a row of pins, if you ask me. Not even when we were kids."

"Did he ever mention joining any clubs or groups . . . or cults . . . of any kind?"

"Bertram?" Just from her tone of voice, Paavo knew she didn't think her brother had joined any cults. "He never mentioned any such thing to me, that's for sure."

"I see." This line of questioning was getting nowhere. "Your brother was found with goggles that we suspect are old and of military origin. Do you know about them or anything like them?"

"No."

"Was your brother ever in the military, or have an interest in military kinds of things?"

"Not hardly. He despised everything that had to do with the military or killing. He was the gentlest man I've ever known."

"Thank you, Mrs. Hazan. I'll call you as soon as we learn anything." Paavo quickly hung up. Maybe Janice Hazan didn't know why Bertram Lambert kept traveling, but Paavo had a good suspicion.

5

Angie scowled impatiently at the red light as she drove her Testarossa toward Tardis Hall. After leaving Wings of an Angel, she'd gotten into her car, grabbed her cell phone, and made a call. But Connie was tired and wouldn't budge from her home. *Honestly,* Angie thought, *some people just don't appreciate the things their friends try to do for them.* As soon as the light changed, she zigzagged through the traffic, making up for lost time.

She was going to the lecture anyway. It wouldn't hurt to learn something about UFOs for her dinner party. Or to learn more about Derrick for Connie's sake. Angie had to admit as well to being curious as to why her NASA scientist was suddenly so interested in extraterrestrials. Her tires squealed on the rain-soaked pavement as she pulled into a parking lot.

Before shutting off the engine, she ran her windshield wipers a couple of times. The rain had stopped, but a heavy mist had quickly settled. Clean windshields didn't improve the looks of Tardis Hall. Four stories tall, it was boxy and warehouselike, with few windows. Although the entrance was well lit, the rest of the building looked dirty and uninviting.

All of a sudden, she wasn't nearly so curious about Derrick anymore. She wished Connie were with her. But this was no time to get nervous. Bobbing her head this way and that to make sure no muggers or worse were lurking outside the car, she made one last check of her makeup in the rearview mirror, unlocked her car door, and got out.

At the entrance to the hall, four young people waited to buy tickets. They were casually dressed to the point of sloppiness, with pale faces and a flabby appearance.

"You did come!" Derrick hurried toward her. "I stepped outside for a moment and here you are! Where's your friend?"

"She couldn't make it," Angie said.

He cast a sly look her way as he took her arm and led her toward the hall. "I would gladly have escorted you here," he said.

"You think I was lying about my friend?"

"I'm not saying that. I'm sure you have many friends. One of them might even have been interested in coming with you."

She stopped in her tracks. "I'm seeing someone."

"So you've said. A special boyfriend." He gave

her a sidelong glance. His arm tightened on hers, drawing her closer. "Isn't at least some little part of you glad to see me again, Angelina? Aren't you the least bit curious about what I've been up to?"

Angie would have set him straight except that a man sitting at a small folding table caught her attention. Brochures were stacked on it, plus a sign that read:

NEW MEMBERS! FREE DRAWINGS!
$100 TO THE LUCKY WINNER! JOIN TODAY!

The man at the table stood as they neared. He had a round belly, thinning black hair, and a tiny, Hitler-style mustache. He thrust a brochure toward them. The title puzzled her. *Roswell: The True Story.* What was Roswell?

She was about to reach for it when Derrick turned, directing her away from the man and toward the ticket taker. Announcing she was his guest, he whisked her into a stark entry hall. The walls were a grimy yellow color and streaked with fingerprints. The gray linoleum floor was worn and dirty. Facing her was a wall of unfinished plywood with double doors in the middle. She assumed they led to the auditorium.

Hanging by the doors was a poster of a man who looked like the reincarnation of a frizzy-haired Albert Einstein. Across the top of the poster, written with a red felt-tip marker, were the words DR. FREDERICK MOSSHAD—HERE TONIGHT!

"What was that brochure being handed out?" Angie asked, thinking of the stack of flyers outside the hall. "I've never heard of Ross-well."

"*Rahz*-well. It's a fascinating story. I'll get you one of those brochures later, since you're interested. I've got a lot of them. Or we can have dinner again and I'll tell you all about it." He smiled and waited for her response.

"I don't think—"

"You and your girlfriend?"

"Well . . ." She really didn't want to dine with him again, but she did want Connie to meet him . . . and she'd love to hear his UFO stories.

He looked like a cat after swallowing a bird. "I knew you'd agree. Please excuse me a moment," he said. "I've been given the honor of introducing tonight's speaker, and I need to check on things backstage. I'm glad you're here. Tonight's show will be an especially interesting one. Ah! Here's my friend Kronos. He'll watch out for you."

A blond, ponytailed man wearing a faded plaid shirt and loose, dirty jeans turned at Holton's words. He wore thick wire-rimmed glasses. Angie shook his hand as Derrick introduced them.

"Kronos takes care of lights, sound, and tapes if we need any," Derrick said, backing up. "Will you watch Angelina for me?" he asked Kronos. "I've got to check on Mosshad."

"Of course, Sir Derrick. 'Twill be an honor most joyous."

Angie chuckled and expected Derrick to

laugh or somehow react to Kronos's bizarre way of speaking. Derrick didn't bat an eyelash and disappeared into the crowd. Kronos gave Angie a big smile. His teeth were as gnarled as his speech. She gave serious thought to chasing down Derrick.

"So you share Sir Derrick's interest in things skyward, m'lady?" he asked.

What was with this guy? Angie looked around to see if people were laughing at them. Maybe Kronos pulled this as a joke on newcomers. "Not exactly," she said. "This is my first time here."

"Ah! 'Tis well chosen that you come this eve. A fine presentation we will hear. The learned Dr. Mosshad will speak of what the astronauts on Mir really saw"—his voice dropped to a whisper and he pushed his glasses back up the bridge of his nose—"and the classified material they have been so ignobly forced to keep secret."

"They've kept secrets?" She thought the whole purpose of space flights and stations was to collect data, not to hide it.

"Of course they've kept secrets, m'lady! All the astronauts have. Did you not know that?" He gaped at her as if she were the odd one of the two. "The hair on your head would stand on end if you heard of what they have seen."

Once more, she found herself wondering if Kronos was serious or if this was all one big practical joke.

"It is one of my favorite matters for discourse. Someday the government will be forced to give up its secrets. Then 'twill be as all the demons of hell loosed upon the land. Do you not agree?"

"Could be." She couldn't argue with what she couldn't understand. Where the hell was Derrick?

His eyes shifted from side to side. "That means you are smarter than most here, m'lady. Therefore, you must beware. They think they know the answers, but they know not!"

"Well . . . forsooth!" she said. Wait until she got her hands on Derrick for leaving her with someone clearly certifiable. "If you'll excuse me, I think I'll go find the ladies' room."

His jaw tightened. "I beg your indulgence as well. Sir Derrick forgot, as is his wont, that I must go set up the projector. Dr. Mosshad will require it."

Kronos pushed his glasses high on his nose again and marched off.

"It was nice meeting you," she murmured. *Real nice. About as nice as having a tetanus shot.*

She shuddered and turned away.

"Hello, lovely lady." A gaunt man wearing a black beret, a black turtleneck, and black slacks gave her a jaunty nod.

Angie stepped back. "Hello." The man's steel gray hair was so long and thick it looked like a helmet, bizarre thick eyebrows nearly covered his eyes, and a thin gray mouth peeked out from a bushy beard and mustache. Was the entire hall filled with nothing but oddballs?

"Is this your first time at a NAUTS event?" he asked.

"Naughts? As in zeros?" Angie asked.

He chuckled. "Not exactly. More like astro-NAUTS. It stands for the National Association of Ufological Technology Scientists. A mouthful, I admit."

"I hadn't realized this was anyone's event. I thought it was simply a lecture."

"It is, but NAUTS is sponsoring it." He clasped his hands, much like a teacher about to give a presentation. Or, considering how gaunt, bushy-bearded, and black-clad he was, a preacher of some back-to-basics-and-not-much-food religious group. "They're a fairly new group—a splinter group—seeking the truth."

"A splinter of what?" Angie asked.

"It was quite distasteful," the stranger said, dropping his voice and moving closer. "NAUTS is an offshoot of the Prometheus Group, made up of those members who considered themselves to have a scientific bent and didn't approve of the paranormal inclinations of the Prometheans. The two fought and eventually broke apart."

"Really?" It was odd that Derrick hadn't mentioned anything to her about NAUTS or the Prometheans. "I've heard of the Prometheus Group and Algernon," she said, thinking fast. If there was bad blood between the two groups, that explained why Derrick had grown so heated when he called Algernon a fraud.

"Algernon . . . yes." A strange half smile touched the gaunt man's lips. "Have you met Algernon?"

"Not yet. I hope to someday soon."

He nodded. "Well, Algernon leads one sect and tonight's speaker, Dr. Mosshad, leads the other."

"Sect? You make it sound like a religion."

He smiled. "It is rather. Sort of like the Protestants and the Catholics. Variations on the same theme. Perhaps because so many people refuse to believe in God, they now search for other things to believe in. My name is Malachi, by the way," the gaunt man said.

"I'm Angie." Her nerves grew edgy. She didn't know if it was because Derrick had abandoned her, or because of this man's strange conversation. She turned her head and spotted a vaguely familiar man wearing black sunglasses and a black suit. He couldn't be the same man she'd seen outside Connie's shop the day before, could he? He stood alone, his back to the wall, his head turned in her direction, as if he was watching her. The same way he'd done the previous day.

That did it. "Excuse me," she said softly. "I'm not up to a lecture tonight."

"You can't leave," Malachi said with a nod toward the auditorium doors, now opening. "The show's about to begin."

* * *

Bertram Lambert had lived in a modest house just off Lake Street in the city's inner Richmond district, a neighborhood of single-family homes and two-story flats surrounding shop-lined Clement and Geary Streets. The house was brownstone with sparkling white trim and white grille-covered windows. An overhang at the entry protected Paavo and Yosh from the rain as they stood in the darkness. Across the street, some of the houses had colorfully lit Christmas trees visible through the front windows and cheerfully twinkling lights strung along the roofline. Here, the street lamp's glow barely reached Lambert's door.

Paavo knocked, as both a courtesy and a caution. Sometimes people the police thought were living alone were not. And sometimes those closest to the victim were the least happy to have homicide inspectors come to call.

No one answered.

The lock was a deadbolt. Yosh held a penlight on it as Paavo used a curved tension hook and a sawtooth comb. A couple of minutes later, the lock clicked open.

After putting on latex gloves, Paavo swung the door wide.

"Will you look at this place?" Yosh exclaimed as he stepped into a large, sparsely furnished room. White rugs lay on glistening golden oak hardwood, and bright, abstract oils hung on stark white walls. Yosh stopped and peered down reflexively at his loafers, then up at Paavo.

Paavo shrugged. Lambert wouldn't care about dirt in his house anymore.

The old house had had the guts torn out of it, Paavo thought, then winced at the involuntary memory of Lambert's death that came with the thought. The remodeling had removed the walls separating the dining room, kitchen, and living room. A teak dining table, a white and black marble counter, and a Japanese shoji marked the different living areas.

Paavo gave the house a once-over, glancing into the bedroom, with a king-size bed, the bathroom, and two closets. The house had all the homeyness and personal warmth of a spread in *Architectural Digest.* Not a washcloth, not even a newspaper, was out of place.

"I'll take the kitchen," Yosh said. "I want to see what this guy used to eat. What in the world could he find that wasn't messy? I'll bet you he's got hand-painted, exotic plates and glasses in the kitchen. Not anything anyone uses. Maybe fancy European pots and pans, too. Just like someone we know, right, pal?"

"I'll start in the bedroom," Paavo said, ignoring what he knew to be a jab at Angie's money and possessions. Joking about Angie's money was a favorite Homicide pastime these days. He didn't find it funny.

He continued on with his inspection. He wasn't looking for anything specific, just something that felt out of place, offbeat, or somehow significant to the mystery of Bertram Lambert's death. He began with the bureau, pulling out drawers one by one, going through socks and underwear. Most drawers were empty. The walk-in closet had one suit, two sports coats, slacks, shirts, sweaters, shoes, and ties, all arranged by style, then color. In the back was a clothes hamper. He opened it. A shirt, boxers, T-shirt, and one pair of socks, all folded, lay in the bottom. Who in the world folded dirty clothes? This guy was beyond anal.

Empty suitcases were stacked on a shelf, along with a shoe box of photos. He flipped quickly through them. They were all old. One in particular, though, caught his eye. A young, unsmiling Bertram stared at the camera while his older sister gripped his hand and frowned, as if she was already displeased with him. He put the shoe box up on the shelf once more.

He had saved the desk for last. It was Scandinavian teak, with only a single drawer below the desktop. Lambert obviously wasn't one to fill his home with clutter. Slowly and methodically Paavo went through Lambert's personal papers, address books, day planners, and the few scraps of loose paper he could find.

He found the names of very few people, men or women, who might have been friends. It seemed that, whatever Lambert's hopes had been in coming to San Francisco, they hadn't been met.

6

Angie searched a bit for Derrick before entering the auditorium to hear the lecture, but she still couldn't find him. Malachi continued to hover nearby. She would have left, except that Derrick's telling her the lecture would be especially interesting and Kronos's telling her she'd hear what the astronauts really saw from the Mir space station had made her curious. She knew curiosity—or nosiness, as her mother, Serefina, called it—was a fault, but sometimes she couldn't help herself. Anyway, staying an hour or so more wouldn't matter in the least.

When she took a seat in the auditorium, Malachi pointed at the empty chair beside her. "May I?"

"Of course." She glanced at the clock to the right of the stage. Nine o'clock already? She checked her watch. Yes, the time was right. So much for getting home early to spend the evening with Paavo—if he showed up. She turned to Malachi. "May I ask you," she said, having decided the man knew his subject, "if you have ever heard what aliens eat?"

He stared at her blankly for a moment, then his lips curled into a smile and he stroked his chin. "That's a matter of considerable speculation," he replied gravely, "but no definitive answers."

It figures, Angie thought.

"What little we know, we've discovered by hypnotizing victims of alien abductions. Some people are abducted over and over, and in time, despite their fear, they develop an understanding of what's being done to them."

Alien abductions? "What is being done to them?" she asked.

"In most cases the abductees—both men and women—are stripped naked, strapped onto a table, and then long needles and probes are stuck into their bodies—eyes, nose, brains, and especially in the, er, groin area."

"It's amazing," Angie replied. Amazing that anyone would believe that if there were aliens roaming around the galaxy, they had nothing better to do than to study human sexuality. The idea gave voyeurism a whole new dimension.

Derrick had talked about the sexual angle, too, which made her wonder about him. Was this stuff just erudite porn for the wigged-out? Derrick used to be so normal.

That reminded her. She turned in her seat, searching again for him. Where was he? The small audience of about twenty people, a few college-age, many middle-aged or older, was growing restless. She checked her watch. Nine-fifteen. The eight-thirty starting time for the lecture must have been MST—Martian Standard Time. It certainly had nothing to do with the Pacific Time the rest of the West Coast used.

She realized Malachi was still talking to her. ". . . and the government won't admit to any of this because they want to keep it hidden from their enemies."

Angie began to hope desperately that Dr. Mosshad would be a lot more interesting than old Malachi was.

"Of course, it's a conspiracy of our government," he continued, "that whenever anyone discovers proof that aliens exist, the proof is immediately spirited away to Area Fifty-one—Dreamland—in the Nevada desert."

Angie could understand the Dreamland name. His long-winded discourse was making her sleepy. He didn't have anything useful to say about what aliens ate, either.

Where was Derrick? When would the show begin? She wanted to go home. She stretched, half rising from her seat, straining to look at the sides of the stage for Derrick to tell him she was leaving.

A blinding white light flashed onto the stage, covering the lectern and microphone, before it pulsated out over the audience. At the same time, a painfully high-pitched squeal blared into the room from all sides. Angie cried out as she squeezed her eyes shut, her hands pressed hard against her ears. The light and sound seemed to go on and on, growing more unbearable with each passing second.

Paavo picked up the wastebasket by the side of the desk and overturned it onto the bed. A PG&E bill. A phone bill. A flyer that said *Roswell: The True Story.* Opening it, he saw it was about an alien spaceship that was supposed to have landed in New Mexico in the summer of 1947. No wonder Lambert had thrown it away. A Macy's bill showing he'd bought a $150 pair of shoes. Paavo dropped everything back into the trash except the phone bill. It would show whom Lambert had phoned out of town. The information might be useful. He put the phone bill into a small plastic bag to become part of his file.

He scrutinized the room once more. Unless Lambert's murder was strictly a random act, the reason he was killed had to be found through a careful study of his life—his job, his home, his hobbies. The answer was very likely somewhere in this meticulously tidy home, and Paavo intended to find it.

As suddenly as it began, the bright light vanished and the room became quiet as death.

Angie lifted her head. "What was that?" She turned to Malachi, gripping his arm. He sat rigidly facing the stage.

A buzz of voices began spreading throughout the hall.

"I must think," he said.

I must leave, she thought.

The din in the room grew louder as she picked up her purse and her coat, which had fallen to the floor.

"Look at the time!" came a shout from the front.

"The time?" Angie glanced up at the clock to the right of the stage—nine-thirty—then at her watch. She tapped it a couple of times. "My watch says nine-twenty. Has it stopped? My two-thousand-dollar unstoppable Movado has stopped?"

"Mine did, too," Malachi said. Suddenly an expression of almost beatific vision came over him. He climbed up on his chair and threw his arms high overhead. In a loud, booming voice, he cried, "They're here! The aliens! Look at the clock, then at your watches! Time stopped for us. It was an alien abduction—of us!"

First the auditorium turned absolutely still, then a woman screamed. Another stood up, then fainted. The man with her grabbed her and half dragged her out of the hall.

"What's going on?" Angie cried, also standing now.

Ignoring her, Malachi shouted at the small crowd, his voice booming. "Where is Dr. Mosshad? He needs to explain this to us!"

A cry rose from the audience as people began to clamor for Mosshad to tell them what had happened, to assure them that everything was all right.

Time to go home, Angie decided. She was trying to step past Malachi when he got down from the chair and grabbed her arm, holding it tightly. "Let go of me!" she shouted.

"Holton's onstage. He'll tell us what's happened. You'll see. Stay and listen to him."

The audience grew hushed, expectant. People sat and waited. Finally, Angie too sat back down, Malachi's hand still on her arm.

"My friends," Derrick began, his voice softer than Angie had ever heard it, "something just happened backstage. Something strange and something very extraordinary. There was a light, and a ringing that went on for a long, long while. When it stopped, those of us back there discovered that we all had been given a message—the same message. I can't say we heard it, because we didn't hear it with our ears. We heard it some other way, and it became embedded deep in our brains. Those of us backstage confirmed it with each other. I know it's hard to believe, but friends, I will share with you now the message we were given."

Derrick drew in a deep breath and looked out over the hall, his gaze meeting those in the audience one by one.

"We have been told that Dr. Mosshad has—" He swallowed hard before continuing. "Dr. Mosshad has been abducted by a life force from another world."

7

As Paavo and Yosh rode back to the Hall of Justice after spending over an hour at Lambert's house, they swung by the top of Mt. Davidson to view the disturbance being reported on the police band.

One of the city's many millennium cults had gathered on the hilltop and built a bonfire. Paavo wondered how many years it would be before all the people worrying that the millennium would bring about changes to the planets, visitors from outer space, the Second Coming, Armageddon, or God only knew what else would find something new to worry about. He didn't know if most cults were in fear or awe of the change in millennium, only that talk of the end of the world was running high. That worried the police. Fear of retribution and punishment was usually the easiest way to maintain order, but when people think the end was near, anything goes. Although some people thought mankind was naturally "good," years of police work had taught him otherwise.

Since there was a new moon that night, the cult had decided it meant their friends in outer space could see a welcoming bonfire. The top of Mt. Davidson was one of the few areas in the city that didn't have nearby buildings. It consisted of a small parklike setting with a large Christian cross that for years had marked the highest spot in the city until the seventies, when the Sutro television and radio tower dwarfed it. Considering the ungodly reputation the city had acquired since that time, the displacement was probably fitting.

Behind the cross, an enormous bonfire burned, silhouetting it. Paavo had never been a religious man and only went to church now and then to accompany Angie, but the contrast of the pagan bonfire and the cross was startling. The change in millennium was causing many people to search and to question. Even if they didn't know what they were searching for.

Paavo remembered the UFO brochure in Lambert's house. He wondered if Lambert, too, might have been seeking answers to the loneliness of his life. If so, he hadn't found them.

The two inspectors saw that the police had the situation under control and the reveling stargazers were being dispersed, so they continued on to the Hall of Justice. In the parking lot, they got out of the city-owned vehicle.

"I'm calling it a night, pal," Yosh said, turning

toward his Mercury Sable. "Nancy's been making noises about never seeing me anymore. She's right. She's been busy, and I haven't even had the time to find out what she wants for Christmas. That isn't good for either one of us. If I get the wrong gift, I'm dead meat. I think leads on this case are pretty dead, anyway. A good night's sleep isn't going to kill them any more than they already are."

"You may be right," Paavo said. He looked at the Hall, then thought of the bonfire he'd just left. Some people were out there having fun even in their anxiety, feeling alive, while he was supposed to go up to the fourth floor to deal with death. Maybe Yosh was right. The next day would be soon enough. That night, he had something else to do.

Visions of Angie came to mind, along with how he'd felt when her loathsome neighbor said she'd gone out with another man. He needed to see her.

"Going to get some shut-eye yourself, Paav?" Yosh asked.

"Not hardly."

Yosh's eyebrows rose, then he laughed out loud as Paavo waved good-bye and headed for his car.

Angie pulled open the door at the first of Paavo's light taps. He had a key to her apartment—as she did to his house—and he would have used it to let himself in if she were sleeping.

He fixed his attention wholly on her, waiting for the shift of an eye, a flinch, the slightest nuance that might tell him he should be in any way concerned about her neighbor's words. Even if Angie had gone out with an old boyfriend, though, it wouldn't mean anything. He knew her, trusted her. Hell, he'd even told her he loved her, something he'd never told any other woman.

"Thank God you're here." She threw herself into his arms. "It was so exciting, Paavo! I couldn't believe it. It was so incredible! How did you find out already? Is it already on the news? Oh, of course! The police-band radio."

He held her close, shutting his eyes a quick moment in relief at her greeting and in disgust at himself for having allowed the slightest flicker of doubt to enter his mind. "Angie, hold on." He lifted his head to look into big, brown, smiling eyes. "Find out what?"

His hands held her waist. She wore a soft, fluffy yellow bathrobe that brushed the floor, and had washed off her makeup, making her look and feel so desirable it was all he could do not to stop her words with kisses. But she clearly was a lot more excited about something other than him just then.

"You really haven't heard?" A small furrow formed between her eyebrows.

"I came here to see you," he said softly. He couldn't help but lift one hand to her face to feel the soft, smooth warmth of her skin. As

their eyes met, his hand rested a mol·
her shoulder, then slid down her back, pas·
waist to her hips, pulling her closer, pressing h·
tight against him.

"Oh well . . . I . . ." Her gaze drifted from his
blue eyes to the deeply shadowed lower lids,
high cheekbones, and angular nose, and rested
on his mouth. Her mood shifted, and suddenly
the reality of the handsome man in her arms
was a lot more interesting than the peculiar
events at Tardis Hall. She lifted her arms to his
neck. *Who cares about some old aliens,* she thought.
His head lowered to hers, and their lips met. In
minutes her robe lay on the floor of the living
room while his clothes left a bread-crumb-like
trail straight to Angie's bed.

In the bedroom, his touch, his kisses, his
caresses sent her spinning higher and higher
until she arrived at a spot in outer space far
beyond mere UFOs and Martians. He was her
universe.

Afterward, they lay on the bed, arms and legs
intertwined. He ran his hand along her spine,
enjoying the feel of her body against his.

"So," Paavo said, his mouth near her ear, his
voice low, "what was this exciting thing you
thought I came over here to learn about?"

She inched even closer, her head on his
shoulder and one arm draped across his chest.
This was not the best time to tell him about Derrick, her new business, or anything else that
might prompt enough questions to break the

spell of the moment. Three nights and two murders since she'd last seen him meant she wanted
all his attention on her for a while. Since he
might find it odd that she would go to a place
like Tardis Hall alone, she decided to pretend
her girlfriend hadn't abandoned her.

"Connie and I wanted to hear a lecture
tonight," she said casually. "But we weren't able
to because the lecturer was abducted by aliens."

"Aliens?" He cupped her breast and lightly
kissed the furrow on her brow that had intrigued
him earlier. "You mean illegal aliens?"

"I mean little green men."

He lifted his head and stared at her. He
should have been past being surprised by things
Angie said and did. But he wasn't. "You're joking."

"Well, I'm not saying the roof opened up and
Leonard Nimoy grabbed the guy, but someone
made an announcement telling us that was what
happened."

At Paavo's smirk, she quickly added, "It was
probably a publicity stunt."

"I'd say so."

"You may be right. Let's forget it." She nib-
bled his ear, raising herself as he rolled onto his
back. Her hand rubbed his chest, then his stomach.

"You said you went with Connie?" he asked.

"Mmm-hmmm," she murmured, kissing his
jaw, his neck, his shoulder as her hand drifted
lower.

"Just the two of you?"

Her hand stopped. He couldn't know, could he? Earl wouldn't have called him and said anything. No, she was just feeling guilty for no reason whatsoever.

"Just"—her mouth hovered over his—"the two of us."

As she kissed him, her hand found its destination and he asked no more questions.

8

"Look at this," Yosh said early the next morning. "Someone's stuck a Post-it to the autopsy schedule. Who's Marcella?"

"I don't know," Paavo said, glancing over at the schedule. *Merry Christmas from Marcella.* Incredible.

"She must be someone in the coroner's office," Yosh said, reaching for the phone. "I've got to talk to anyone brain-dead enough to put Christmas cheer on a coroner's log."

He punched in the number. "I'd like to speak to Marcella," he said. Then, "Oh. Oh, I see. Okay. I'll call back. Thanks." He hung up and chuckled. "She's one of the clerks. Does typing, filing. Called in sick today, though. God, I've got to meet her."

"She's probably just a nice kid," Paavo said. "Leave her alone."

"I'll bet the note was for you, pal. She probably took one look at those baby blues of yours and fell madly in love."

"Not hardly," Paavo said, turning back to his reports. Fending off lovesick females was about as far removed from his reality as . . . as being liked by Angie's father.

The funny part was, he was more used to being disliked by someone like Sal Amalfi than he was to being loved by someone like Angie. Throughout his life, the only one who ever professed to care about him and didn't die or leave him was his stepfather, Aulis Kokkonen. Everyone else seemed to die or run off first chance they got. Including his father—who had never even acknowledged fathering a child, as far as Paavo knew—and his unwed mother, who had abandoned him when he was four. What a pair.

No wonder he had no interest in marriage or lasting relationships. What firsthand experience did he have with either of them?

Maybe that was why he had been so ready to jump to the wrong conclusion about Angie's faithfulness. He was still kicking himself over the way he had quizzed her about going to the lecture the previous night. She'd said she'd gone with Connie. Stan had said she'd been with an old boyfriend. Which one should he believe? No contest. She had hesitated in her answers to some questions, but that was probably because she'd been shocked at his persistence.

He should get her something really special

for Christmas. Something that would show her how important she was to him. But what?

Yosh initialed a couple of circulating memos and put them in Paavo's in tray. "Isn't that how it was with Angie?"

"What was that?" Paavo asked, breaking away from his musings.

"One day Angie was just another case," Yosh said, "and the next she had a case on you."

Paavo scowled. "There was a lot more to it than that. And anyway, Angie's different."

"Ain't that the truth!" Yosh laughed.

Inspector Luis Calderon pushed the door open and stomped heavily to his desk. In his forties, he wore his thick black hair heavily pomaded in a pompadour, and sported a closely trimmed mustache.

"What's the joke?" he asked, his voice low, his tone grumpy.

"Nothing," Paavo snapped, turning back to the autopsy.

Calderon's eyebrows shot up.

"You had to have been there," Yosh answered. "Say, do you know a clerk named Marcella in the coroner's office?"

"What do you care?" Calderon asked warily.

"Just wondering who she is," Yosh said.

"Well, I never heard of her. What do you think, I spend my time checking out all the women in the place?" Calderon tossed a newspaper onto his desk and sank heavily into the seat. "Just because my wife took off doesn't mean I play around, for cryin' out loud. Maybe she'll come back."

"To add some sunshine to her life again," Yosh said.

"Go to hell." Calderon pushed aside a stack of papers and logged onto his computer. "One of these days she'll wise up," he said, drumming his fingers as the network went through its security checks. "I should have seen it coming, though. She was always out when I tried to call. Out early in the morning, stayed out late at night. Had girlfriends to do this with, and that." Behind Calderon, Yosh caught Paavo's eye and pretended to play a violin. "Then some guys starting hanging around," Calderon continued, more to himself than the others, especially since they'd already heard his story many times. "Not boyfriends. Just guys who were into the same things she was. Things I didn't care nothing about. Then one day, I walk home and the place is empty."

"It's tough," Paavo said.

"You got that damn right. The thing that makes me mad, though, is I never even seen it coming. Not a damn hint. Not a clue. She was always understanding. 'Oh, you gotta work late? No problem. You got a big, important job to do. Do it. Me and the kids, we're proud of you.' Yeah, proud of me right out the door."

"She'll be back," Yosh said quietly. He had suddenly stopped clowning and picked up another memo. "At least there's no other guy," he added.

"That's the damned part of it." Calderon shook his head. "No guy. She just got tired of me. Women!" He poured black coffee from a thermos into a cup coated with the crud from coffee of ages past. "What's to be tired of?"

Yosh didn't respond and the question hung in the air. "Beats me," Paavo said, casting an eye on his partner. Calderon's question had been a perfect setup for another one of Yosh's shots at Calderon's dour personality, yet something in Yosh's demeanor had changed as the conversation continued. Now Yosh seemed engrossed in the report on the visits to the people who lived around Sigmund Stern Grove.

Paavo glanced at his partner, a coldness settling in his stomach. *There couldn't be anything wrong in Yosh's marriage, could there?*

When Angie awoke that same morning, she was alone. Paavo must have gone home to shower, change into clean clothes, and go back to Homicide. She knew he was working on some sort of horrible case. As she waited for her coffee to brew, she opened that morning's *Chronicle*. There, on page five, was the story.

Lecturer Disappears—Alien Abduction?

Dr. Frederick Mosshad, astronomer and lecturer with the National Association of Ufological Technology Scientists, was abducted by space aliens, according to a NAUTS spokesman. That message was given to a group of several hundred people waiting to hear Mosshad's lecture last evening at Tardis Hall.

Dr. Derrick Holton, spokesperson for NAUTS and a former NASA scientist, said several attendees reported seeing a flash of light and hearing a strange sound fill the auditorium just before the lecturer's disappearance. Such abductions are common, Holton stated, but usually are not so public.

The police have not been asked to investigate. "This isn't a police matter," Holton said. He added that the faithful will gather again at Tardis Hall in two nights to see if Mosshad returns.

Angie stared at the article. *Former* NASA scientist? Why did it say that? But then it also said several hundred people had been there when to reach thirty would have been a stretch. Maybe the reporter had both facts wrong. She tossed the paper aside. If this was a plan for publicity, it had worked very well indeed. She wondered how many more people would show up at Tardis Hall for the next lecture. Perhaps she should hire Derrick to do PR for her Fantasy Dinner business. It certainly needed a shot in the arm.

She started up her computer to check her e-mail, hoping against hope that someone else had contacted her about a fantasy dinner through her Web site: fantasydinners.com. It would be nice to know there was at least one other person in the world who wanted a fun party. But the *You've got mail!* voice didn't sound for her that day. Not even a lousy piece of spam. So much for potential clients beating a path to her door, or her computer.

Just then her telephone rang.

"This is Triana Crisswell," the woman said in response to Angie's cheerful hello.

"Mrs. Crisswell, I was just thinking about you," Angie said.

"Good, because I've just got to tell you, sweetie, you'll need to come up with an idea that's a lollapalooza. This party is simply taking off!"

"What do you mean?" Angie asked.

"I mean the abduction!" Angie had to hold the phone away from her ear. "Didn't you hear about it? It's the talk of the whole city."

"I was there," Angie said.

"You saw it? I can't believe this. How I envy you!" Triana lowered her voice and said, "So you must realize what this means, sweetie."

"No, I'm afraid I don't," Angie said.

"It means this party will be so hot, I can't tell you! Already I'm getting calls from people who want to be sure to be included. We're going to have at least two hundred. Maybe more. It won't be held at my house. This place is simply too small. And I don't want to wait. I want the party now. Immediately."

Now Angie was the one shouting into the phone. "That's impossible."

There was a pause. "A week from Friday, then."

"That gives me no time," Angie wailed. "I need a theme, catered food, special decorations—these are supposed to be fantasy dinners, after all."

"Fantasy, shmantasy. Forget the dinner. All I want is a party, right away, with something to munch on. Heck, I don't care if you serve hot dogs!"

"We need to talk about this," Angie said, desperately attempting to calm her first—and maybe her last—client. "Keep in mind that the best caterers are already booked for next week. In fact, all the caterers are booked. This is the time for holiday parties. Also, to cook for two hundred people is no small potatoes. You do want the best, don't you?"

"Honey." Triana sounded even more annoyed. "You think this is about food? It's about publicity. Getting people to join our cause. It's about making a great name for Algernon."

"I haven't even met him yet."

"I suppose you have a point," Triana said, her tone suddenly hard as chipped ice. "He should be at a meeting of the group Thursday night. I'll meet you there and introduce you."

Angie sighed as Triana brusquely gave her the address. If Triana didn't care about the tastiness of the food or the imaginativeness of the fantasy, why should she? Except that it was her first fantasy dinner, and she had hoped to use it to build her reputation. But she was a clever person, and if this is what her client wanted, she would find a way to deliver it. "Thank you, Mrs. Crisswell. I'll see you tomorrow night. Tell me, since the dinner is now too big for your home, where will it be held?"

"There's only one place. Tardis Hall, of course."

Criminologist Ray Faldo reached his gloved hand into the evidence bag and took out the heavy goggles that had been found on Bertram Lambert's body. Blowing on them to remove a trace of fingerprint powder, he placed them on the table in front of the two inspectors. Faldo was a pro. Even though he'd worked in the crime lab nearly fifteen years, he didn't simply put in his hours and go home at the end of the day. He still approached his work ready for the excitement that discovery could bring. For that reason, Paavo had gone to him about the goggles in the first place. "Do more than test for prints," Paavo had said. "Find out what in the hell they are."

When Faldo had called a few minutes earlier and asked Paavo to come down to the lab when he had time, Paavo made time right then. Yosh joined him.

"They're old," Faldo said as they peered down at the heavy black object. "Fifty years, at least." He picked up a black lacquer Japanese chopstick and used it as a pointer. "You can tell that from the way they were made, and the way the glass and metal

sheathing have become scratched and worn from
handling. For the longest time, I had no idea
what the goggles were supposed to be used for,
until I happened to have them on at the exact
right moment."

He picked them up and gave them to Paavo.
"Take a look."

Paavo peered through the goggles. The lab
looked fuzzy and distorted. Faldo switched off
the light.

"Hey!" Yosh cried. "What's going on? I can't
see a thing!"

But Paavo could.

"Don't reach out that way, Yosh," he said.
"You're about to hit a beaker."

"What?" Yosh pulled back his hand. "You can
see in the dark with those things?"

Faldo spoke. "That's what I discovered. I was
looking through them when the lights flickered.
That's when I realized the view had changed. I
didn't understand how it changed—but it had
to do with the light.

"I turned off the lights in the lab and put the
goggles on. What Paavo sees is what I saw.
They're not as sophisticated as the night-vision
glasses the military has now, of course, but an
early version of that very technology. Something
is strange about them, though."

Paavo took the goggles off and handed them
to Yosh.

"Holy Toledo!" Yosh cried. "Will you look at

that! You know, Paavo, we should use something like this when we travel around at night in the city. Can you imagine? We could see the crooks but they couldn't see us. It'd be great! Maybe I should ask Nancy to get me a pair for Christmas. I wonder what they cost."

Faldo flicked the lights back. "There you have it."

"You said there was something strange about them," Paavo said to Faldo as Yosh took the goggles off and gazed at them admiringly.

"I looked through catalogs and manuals about old military gear—early night goggles and such. The earliest versions were very poor. Huge, bulky things. The current generation of them, issued during the Vietnam War, used a very different technology—they were slimmer, more reliable, easier to use and see with. These seem to be a prototype of the current generation. What's strange is that they've never shown up in a catalog or anywhere else. I could find no documented history of the evolution from the early ones to the night goggles of today. It's as if there was a missing link in night-vision technology. These are that missing link—a secret prototype, from all I can tell. But I have no idea where they're from or who made them. Nada."

Paavo and Yosh stared at the strange goggles. "Did you find any prints on them, or anything that might help us find out where they came from?" Yosh asked.

"They've been wiped spotless," Faldo said.

"Still, thanks for all you've found out," Paavo said.

"Thank PG and E. They caused the electricity to go haywire. Messed up my VCR at home, but gave me the clue to the goggles. The electric company giveth and the electric company taketh away—too often these days."

9

Derrick Holton opened his eyes. The bedroom was dark, but a flickering light had awakened him. He heard a high, whining noise. He covered his ears with his hands and at the same time struggled into a sitting position. It didn't help, though, because the sound wasn't coming from the outside. It came from within him. *Not again,* he thought.

He was fully awake now, his eyes wide and fearful. He knew with absolute certainty what was causing the lights, the sounds in his head. And he was afraid.

A white light shone into his window, dim at first, quickly growing brighter.

His mind screamed in fright. Knowing that they were back and were out there, taking people, he could think only of hiding.

He had believed he'd managed to hide from them. He was wrong. He had to get away from

them. He had to run. As he got off the bed, he
fell, tangled in his bedcovers. The clothes he'd
worn the day before were lying in a heap on a
chair. He crawled to them, ignoring the pain in
his ears.

He wouldn't let them take him. He'd die
before he let them touch him again.

Clutching his clothes and shoes in his arms,
he ran out to the hallway, pulling the door shut
behind him. Not that it mattered much. A
closed door meant nothing to them.

He took the stairs down three flights to the
street level, then kept going, down to the basement parking garage. To his car.

He had to go somewhere they couldn't find
him. Somewhere until he came up with a way to
stop them. Somewhere to be safe. First, he had
to run. Run as far and as fast as he could, now
that, once again, they were here.

"I felt terrible lying to Paavo about Derrick,
Mamma," Angie said as she sat across the table
from Serefina in her mother's kitchen. "What if
he finds out Connie didn't go to the lecture
with me?"

They huddled over black coffee and little
round Italian cookies with white icing that were
so hard that if you didn't dunk them in the coffee, they could easily crack a tooth. Angie didn't
know if the cookies were good or not, only that
she'd eaten them from the time she was a child
and they comforted her.

"When did I teach you to be such a liar, Angelina?" her mother cried, distress evident in her voice.

"It wasn't a lie lie. It was a white lie. I said it so I wouldn't hurt him."

"It was a lie!" Serefina jumped up, went into the pantry, and came out with a bottle of what she called her cooking brandy. She poured a splash in her coffee to make a coffee royal, another fine Italian tradition. Or was it Irish? Whatever, she enjoyed it. "One lie here, another there," Serefina continued, "and pretty soon, you bring down everything. *Capisce?* Tell him the truth. He'll understand."

"But then I'll have to tell him about my business. What if it fails?" Angie put her elbows on the table and hung her head. "He'll think I'm an idiot!"

"He doesn't like you for your business sense, Angelina. I'm an old woman, but I'm not so old I don't remember what it's like between a man and a woman. If the business fails, it's all right."

"Not to me." Pouting, Angie dropped another cookie into her coffee. It floated, so she held it down with a spoon until it softened. "I definitely don't want to tell him about Derrick. Paavo worries that I might change my mind about how I feel about him. I tell him he's wrong, but if he finds out that I changed my mind about Derrick, he might see me as frivolous again."

Serefina peered long at her daughter. "You were in love with the idea of Derrick. You brought home your fancy, intelligent NASA scientist for all of us to admire. You were so proud of yourself for getting him interested in you, you strutted around here like a peacock."

"I did not, Mamma!"

"You did. With my own eyes, I saw you!" Serefina could shout even louder than Angie. "But you never loved the man. You liked what he was, not who he was."

"Now it's my fault! I give up!" Angie threw her arms wide, her face upturned like a martyr. "I thought you and Papà wanted me to marry him."

"Maybe your *papà* did. He was like you, boasting to his *amici* about Dr. Holton dating his daughter. Your *papà* never even finished high school, so of course he was impressed. He's always wanted the best for his girls. Since you're the baby, Angie, he wants the best of the best for you. You know that. I hoped you'd realize Derrick wasn't the man for you before it was too late."

The realization that her mother had given so much thought to her relationships made her want to know more. She was almost afraid to ask. "Do you feel that way about Paavo, too?" Her voice was soft now.

Serefina smiled wisely. "It's different with Paavo. With him, you've grown up a lot. You would love him—the man—no matter what his job was."

"I do. And that's why I want him to be proud

of me. I'm going to put on a fantasy dinner about aliens and UFOs that will wildly impress the ufologists of this city and anyone else who wants to attend."

"Testa dura!" Serefina cried. "Did you hear a word I said?"

"I know what I'm doing, Mamma." She stood up. "Excuse me while I call Connie. I'm going to somehow convince her to come with me this afternoon to a science fiction and fantasy convention down at the Moscone Center. It should give me other insights into the world of time and space."

As Angie headed for the phone, Serefina called after her, "Ask Connie if she'd like to come here for Christmas dinner with the family. And remember to tell Paavo he can't work that day." Then, shaking her head at her single-minded daughter, she made herself another coffee royal.

Angie and Connie hadn't yet entered the science fiction and fantasy convention at the Moscone Center when they saw two men with gray bodies, huge heads with bulging almond-shaped black eyes, and three fingers on each hand standing in front of the building, smoking cigarettes. Apparently the San Francisco no-smoking-indoors-in-public-places ordinance applied even to beings from outer space.

Not far from the entrance, Angie saw a table just like the one that had stood outside Tardis

Hall the night before, with the same heavyset man with the stubby black Hitler-like mustache hawking free drawings for hundred-dollar prizes. Going over to get a brochure crossed her mind, but he was busy talking to several young men, and she was more interested in what was happening inside the convention.

She and Connie headed past the smokers and paid their way into the center.

The aliens they had seen outside were dull compared to the ones inside. Sorcerers, gnomes, and princesses made up the bulk of the fantasy side of the con, while the science fiction crowd saw fleets of Martians, Klingons, Han Solos, and Darth Mauls, at least a dozen Mr. Spocks, and an equal number of Datas, although *Deep Space 9* and *Next Generation* captains vastly outnumbered Captain Kirk. She also saw at least twenty men in wildly colorful suits carrying miniature old-fashioned telephone booths.

"Who are you?" she asked one of them.

"Exactly! Yes, I am!" he cried. His hair was thick and curly—almost like Shirley Temple's.

She stared at him as if he truly were from another planet. "Wh-What?" she stammered.

"Not what, who! Dr. Who, I should say!" He giggled. "I love doing that. Just like an Abbott and Costello routine. And you're saying you don't know me?"

She rubbed her head. "I'm afraid not."

"I'm a time lord. When not on the BBC—and I'm afraid I was canceled after a run of over twenty years—I travel through time and space in my tardis."

"Your tardis? What's a tardis?" Angie had thought Tardis Hall was named after someone—some wealthy Mr. Tardis. She had no idea it was something a British television time lord used.

"This is a miniature version." He held up the phone booth. "Although it looks like a simple old-fashioned phone box, when you go inside it turns into my spaceship."

"Uh . . . right." Angie backed away. "Thank you." She'd just found out a lot more than she ever wanted to know about British science fiction.

Angie pulled Connie toward the National Association of Ufological Technology Scientists' booth. "Hi," she said to the serious young man behind the table. He was dressed like a college-prep student—white shirt, red tie, no jacket, neatly trimmed reddish brown hair, and a plain, nondescript face. He didn't fit in with this weird crowd at all. It was embarrassing to ask someone so normal-looking her question. "Excuse me. Can you tell me a bit about UFOs?" she asked.

"Why, most certainly, ma'am, my pleasure." He had a thick southern accent, and he kept giving her strange looks. "Say, didn't I see you at Tardis Hall the other night?"

Angie was surprised she was so recognizable. "Yes. I was there the night of the abduction."

His smile disappeared. "Oh, I know what night

it was, that's for sure. My name's Elvis, by the way."

Angie and Connie both took a step backward.

"Don't worry," he said with a long-suffering sigh. "I'm not crazy, my mama was."

Angie's and Connie's eyes met.

"You asked about UFOs." He picked up a large book from the display in front of him. "Here's a book with photos of them taken all over the United States. It's on special today. Only twenty-nine ninety-five. It's usually ten dollars more."

She glanced at the book he'd stuck in her hands. It was filled with pictures of small shiny objects in the sky. She put it back on the counter. "I don't mean UFOs as such—I mean, what makes them interesting? What real, tangible things come to mind when you think about UFOs?"

He pondered a moment. "Well, as far as what's real, the first thing I think of is Roswell."

"Roswell?" Maybe she should have stopped and picked up a pamphlet from the guy outside the Moscone Center. "Why?"

"Simple. It's the only place in the United States where it's well documented that an alien spaceship crashed."

"It's a fact?" she asked. Was he putting her on? The man looked quite serious. And normal, despite his name. In fact, Elvis was the most normal-looking person she'd met connected with all this ufology. And what did that say about it? "Where is Roswell, by the way?" she asked.

"Are you serious?" He acted as if he was wondering whether she was putting him on. "It's in New Mexico. I thought everyone knew that. Here, take these books and brochures." He pulled a paperback out of his briefcase and several from boxes on the floor, plus a number of pamphlets from the tabletop. "There's no charge. Just read them. No one should be ignorant about what's really important in the world."

"I agree," Angie said as he loaded the books into her arms. She might not agree that Roswell was at that level of importance, but to him, obviously, it was. She was so stunned by the man's reaction to her ignorance, it took her a moment to realize that the shaking she was feeling wasn't the ground moving, but Connie yanking on her arm, trying to get her attention. "What is it?" she asked.

"Look at the picture of the president of this group," Connie whispered. "He's a dream!"

Angie peered at the flyer Connie was holding. Smiling up at her as president of NAUTS was her old boyfriend, Derrick Holton. Why hadn't he told her he was president? Was there some reason for keeping it secret?

After telling Connie his identity and watching her stunned reaction, Angie continued to wander around the convention floor, Connie in tow. She saw a sign reading Prometheus Group. Here was her chance to find out something about Algernon's association. When she reached the booth, she saw two men and a woman in their late teens or early twenties. They were dressed more like skateboarders than people interested in science fiction or fantasy. She hoped none of them was Algernon.

Angie stepped up to the orange-haired fellow who smiled at her, while Connie hung back and watched warily. "Hello," Angie said. "Are any of you Algernon?"

He grinned. "Don't I wish!"

"Is Triana Crisswell around?" she asked.

He glanced over at his friends. "Hey, you dudes know Triana Crisswell?" He scratched the chest of his *X-Files* T-shirt as he waited for their response.

"I've heard her name, but I don't know her." A tall, pudgy young woman, dressed in baggy jeans, a long green shirt, and a shorter, bulky Levi's jacket, spoke and chewed gum at the same time. She even snapped it.

"She's not here," the other fellow replied. He wore a baseball cap on backward and a T-shirt that said The End Is Near.

"Well, duhhhh," the girl said, rolling her eyes. "That's pretty obvious." She took her gum out, looked at it, then stuck it back in her mouth. Angie wondered what she'd expected to see.

"I think she was here yesterday," End-Is-Near added. The others shrugged.

"I'm going to be helping her with a dinner for Algernon to launch his new book. Have you read it yet?"

"I didn't know he had a book. He's not a

writer," X-Files exclaimed indignantly. "He's got brains. A scientist. Some people say he's a vision . . . vision . . . vision-something-or-other."

"Visionary?" Angie offered.

"He's the true one," End-Is-Near replied. "Everybody else just fakes it. For the money. Like that Mosshead freak. What a rip-off artist."

"You mean Mos-*shad*?" Angie said, pronouncing it as she'd heard Derrick and the others say the name.

"I mean *Moss*-head," he reiterated. "That's 'cause he's got moss instead of brains."

"Hey, did you guys hear about his botched-up abduction?" The gum chewer stopped chomping long enough to ask the question. "People said he just walked out of the building, and most people saw him leave, but now the press is making a big deal out of it."

"Gross," End-Is-Near said. "Junk like that gives us all a bad name."

"He's such a phony, dude," X-Files said. "So is that jerk he hangs around with. The pretty boy. You know the one."

"Holton," the gum chewer said. "He's sooo cute." She made a strange squealing sound. "Too bad he's on their side. He calls himself their president now."

"He's a phony, dude, if I ever saw one," X-Files said.

"He's so phony he gives fakes a bad name," End-Is-Near pronounced.

As they chortled, the gum chewer swallowed

her gum. "Oh shit," she muttered, pounding her chest.

"Why do all of you think he's a fraud?" Angie asked.

They looked at her as if she were the alien. "We just know, dude," X-Files said. The other two nodded.

"Algernon's no fraud, though. He's the real thing."

"He's cute, too. If you like older men," the former gum chewer said.

Angie wondered what the girl thought older consisted of. Probably anyone over thirty.

"So, you interested in anything in particular?" End-Is-Near leaned forward, elbows on the counter. "Maybe we could help you out."

Angie looked back at him. Well, she'd asked everyone else—why not them? "I do have a question. What do aliens eat?"

The three glanced at each other, then X-Files leaned close and said in a hushed voice, "Earthlings."

10

Paavo couldn't say that Thai food was a favorite cuisine of his, but it was one of Angie's. That was why they were seated in the Rose of Siam restaurant and he was chasing clear, slippery rice noodles around his plate with a fork. At least in this restaurant he didn't have to fight his food with chopsticks. He wasn't very good with those, either.

He'd been feeling guilty ever since he'd questioned Angie because of Stan's crack that she had gone out with an old boyfriend. *Damn that man, anyway. Why, out of all the millions of people who could be living next to Angie, does he have to be the one?*

Paavo was going to make it up to her, though, first with this dinner, and then with a play in the little theater area of the city just off Geary Boulevard. He also needed to find her something especially nice for Christmas. What that was—that he could afford—he had no idea. Christmas was only two weeks away. He'd better come up with something.

"The green curry prawns are excellent," Angie said. "The curry is hot, but the varied tastes are clear and even the delicate flavor of the prawns isn't overwhelmed."

"I'm glad you're enjoying it."

"It's good you decided to take a break. This case seems to be getting you down."

He nodded. "The victim was practically a hermit. We contacted people whose names he had written down in his address book, and most of them hadn't heard from him in years. They didn't even exchange Christmas cards. It made me wonder why he still had their names in his book. Unless it was simply because he didn't have anyone to replace them with. Even looking at his phone bill, the only long-distance calls he made were to businesses. Not even his sister cared much that he was dead."

"How awful for him. There's been little mention of the death in the papers. It was murder, right?"

"It's a good thing it's stayed out of the papers. The guy was mutilated. Badly. We don't want the gory details published."

"What was his name again?"

"Bertram Lambert."

"Great name." The singsong quality of the name made her want to smile, but due to the gravity of what had happened to the man, she kept a straight face. "Well, with that gory a murder, I guess whoever did it must be nuts. If he's still in the city, you'll find him. Someone that crazy can't stay hidden for long."

"Let's hope not." The subject died. "What have you been up to?"

The waitress cleared their plates and brought them tall glasses of iced and sweetened Thai coffee. "Let's see. Connie and I went to a science fiction convention this afternoon," Angie said, using her straw to stir the milk through the syrupy coffee. "It was fun. That's about it."

"Science fiction? I didn't know you liked that."

"It's so new-millennium," she said. "Thought I'd try it." She hoped he couldn't tell she was lying through her teeth.

"What gives, Angie? All this millennium stuff isn't like you."

She bit her tongue, literally. That was the only way she could stop herself from telling him about Triana Crisswell and her fantasy dinner— or fantasy party—for two hundred plus people. Despite her mother's advice, she couldn't tell him about a business that might fail, and she simply wasn't sure that she could pull the party off—or that Triana wouldn't back out, or that some other last-minute disaster wouldn't occur and cause the entire job offer to go belly-up. She was tired of telling Paavo of her excitement over new job prospects, only to watch them blow up in her face. So, despite everything, she decided to keep this a secret until she was certain the Fantasy Dinners enterprise was everything she intended it to be.

"What can I say, Paavo? I want to be with it. Just like everyone else these days. After all, I probably won't be around for Y3K."

The next morning Paavo found the official write-up of Bertram Lambert's autopsy on his desk. Even though he had watched the autopsy take place and had a preliminary indication of what had happened, the complete report could still hold some surprises. As he read, Yoshiwara came in and sat, looking up from time to time to gauge Paavo's reaction.

Based on pattern impression and calculations of the shape and dimensions of the implement used on Lambert's skull, the coroner determined a hammer had been used. Paavo remembered seeing a well-stocked toolbox in the garage. The tools in it were so shiny, he had doubted they had ever been used. The cut to the carotid artery had apparently been made with a broad-bladed steel knife such as the kind used by hunters. Gastrointestinal tract contents were described. The crab, liver, crackers, and blood alcohol caused Dr. Ramirez to unofficially suggest in a Post-it to Paavo that the deceased had eaten crab mousse, paté, and wine. If she was right, an elegant little party had been taking place before things turned ugly. Whom would a pariah like Lambert have been partying with?

"I've never seen anything like it," Paavo said when he finished reading.

"It's crazy." Yosh rolled his chair away from his desk and turned toward Paavo. He had already read the reports. "There's barely a drop of blood left in the guy's body, his wounds were made with a fine cutting instrument, and they've been cauterized. It doesn't make sense."

"The crime lab suggests some kind of laser was used," Paavo said.

"Who'd get access to a laser?" Yosh cried in frustration. "And why bother? The guy was dead. What was the killer trying to prove?"

Paavo flipped through the pages to the description of the cauterized tissue. "Say, have you figured out what you're going to give Nancy for Christmas?" he asked as he read the gory description.

Yosh slid his chair back to his desk and picked up a memo from the bureau chief talking about holiday leave and the need for staff coverage. "I don't know what I'll do this year. Last year I had her gift all picked out. She'd been hinting, so I knew she'd love it."

Paavo looked up, interested. "Really? That good?"

Yosh nodded, a big smile on his face. "It was perfect. Hey! It's something Angie might like."

"Really? What was it?"

"An electric bread maker. It cost a bundle, too. Over eighty bucks!"

So much for that idea. Paavo tossed the autopsy report on his desk. "I'm going to send the CSU over to Lambert's house. We have no indication that it was the scene of the crime, but he had a nice store of wines, paté in the refrigerator, and a hammer in his toolbox. He might have invited the killer over. The doer would have had plenty of time to clean up, since Lambert's neighbors never paid any attention whatsoever to him."

"Do you realize how boring that means he must have been?" Yosh said with a shake of his head.

"If you guys are done talking about all that gore," Calderon barked, "I want to know who's going to handle Christmas duty. I want to make sure you don't expect me to do it just 'cause I'm alone this year."

"You planning to sit home singing carols?" Yosh asked. "With visions of sugarplums dancing in your head?"

"Real funny. I'm going to try to see my kids," Calderon said. "Why don't you take it, Paav? You don't have kids or family. Christmas can't mean anything to you."

Paavo's head jerked up at Calderon's words. Here he'd been thinking of what a loner Lambert was. He wondered if others saw him the same way. "I'm supposed to go to Angie's parents' house. I guess—"

"Go ahead, pal," Yosh said. "I'll do it."

Paavo stared at his partner. Yosh was the biggest family man in the department. "But—"

Just then Lt. Hollins, head of the Homicide Bureau, stepped into the big room where the inspectors had their desks. All talking stopped. He seemed even more worried than usual. "Paavo, Yosh, come into my office."

The lieutenant was in his early fifties, with thinning gray hair and a thickening waistline. He'd been a cop for over twenty years, starting as a beat patrolman at Central Station in North Beach. His dream had been to become the head of Homicide, and five years ago he'd made it. He'd been nursing an ulcer ever since. Even though his job had become, for the most part, administrative instead of investigative, he still had a nose for crime scenes and knew how to follow up on a good lead.

As they entered his office, he walked to the windows and stood in front of them, one hand rubbing the back of his neck.

"Hey there, Chief," Yosh said exuberantly. "Why the long face?"

"Sit down," Hollins said, his voice grim.

They sat. Yosh clamped his mouth shut.

Hollins drew a deep breath. "I just got a call from the Southern station," he said. "There's been another murder. A man, probably in his mid-thirties. It's hard to tell exactly what was done to him, but it sounded a lot like the Stern Grove victim. Our boy—or whoever's responsible for this—is at it again."

Hollins paused, then stared them both in the eye. "You two need to get out there right now and take over. Keep it quiet. I don't want the press involved. We managed to keep any details of the first mutilation out of the newspapers. If the press gets wind of this second one, it could throw the city into a panic. Especially with all the kooks already running around sure the millennium means the world is coming to an end."

The two inspectors stood up. "Where are we going?" Yosh asked.

"The Giants' new stadium. The groundskeepers found him. Right behind second base."

11

"I wonder if I'm overdressed for a lecture," Connie said, her voice giving away her nervousness as she checked her face in the mirror of Angie's Testarossa. "I kept thinking about how handsome he was in that picture, and I might have gotten a bit carried away." Under a heavy coat, she was wearing a kelly green cocktail dress, sleeveless, with a plunging neckline.

"You said you wanted Derrick to notice you," Angie said noncommittally as she turned into a parking lot by Tardis Hall. "Once you take that coat off, he definitely will. Anyway, I told you how lonely he seems. He needs you, that's all there is to it."

As they walked toward the entrance to the hall, they saw that a line had formed to buy tickets. It was considerably longer than the first time Angie had been there, and the crowd was considerably more conservatively dressed. "It looks popular enough," Connie admitted.

"Didn't I tell you?" Angie said, trying to hide her own amazement.

The same man Angie had seen the first time she was there, and at the Moscone Center, again sat behind a small folding table with brochures stacked tall. The same sign stood in front of him:

NEW MEMBERS! FREE DRAWINGS!
$100 TO THE LUCKY WINNER! JOIN TODAY!

Angie and Connie joined the line to buy tickets for the lecture. The wait wasn't long, and soon they were in the dingy entry hall, milling about with others and waiting for the auditorium doors to open.

"Back again, Angelina?" Derrick said as he reached Angie. He gave her a hug. "What a wonderful surprise! You must like our message."

He tried to put his arm around her, but she stepped to the side. "I'd like you to meet my friend, Connie Rogers. Connie, this is Derrick Holton," Angie said. Derrick held out his hand and said it was nice to meet her. Connie took a moment before she placed hers in his and, with a look of sheer bliss, she checked him out from his neatly trimmed brown hair to his black oxfords, then murmured something that sounded a bit like "Same here."

"The doors should be opening anytime now." Derrick clapped his hands together and rocked onto his toes as he excitedly scanned the area. "Isn't this crowd fantastic? They're here to see if Mosshad shows up tonight. I think he will, but he's not here yet. I've got to go wait for him. If you can stick around after the lecture, I'd love to take both of you out for a drink. How would that be?"

Angie turned to Connie, who nodded enthusiastically. "That would be quite nice," she said. Derrick rushed off as quickly as he'd arrived.

"My, my!" Connie said, fanning her face. "I see what you mean about him."

"Ah! Sir Derrick's lady fair." Angie jumped as a man came up from behind her. Even before turning to look at him, she knew such words had to belong to the blond, long-haired fellow she'd met last time.

"Kronos, right?" she asked.

"At your service. And who is the lovely wench with you?"

Connie had been gaping at the strangely speaking fellow with the loose bleached-muslin overshirt and grubby jeans.

"Connie," Angie said, "meet Kronos."

"Hello." She cautiously held out her hand.

Instead of taking it, he bowed from the waist with a great flourish. "Greetings and salutations."

Elvis, from the science fiction and fantasy convention, joined them. He was still conservatively dressed in a white dress shirt, blue tie, and gray slacks. "Remember me? I gave you books on Roswell."

"You're pushing Roswell again, young knave?" Kronos asked. "Haven't you learned there are some things better left unspoken?"

"We've got to talk about it," Elvis exclaimed. "Roswell is where it all began for us. Even Algernon can't break away from it, as you well know."

"I hate Algernon. I hate Roswell. And I hate your talking about them!" Kronos cried, forgetting his phony Elizabethan speech for the moment.

As the two men glared at each other, Angie said, "Why does everyone seem to dislike Algernon so much?"

Two heads swiveled toward her with surprise. Elvis's expression changed first, his mouth curving into a lopsided grin. "You don't know much about us, do you? Algernon and Mosshad were on the same side until Holton entered the picture. Then it was Holton and Mosshad on one side, Algernon on the other. Along with Kronos's ex-wife."

"That's old history, swine. I have better things to do than stay and listen. Excuse me, fair ladies. The truth about Algernon is simple. He is a fraud and a liar. And a home wrecker. If he were dead, everyone would be better off."

With that, he spun away.

"Go play with your implant," Elvis said to Kronos's disappearing back. He faced Angie. "Have you met Algernon?"

"I meet him tomorrow night. I think it'll be most interesting," she said with a glance in the direction Kronos had taken.

"To understand Algernon is to understand NAUTS and Derrick Holton. Even though they are opposite in almost every way. And deadly enemies." He glanced at Connie. "It seems to me that meeting Algernon would be well worth your while."

Connie's eyes met Angie's. "Perhaps so," she said.

"Well, excuse me, please," Elvis said. "I've got to help my friend Phil over there with the tickets. We're getting a good crowd due to all the publicity about Dr. Mosshad."

Angie watched Elvis walk over to the man he had referred to. The name Phil had a strangely normal sound for this crowd. Phil himself, however, fit in with the others. He was an older man, his black hair streaked with gray. He was almost bald on top, though his hair was thick and bushy at the sides and back. He had a full beard and wore love beads and Birkenstock sandals with no socks. A true child of the sixties, most likely still searching for the Age of Aquarius.

Angie turned back to Connie and the two were quietly commenting to each other on the bizarre people there when Angie noticed another man hovering nearby. He was a pudgy twenty-something fellow with a little Hitler-type mustache and thin black hair combed forward onto his forehead. He was the man who had been sitting outside the hall and giving away Roswell brochures. She frowned and turned her back to him.

Instead of taking the hint, he moved in front

of her. "Are you a member of NAUTS?" he asked nervously.

"I'm here to learn," she said coldly.

The chubby fellow stepped closer, twisting his fingers. "It's nice that you're here. Both of you." His voice was soft. He smiled at Connie, who looked even more alarmed. "You should both think about joining us. You might even win a hundred dollars." His smile made his cheeks dimple deeply. "My name's John Oliver Harding. Everyone calls me Oliver—Oliver Hardy." He gripped his shirt as if it were a vest and waggled his fingers. "I'm into old movies and comedies."

"Ah, I see," Angie said. She looked around for Stan Laurel. He had to be nearby.

Just then the doors opened. "Good-bye, Mr. Hardy. We've got a lecture to hear."

"It'll be about the men in black. You should enjoy it."

Better than men in Oliver Hardy disguises, Angie thought as Connie tugged her to the front row for a better view of Derrick Holton.

Another male. This one seemed to be in his forties. His lips, nose, ears, genitals, and rectum had been removed as cleanly and bloodlessly as those from the victim found in Stern Grove. The number 5 had been carved into his chest.

Paavo stood on the infield of the city's new ballpark and looked down at the victim. He had come from the dugout, where he'd talked to the security team and the groundskeepers who had found the body. They'd given him a good idea of what he'd see when he got there. Maybe that was why, as he crossed the field, he'd made a detour to the pitcher's mound, stood on the rubber a quick second, and stared at home plate. When he was a kid and would go to Candlestick Park to watch the Giants with his stepfather, he had dreamed of standing on the mound one day. He guessed this was as close as he'd ever get. Then he turned and continued toward the crime scene.

As Yosh joined him, he looked once more down at the body. This one hadn't been dead a couple of days like Lambert. He was so recently dead his skin still smelled burnt where the cuts had been cauterized. Paavo held his breath as he squatted down. There was no lividity. Finger pressure could not turn the skin any whiter than it already was. It looked as if this victim, too, had been drained of blood. Rigor mortis was in the early stages of development. Three or four hours earlier, the man might still have been alive.

Beside the mutilated body Paavo saw a small waferlike metal object. He didn't touch or move it until the photographers got there, just in case there was some significance to the way it had been placed at the victim's side. It seemed to be some kind of computer circuitry, but neither Paavo nor Yosh, nor any of the patrol officers around them, had any idea what they were looking at.

"It's got to be the same doer," Yosh said. "I don't want to think there's more than one psycho going around hacking up people like that."

"What worries me," Paavo said, "is that there was only about a week between this murder and the earlier one—depending on how accurately we estimated the day of Lambert's murder." Anyone who killed so brutally usually took a few weeks, even months, between crimes. Past studies of serial and spree killers showed that such killings often accompanied a kind of sexual frenzy on the part of the killer. Those who mutilated their victims, in particular, always went into a profound exhaustion for days thereafter. It was considered nearly impossible for someone to kill again in such a lurid way after only a few days. Nearly impossible, but obviously not completely so.

Or—the thought was chilling—there might be more than one killer. A cult, perhaps? One that had a sick fascination with death.

Equally grim was the possibility that these killings were being done without the frenzy and emotional involvement and release such horrid crimes usually entailed. Was it possible for a man to commit crimes like that without passion? To do it with indifference? Not if the killer had any humanity at all.

Paavo slowly circled the victim. Needle marks speckled his arms. He was so skinny his ribs showed. The corpse's unkempt and dirty hair, battered and scarred hands with dirty nails, and callused feet with ragged toenails were the markings of a man who had lived hard and lived on the streets, the antithesis of the immaculate Bertram Lambert.

Just as with the last victim, something about the mutilation and the way the victim lay cast a ritualistic tinge over the murder. All the flesh that had been removed had surrounded an orifice of the body. It was significant—but why?

"Number five," Yosh muttered, as much to himself as to his partner. "What the hell does it mean? The other guy had a seven. Seven, five? Seventy-five? I don't get it."

"It might be the start of an even bigger number," Paavo said.

"Let's hope it's not too big a number," Yosh said, his voice low. "I don't want to see any more vics end up like these last two."

Paavo silently scanned the empty ballpark. "Something tells me we're only looking at strike two."

12

"I don't know about this."

Angie and Connie peered up at the large, dark, and dreary building on the part of Larkin Street that lay between the gentrified gay area of Polk Street and the seedy porn shops and prostitute haunts of the Tenderloin. Angie double-checked the address Triana had given her. This was where she was supposed to meet Algernon.

Connie nervously hooked her arm in Angie's. "It looks kind of creepy from out here, but I'm sure it'll be fine inside. Can't judge a book by its cover. Ha, ha."

Angie glanced at her friend and grimaced. Still, she was thankful Connie had consented to come with her. "We'll go up there, see what Algernon is all about, then leave," Angie said, mustering her courage.

"That's right. It'll help you in planning his dinner party, plus I need to do this." Connie straightened her back, lifting her chin as she pushed open the main door and entered the building. "If Derrick and I are to have a chance together, I need to understand him and everything he's involved in a whole lot better than I do now."

Angie had to agree to that. After the bizarre lecture about the men in black—a mysterious lot whose job was to intimidate witnesses to UFO activities—she and Connie had gone with Derrick to the Top of the Mark for cocktails. Angie had to admit that Connie couldn't have looked better. Derrick, though, had been troubled and distracted.

Dr. Mosshad hadn't reappeared that night, as expected. Derrick darkly hinted that Algernon was somehow behind the scientist's disappearance. Angie couldn't get him to say why, but as the evening wore on, Derrick had grown increasingly agitated.

When Connie asked if Algernon was dangerous and if the police should get involved, Derrick had laughed. Algernon was no more dangerous than a maggot, he had said. In fact, he added, that was what Algernon was—a maggot to be squished.

Soon after, they had called it a night.

Now, with growing apprehension, Angie walked up the stairs to the Prometheus Group meeting in apartment six. The walls of the stairwell and hallways were painted black and the doors a garish red. No welcoming doorbell was evident. As Connie nodded encouragement, Angie knocked.

The door was opened by a woman wearing a soiled, sleeveless, floor-length Cleopatra-style outfit—except Cleopatra wouldn't have been caught dead in it. Tied around her head was a gold ribbon and sticking up from the center, over her forehead, was a small yellow plastic snake—the type that cost about fifty-nine cents at a toy store.

It was all Angie could do to stop staring.

"Greetings, fellow voyagers," the woman bellowed. "I am Isis, daughter of the Great Pyramid. Welcome."

"I'm Angie, daughter of Sal and Serefina. This is Connie. We're here as guests of Triana Crisswell." The two moved cautiously into the apartment. The furniture was as run-down as the rest of the building—a green Naugahyde sofa and chairs that must have been nearly forty years old. Didn't that stuff ever wear out? It was the most resilient legacy of the fifties. Wooden chairs filled the rest of the room. Three men and four women chatted and paid no attention to the new arrivals. Triana was not among them.

"Here it comes!" someone shouted. Everyone leaped from their chairs and circled a computer monitor.

"We're going to look at some pictures taken by members of our Santa Fe chapter while visiting Egypt," Isis explained. "Santa Fe is filled with good feng shui, so sensitive people such as us can live there. Only a few places are suitable for us, you know."

"Is that so?" Connie asked, bobbing her head to see the computer screen.

"Yes. Santa Fe, Sedona, and of course, San Francisco and Berkeley."

There was nothing in the least bit spiritual or ethereal about Berkeley to Angie's eye. She wondered if that was feng shui humor.

"It's beautiful!" one of the men shouted when the photo came clearly into view. Connie moved in close to get a better view. To Angie, though, it looked like all other photos she'd seen of the Great Pyramid.

Angie watched the changing images for less than a minute, then stepped back to Isis, who remained near the door. Connie seemed to be as engrossed as the others watching the photos and listening to a running commentary about the chambers inside the pyramid.

"Why does it mean anything special to you?" Angie asked Isis. "Does this have to do with pyramid power—putting things inside little pyramids to make plants grow better, or whatever?"

"Not at all," a voice behind them said.

Angie turned toward the man who entered the room. He was tall and darkly handsome, with flowing black hair and a black suit that bore a close resemblance to the old Nehru jackets of fleeting popularity. "That was New Age nonsense," he said. "This is real. The Great Pyra-

mid is so large it can be seen from the moon."
His gaze fixed on Angie. "Were you aware of
that?"

"No, not really." She took a step back, as if
pushed by the power of the man's eyes. "I don't
see that that matters."

"The Great Pyramid's base is equal to thir-
teen acres. Its weight is so great, only a solid
stone mountain would be able to hold it—and
the ancients built it right on top of solid granite.
You must be a new member of our group," he
said, taking her hand in both of his. His middle
finger bore a heavy gold ring in the design of a
cobra. "Tell me, little skeptic, how did such
primitive people know that deep within the
earth, far below the sand they chose, stood a
mountain of solid granite?"

Mesmerized, Angie's gaze flitted between his
black eyes and the gold snake that coiled round
and round his finger. "How did they?" she
asked. This man had to be Algernon. There
couldn't be two such powerful personalities in
one group. She glanced toward the entrance.
Where was Triana?

The man was already speaking. "It took a special knowledge impossible for them to pos-
sess"—his voice dropped dramatically—"on
their own. It also took a special knowledge for
the ancients to place the Great Pyramid in the
exact center of the Earth's land mass."

Angie's eyes widened. "The exact center?"

"Come." Holding her hand, he led her away

from the others, across the room to a desk with a globe of the world. She turned toward Connie, wanting to gesture for Connie to come with her, but Connie's attention was glued to the computer monitor.

With his right hand he slowly spun the globe. "East to west, the pyramid's axis corresponds to the longest land parallel across the Earth." He stopped the globe with Egypt facing them. "North to south, it passes through the longest land meridian on Earth. In other words, out of three billion places on this planet where the Great Pyramid could have been built, the spot chosen was the one place where the greatest north-to-south and east-to-west land masses cross." He whispered in her ear, "How could the ancients have known that?"

She swallowed hard, both intrigued and somewhat alarmed by this man and the sexual energy he exuded. "I don't know."

He wore a closed-mouthed, indulgent smile as he turned her to face him. Gazing down at her, he kept his hands on her arms as he spoke. "The total length of the Great Pyramid's base is a precise fraction of the Earth's circumference, and the ratio of the height to its base perimeter is the same as the Earth's radius to its circumference. How could the ancient Egyptians have known that?"

She couldn't even follow what he said, let alone be able to answer. Where were Triana and Connie?

"When you look at the stars, little skeptic," he said, placing his hand on her chin to tilt her head upward as if toward the heavens, but in fact toward him, "the positioning of the pyramids is mathematically proportionate to how the constellation of Orion would have appeared in the sky in 10500 B.C."

"That's very long ago," she murmured. She felt as if her body had turned to Jell-O.

A harsh female voice broke the spell being cast on her, and the stranger dropped his hands. "Old doesn't begin to do it justice," Isis said, stepping up to them both. Her eyes burned. "The pyramids were built at that time, you know."

Angie faced her. This was something she did know. "The pyramids were built twenty-five hundred years before Christ, not ten thousand."

"That's old thinking," Isis said with a sneer. "The new places them much earlier. Archaeologists discovered that a vent in the King's Chamber points to Orion. A vent in the Queen's Chamber points to Sirius—the star sacred to Osiris's consort, Isis. Orion, as you probably know, was the sacred home of Osiris, the Egyptian god."

"Isn't Osiris the god of the dead?" Angie asked, her gaze drawn again toward the dark stranger.

"Life and death spring from each other," he said. "One could say the pyramids, too, are as connected with death as with immortality. In that sense it is, in all, a death cult."

Isis held her chin high. "We are its priest and priestess. Osiris and Isis, the lovers." She gazed fondly at the man, then back to Angie. "Let me introduce Osiris."

Angie glanced up at him. He gave her a small bow and that same haunting smile. "In a past life I was Osiris, little skeptic," he said. "In this life, I am also called Algernon."

13

"Algernon! You're the person I'm here to meet," Angie said. "I was hired by Triana Crisswell to put on a dinner party for your new book."

He chuckled and took her hands. "Well, no wonder you are so skeptical, then. I was wondering how someone such as you had found her way here."

"Triana Crisswell invited me here to meet you. I wonder where she is. With me is my fr— my assistant. Let me get her."

Connie chose that moment to look up, and she saw Angie waving her over. Her eyes widened when she noticed Algernon.

As the two met, Angie took the opportunity to better study the man now that she knew for sure who he was. He was a lot older than she had first assumed. His skin had the too-tight look usually associated with women who'd had face-lifts, and his hair was too black to be natural. His neck and hands most gave his age away. Still, natural or not, he was a handsome man and—she had to admit—he had a lot of sex appeal. Just as Triana Crisswell had told her.

"It's so nice to meet you," Connie said. "Angie and I went to a NAUTS lecture yesterday. I heard so much about you."

A hard look passed over his eyes and then was gone. Angie hoped she had imagined it. It was chilling. "You went to a NAUTS event and learned about me?" Black eyes darted from one to the other. Then he burst out laughing. "That was like going to Rush Limbaugh to learn about Bill Clinton. Did they have anything good to say?"

"Are you rivals, or what?" Angie asked, careful not to answer his question.

"*Rivals* denotes equals," he replied. "I'm afraid jealousy has more to do with our differences than anything. When the first leader of the Prometheans died, I took over. That was how he would have wanted it. Others—Derrick Holton in particular—couldn't bear to be second to anyone and left the group. NAUTS is small and weak and wrong. That's why they have no followers, why they must resort to stunts like that ridiculous alien abduction of Mosshad to get attention. It makes us all look silly."

Angie remembered that Derrick was convinced Algernon had something to do with Mosshad's being gone so many days. Listening to him now, though, she doubted Derrick's assumption was correct.

"What if Mosshad's disappearance wasn't a sham?" Connie asked. "Mosshad didn't return for the big NAUTS meeting when he was supposed to."

Algernon shrugged. "More drama? Who cares? The Prometheans and I know the truth about the universe and the future. There is more to the universe than most men can imagine. The ancients, the Egyptians, understood it, and so do I. I am followed by many. I am the truth."

"And Derrick Holton?" Connie asked.

"A gnat. To be swatted."

A maggot and a gnat, Angie thought. How she'd gone from astronomy to entomology she'd never know.

The next morning, Paavo did something he'd never done before. Instead of throwing away the Macy's advertising supplement to the *Chronicle*, he went through it page by page, studying jewelry, dresses, suits, blouses, sweaters, pots, dishes, knives, and even bedding in hopes that something—anything—might trigger an idea of what to buy Angie for Christmas.

Inspector Bo Benson passed by his desk, dropped some memos in his in tray, and focused on the underwear ad Paavo was reading. "I'm not sure which will look better on you, Paav," Benson said, "the red lace or the black satin."

He howled with laughter as he continued on to his desk.

Paavo shut the paper and dropped it into the wastebasket. Benson was Homicide's man about town. A tall, thin, handsome African-American, he always wore fashionably cut, elegant suits in a homicide bureau where most inspectors had readily adopted California casual. As if the suits weren't enough to set him apart from the others, he topped them with a fedora. On him, the hat looked cool. If Paavo had tried to wear one, he'd look like he was auditioning for a 1930s role with central casting.

Paavo's gaze followed the inspector. Benson had a lot of experience figuring out what women liked. "Bo, have you ever given a woman a Christmas present?" he asked.

"Every year, bro. This year, I've outdone myself. I've got three women to please."

"Do you know what you'll give them?"

"Sure. I've given every girlfriend the same thing for years now—ever since I first discovered the reaction I got. They love it."

That sounded perfect, Paavo thought. "What is it?"

"Two dozen roses and a two-pound box of Godiva chocolates. They even let me eat most of the chocolates. The secret is, see, I get them two dozen and two pounds. Then I tell them it's because I love 'em twice as much." He smiled broadly, well pleased with himself.

Paavo pulled the Macy's ad out of the waste-basket and went back to studying it again.

When Angie awoke, she was nearly as tired as when she had gone to sleep. Things just weren't working out the way she had hoped they would. The man who would be the star attraction for her first fantasy dinner troubled her greatly. He was fascinating, intelligent, even charismatic. But he came on too strong with her, and the issue of the worship of death, even if it was in the classic Egyptian form of Osiris, was disturbing to her on many levels, both social and spiritual.

The bad blood between him and Derrick also concerned her. Derrick had changed a lot since she'd known him, but basically he still seemed to be the good person she had once dated. She gave store to his feelings about Algernon.

She needed to rethink her involvement in Algernon's party. The people around him were too strange for her taste. She would call Triana and bow out.

Just then her phone rang.

"Hello," she said.

"Angie? This is Triana Crisswell."

She could hardly believe it. "Hello, Mrs. Crisswell, I missed you last night."

"I would have been there except my husband came home early and started up again about my friends. He just doesn't understand the Prometheus Group. He gave me such a headache, I had to take to my bed! In any event, I talked to Algernon this morning. You made such a hit with him, I can't tell you! I've rarely heard him so excited about anyone. Not only was he impressed with you, but with me, too, for finding you. You're a pro, Miss Amalfi. I'm going to tell all my friends about you."

"Oh." How was she going to bow out now? "Thank you, but—"

"No need to thank me. We're up to three hundred people already! And I haven't done any publicity to speak of. This party is going to be bigger and more important than ever."

"I'm really sorry, but—"

"Don't be! It's so much more exciting this way! It means your hard work will be seen and valued by even more people. Your name will be made with this event, sweetie. You better believe it."

That was exactly what she was afraid of.

"One more little thing," Triana continued. "Algernon wants to get together to discuss this party with you personally."

"He does?"

"This is such an honor! He's even willing to come to your house. He, uh, suggested that since I'm so busy, I don't need to be there, so don't worry about me. What would be a good time for you?"

So that's his game. "Why, Mrs. Crisswell, I couldn't possibly meet with him unless you were there as well," Angie said. "I wouldn't dream of it."

"Oh, isn't that sweet of you, Angie! I'd love to join you both—if you're sure. Algernon sounded as if he thought I might not be needed, and I certainly wouldn't want to be in the way."

"Don't be silly. You couldn't possibly be anything but a welcome addition. Maybe in a couple of days? Give me a call when you both settle on a time."

"I'll be in touch, Angie. One last thing: How is the planning coming?"

"Wonderfully, just wonderfully. We'll talk about it when you're here," she added quickly, hoping Triana wouldn't ask for details.

"I'm so pleased. Call me if you need me. Ta-ta!"

With that, she hung up.

Angie just sat for a few minutes staring at the phone. How had she gotten into this fix? All she wanted to do was to have a simple little business. Cater some fun dinners for people. Throw a few parties. That was all. Instead she was going to end up feeding all the nut cases in the Bay Area.

And one very sexy Egyptian god.

Triana was right about one thing, though. The people attending this party would be the crème de la crème of San Francisco. They might be wacko crème, but crème nonetheless. And crème always gave big dinner parties, needing to hire people just like her to help out.

She might make a go of this business yet.

She wandered into the den and saw the stack of Roswell books on a lamp table. She had put them there when she returned from the science fiction convention and hadn't looked at them since. The events there certainly caused strong reactions from people. She thought of Elvis's awe and Kronos's anger at the mention of the name.

She picked out the one the man behind the booth had pulled out of his briefcase, a well-thumbed book with some underlining and some asterisks. She sat down on the daybed, put her feet up, rearranged the pillows, and began to read.

On July 3, 1947, strange sightings began over the vast, empty desert outside of Roswell, New Mexico.

She looked at the date and wondered if the whole controversy had been caused by too much Fourth of July celebrating. She continued reading.

The guided-missile base at White Sands had monitored the bizarre activity on radar, but could not explain it. Two days later, word reached the U.S. Army's 509th airfield of a crash in a remote area. Investigators were sent out, and the next day, the base commander approved a press release saying a flying saucer had crashed. The Associated Press picked up the story.

Angie chortled. There went the base commander's career.

Immediately, the army changed its tune. The next day, they announced the fuss had been a mistake caused by a weather balloon that had broken up. One of the men who had been to the crash site was the base intelligence officer, Major Jesse Marcel. He was neither a fool nor a psychopath. Other weather balloons had fallen and none had ever been mistaken for a flying saucer.

So, Angie thought, the army wasn't any better at covering up things fifty years ago than it was these days. She continued reading.

The army sent a convoy of soldiers to the crash site to pick up every single scrap. That material was sent to Fort Bliss, Texas, headquarters of the 8th Army Air Force. From there, the most important materiel continued on to the Air Materiel command at Wright Field in Ohio: four extraterrestrials. Three were dead, and one was still alive.

She frowned. How could anyone believe such garbage? Nonetheless, she couldn't bring herself to put down the book.

A shave-and-a-haircut knock on the door to her apartment came as a welcome distraction. Stretching as she walked to the door, she was surprised that nearly two hours had passed. Maybe this was true time-warp alien-abduction stuff—wasting time reading made-up, albeit entertaining, stories about UFOs.

"Stan! What in the world?" She stared at her neighbor from across the hall, then backed up as he entered her apartment.

"Angie, I'm desperate. Do you have anything to eat? I can't go to a restaurant looking like this. In fact, not even to the corner grocery. I haven't eaten all day today." In each ear, Stan had stuck a piece of aluminum foil, twisted into the size and shape of a cigarette.

"Tell me, Stanfield," Angie said, "why do you have tinfoil stuck in your ears?"

"I can explain . . . after I've eaten." He gave

her a doe-eyed, hollow-cheeked look, like a starving waif in a Keene painting. Angie knew he was anything but starving, considering that he mooched meals throughout the apartment building, and probably from people at work as well.

"Check the fridge." Angie waved her thumb toward her kitchen, although it was nearly as familiar to him as to her. "My mother—"

"What? You'll have to speak up a bit," Stan said, his back to her as he dashed toward the kitchen. "The foil, you know."

"My mother sent my sister Bianca over with a care package for me—some leftover cannelloni from a big dinner party. If you aren't interested in that, there's some yogurt. Or you can open a can of tuna, throw in some curry powder and sour cream, and—"

"No, no." Stan shuddered at the thought and pulled open the door of the refrigerator. "I have nothing against leftovers." As he stuck his head inside to check out the goodies, one of the pieces of foil hit the side and fell to the floor. He straightened up and reattached it. Then, squatting slightly, he continued his search for the cannelloni—pasta tubes filled with ricotta and Parmesan cheese, chunks of chicken, ground veal, and spices, then covered with a red sauce and teleme cheese—along with any other food that might find its way to his stomach. "I wonder if I dare use your microwave with this tinfoil?"

"I think you'll be fine as long as you don't

stick your head in it," Angie replied dryly. "Why are you wearing those things, anyway?"

"Headaches. I couldn't even go to work the other day because of them." Clearly deciding to brave the dangers of the microwave, he put the pasta in and set it on high for three minutes.

"So you're trying to prove your case for disability benefits, is that it? If you don't get them for physical, you will for mental." With the microwave oven on and the aluminum foil in his ears, he didn't seem to hear her.

He got himself a fork, a napkin, and a glass of red wine. He liked wine with Italian food.

She mixed a green salad with a simple olive oil, onion, garlic, oregano, and balsamic vinegar dressing for him and brought it and the wine out to the dining room table, closely followed by Stan, gingerly carrying the hot plate of food.

He sat down and took a big bite. "Delicious. You're a good cook, Angie, but your mother is really outstanding."

"Uh-huh." She'd heard that before. More times than she could count. It didn't do her attitude about Stan any good to hear him praise the food she'd been saving for her own dinner later that night.

Maybe this was God's way of telling her to start the diet she'd been thinking about ever since she and Paavo returned from a most peculiar cruise to Acapulco.

Although she had more important things to do than to pay attention to Stan, her curiosity got the better of her. "Why do you think tinfoil will stop a headache?" she asked, even while knowing the answer would probably make little sense.

"It blocks radio waves," he said.

As predicted. "Now, wait a minute. You think radio waves give you headaches?"

"I was listening to the radio, Art Bell's show. He was interviewing this scientist about the abduction of some lecturer. One of those millennium things, you know? Anyway, as the scientist was talking, he mentioned all the strange stuff that goes on in the world that we have no explanation for. The explanation, he said, is that it's all being controlled by aliens. They're working with the government. And one of the ways they control us is with radio waves. The more sensitive among us feel them and get headaches."

"And you're one of the more sensitive, I take it."

"I'm afraid so, Angie." He sighed under the weight of all that fragility. "I figured the tinfoil would work like a lightning rod, capturing the waves at the tips and destroying them. Clever of me, don't you think?"

"How do you know it doesn't work like an antenna—sending the waves right through you?"

"Well, if it did that, I'd be hearing programs in my head all day long. Can you imagine what I'd be like if the program was Howard Stern's?"

She couldn't stand it. "Stan, radio waves do

not give people headaches! It's all this new-millennium talk that's making people worry about the craziest things. Including aliens! Has the whole world gone completely psycho?" She tried to calm down. "Listen, if you're getting a lot of bad headaches, that could be serious. You need to find out why. The foil won't help."

"It's helped already," he said. A satisfied look filled his face as he polished off the cannelloni.

She had to change the subject before she smacked him. "You said those people on the radio were talking about a lecturer who was abducted. Has he reappeared yet?"

"Apparently not."

"How weird. Do you remember who was talking?"

"I'm not sure. Some guy. I think they said he was once some big astrophysicist. For NASA or something."

"Derrick Holton?" she asked, troubled by Stan's saying he was once an astrophysicist and not still one.

"I don't remember. Look at it this way, Angie: If a guy like that takes this stuff seriously, there's got to be something to it. Hey, that isn't the guy you went out with the other night, is it?"

"It is. I was there when the lecturer disappeared."

"No shit!" he murmured, staring at her as if she'd turned green with bulging black eyes and little antennae sprouting from her forehead.

She nodded.

"It's dangerous hanging around people like that. Very dangerous." He jumped to his feet. "Sorry to eat and run. I just thought of some important stuff I've got to do tonight. Thanks for the dinner." He dashed out the door so fast he didn't even grab a chocolate-covered macaroon. That meant he was truly upset.

Much as she hated to admit it, Stan might have been right. Derrick and his friends were strange. Could they be dangerous, too? She had thought she knew and could trust Derrick, but now she wasn't so sure.

She particularly didn't want Connie to get more involved in any of this. Connie had been a little too intrigued by Derrick and Algernon both.

She and Connie needed to have a heart-to-heart.

She picked up the phone and called Everyone's Fancy. Lyssa answered. "Connie's gone," she replied to Angie's question.

"Gone? Where has she gone?"

"To buy a new dress. She's going to some meeting tonight and she wants to look good."

"What meeting?"

"I'm not sure. I think she said something about UFOs. I didn't listen. It sounded, like, far out there, you know?"

Angie hung up. What had she gotten Connie into?

14

After someone leaked a report to the *San Francisco Chronicle* on the mutilated body found at the Giants' new stadium, causing more than a little paranoia in an already nervous city, calls about missing persons began.

The homicide inspectors were always amazed at the number of people who had gone missing but whose disappearance had never been reported to the Missing Persons Bureau. People didn't want to hassle with answering all the questions missing-persons inspectors asked, but they were willing to call and ask if the murder victim fit the description of their missing loved one—or not-so-loved one.

Paavo and Yosh followed up on each call, but none matched the victim. They had to wait until a fingerprint ID came in. When it did, it provided a name, Felix Rolfe, but nothing more except that he'd been given a dishonorable discharge from the army.

When people drop off the face of the earth that way, there's usually a good explanation. At the city's social services agency, they found it. Rolfe was a drifter who lived on Supplemental Security Income disability. He'd drifted all through the Southwest and finally came to California, where the weather was milder and the SSI state supplement more generous. Most of his SSI money went to drugs and alcohol, which contributed to the liver disease that gave him the SSI disability, which allowed him to continue with his drug and alcohol habit. The consensus was that all in all, if he hadn't been murdered, he wouldn't have lived much longer anyway.

The only address on record was his mother's— a rooming house on Third Street. As Paavo knocked on the door to her room, he braced himself to deal with a distraught mother. He should have saved himself the trouble.

He sat on a wooden chair with plaid-covered foam rubber cushions on the seat and back. Maureen Rolfe sat on the bed. She was an enormous woman with gray hair cut ragged below her ears. Huge thighs forced her knees wide apart and caused the skirt of her worn blue dress to ride up too high. Black socks and men's shoes adorned her feet, and she smoked the butt of a stogie.

"Felix's killer carved the number five on his chest. Does that number mean anything to you?" Paavo asked after a short talk during which he gave his condolences for Rolfe's untimely death. She shrugged them off.

She sucked on the cigar. "Number five? Why'd anyone want to cut up Fe?"

"That's what we're trying to find out. Did five have any significance you can think of?"

"Nope."

"Where did he live?" The fact that Bertram Lambert lived on Seventh Avenue and the number 7 had been carved on his chest hadn't been lost on Paavo.

"On the streets."

When he asked where she would have looked for him had she needed to find him, she spit into an old coffee can and asked what it was worth to him.

Ten dollars got him the answer: the Giants' new ballpark. Felix Rolfe had found it a good place to panhandle.

"Beware the new millennium!" Oliver Hardy cried to the people passing Tardis Hall. He waved his UFO brochures. "Join us as we seek the safety of a new world. Learn what the government isn't telling you: The end is near!"

A gray-haired African-American man strode by, looking at the hall as he went.

"This is for you, brother," Hardy cried, holding out a brochure.

The man gave Hardy a look of disdain. "I'm no brother of yours unless a miracle happened."

Hardy forced a chuckle. "You pay attention to things of no importance, like the color of skin, when soon our differences will be nothing in the face of the enemy of all humankind. We will be side by side, and we will be brothers. Believe me. It's all here, in this flyer." He waggled the brochure about Roswell. "And you just might win a hundred dollars, besides." He pointed to the sign.

NEW MEMBERS! FREE DRAWINGS!
$100 TO THE LUCKY WINNER! JOIN TODAY!

The man studied the brochure a moment. "Does your group also talk about other things? Area Fifty-one, for instance?"

"Absolutely. Join us. It costs nothing, and even if you never come to a meeting, this is a chance to win a hundred dollars."

The man's brow furrowed as he looked from the brochure to Hardy. "Why not?" He picked up the Bic on the table and filled out a card for the drawing.

Hardy glanced at the address, phone number, and name—Leon Cole.

He smiled. The spirit was truly with him on this day.

"I think you have a wonderful chance of winning, Mr. Cole," he said. "This phone number is good to reach you at, right?"

"You call and tell me I've won, and I'll make any damn phone number you want be the right one."

* * *

The first thing Angie noticed as she entered Tardis Hall was a table with food and beverages spread out on it. Paper cups were next to a punch bowl with lemonade, and platters of thin pretzel sticks and goldfish-shaped crackers were offered. Angie couldn't imagine serving anything so uncreative. If this was the kind of catering a UFO group was used to, she wouldn't have to work hard at all to win praise for the party she was planning for Triana. If she went through with it.

"Hey there! You're back," Elvis said. "This is Phil." He gestured toward the man beside him. "Phil, Angie's a friend of Derrick's."

Still wearing love beads and sandals, his hair long and frizzy, and now with goldfish-cracker crumbs sprinkling his beard, Phil wiped a hand against his jeans, then held it out to shake hers while mumbling something that she guessed was a greeting.

"Nice to meet you," she said, then to Elvis, "Is Derrick here yet? Or my friend Connie?"

"I guess she didn't come back for my company," Elvis said with mock dejection to Phil. "I haven't seen Derrick yet, or Connie. Derrick's supposed to be here. Maybe they're together."

"That's just what I was thinking," Angie said, looking around. There wasn't a large enough crowd there for Connie to be lost in it. No wonder Algernon was so derisive of NAUTS—unless his crowds weren't any larger.

"I'd have noticed if some attractive babe had gone through here, man," Phil said, his words wispy and languid. "Could Derrick be hiding her? Keeping her to himself?"

"I don't think so," Elvis said.

"Maybe she hasn't arrived yet." Angie wasn't sure what to do. "I just want to make sure she's all right—and that Derrick is as well. He was troubled last time I saw him."

"That's his natural state," Phil said with a lazy smile. "He got what he wanted now that Mosshad's out of the way. All the glory. All the women."

"He's not out for glory, Phil," Elvis said.

"No? You could have fooled me, man. Who was here when the Prometheans started? Me, not him. Who knew Neumann personally and worked with him? Me, not Holton."

"Neumann?" Angie asked.

"He was the founder of the Prometheans," Elvis explained. "NAUTS broke off from the Prometheus Group after Neumann died."

"After he was killed, you mean," Phil said, his flat eyes boring into Angie. "The government killed him. Just like they did my buddies in 'Nam. Just like they probably killed Mosshad."

"No one knows the government killed anybody," Elvis said to Angie. She was growing increasingly alarmed by Phil's words, not because she believed them, but because Phil so obviously did. Elvis turned to Phil. "Who said Mosshad is dead? He's apparently hiding out somewhere. He'll show up."

"He's dead." Phil's eyes shifted. "All the good ones are. Algernon or Holton—which will die, and which will live? They'll see to it that the good one dies. They always do. From the time of JFK. It's always that way." His dark gaze met Angie's. "Trust nobody. Especially not Algernon." He glanced at Elvis. "Maybe not even our own leader. Not even Holton."

He walked away.

"Don't worry about him," Elvis said. "He's an example of better living through chemistry. Don't listen to anything he says."

"Is it true Mosshad is still missing, though?" Angie asked.

"Derrick knows what he's doing," Elvis said.

Derrick?

"Hello." Oliver Hardy joined the group. His gaze shifted nervously from Elvis to Angie. He flicked his daisy-patterned tie. "I don't know if you remember me."

"Of course I do, Oliver," she said.

"Who wouldn't?" Elvis said. "I'll see if I can find Derrick and your friend for you," he said to Angie before he walked away.

Angie turned to Oliver. She was alone with him again, and something about him, frankly, made her nervous. She scanned the small group once more for Connie.

"I guess you and Derrick are an item?" Oliver asked, stepping closer.

"We're not." Her tone was curt. "I knew him a few years ago."

"That doesn't mean you can't go out with him now!" He sounded almost angry.

"I'm seeing someone else." She clamped her mouth shut as if to say, *End of story*.

Instead he twisted his head from side to side. "Not that I'd notice. If you were my girlfriend, I'd be with you."

Fat chance. "I'm afraid he's busy. He's a homicide inspector," she said pointedly. "He's investigating those mutilation murders."

Oliver's eyes widened. "Mutilation murders?"

Sheesh, as if the whole city isn't talking about them. "The ones on the front page of the paper."

"I don't read the news. It's too depressing. Especially horrible murders of young women. I keep away from them. I'm too sensitive for this world, I'm afraid."

She seemed to be hearing a lot about sensitive males these days. "They aren't young women, they're men."

His face turned milky white. "Men? Are you sure?"

"That's what the papers say. I don't know the second one's name—but I'm sure it was a man found at the Giants' stadium. The first one, though, had a name easy to remember— Bertram Lambert—sort of singsongy, don't you think?"

She stopped speaking. Oliver had gone from pale to green and now looked as if he was going to be ill. "What's wrong?"

"N-Nothing."

"Did you know Mr. Lambert?"

"Me? No. Never heard of him. Not at all. You said these men were mutilated, but not like cattle mutilations, right?"

Her head began to spin. "Cattle mutilations? Whatever are you talking about?"

"Uh, nothing. Go on."

She didn't want to talk any more to him about this or anything else. "Paavo won't give me the details, and they've been kept out of the paper. All I know is, the mutilations were quite horrible. I can't tell you anything more than that."

"Oh my." He pressed his hand to his stomach. "Excuse me, please. I told you things like that upset me. That's why I don't read or listen to the news anymore."

He turned and rushed away from her, practically stumbling his way into the auditorium. She supposed he was either going to sit down and calm himself or continue through the auditorium to the backstage area, where Derrick and some of the others might be.

The doors were already open, so people could take their seats. She checked her watch—not that it did much good in Time-Stands-Still Hall. After her first visit to this place, she'd had to buy a new watch battery. She still didn't see Derrick or Connie. Where were they? Since they'd probably show up for the lecture, she entered the auditorium. Although she hadn't wanted to listen to more weird alien talk, she didn't want to abandon Connie to the tender mercies of this strange crowd. Connie was too vulnerable now, being divorced and alone, with the holidays approaching. Angie watched out for her friends.

No sooner had she sat down in the back row of the auditorium than a familiar face appeared. "Hello, Malachi," she said to the gaunt, bearded man she'd met at her first visit to Tardis Hall. He was again dressed in a black turtleneck and black slacks. "Are you here to see another abduction?"

"Absolutely." He gave her a wink. "I haven't had so much fun in years." She laughed. She had no idea if he took the abduction seriously or not, but he was having a good time with it no matter what.

"But why are you here again?" he asked. "Surely you have better things to do than to spend time with people who have so much trouble dealing with this world they search for a better one in the stars."

She was surprised to hear him say that. "You're being a little unfair. These are simply people with an overblown imagination."

He grinned. "I stand corrected . . . somewhat."

She was starting to like him. "Last time we talked you told me about the rift between Derrick and Algernon. I met Algernon. What a piece of work."

Malachi chuckled. "Algernon is all show. He

wouldn't know a flying saucer from a turnip. And frankly, I believe he's more interested in women than in any EBE, which isn't to say an alien chick would be safe around him. Why do you care about Algernon? You surely don't want to join the Prometheans, do you?"

She felt a little peculiar telling a stranger something she hadn't yet told Paavo. On the other hand, she wouldn't care if Malachi learned her business idea was a failure. She would care if Paavo found that out. "I've been asked to cater a theme party for Algernon's book launch. Since I have a new business, I wanted to do it right. The right theme, the right food. But with this Algernon, I just don't know. . . ."

"Well, I'll tell you, you won't go wrong with these people if you use the crash at Roswell as your theme. Everyone is fascinated by it . . . and by what happened after the crash."

"After?" she asked. She hadn't yet heard a word about after the crash. From the corner of her eye she saw Derrick step up to the microphone. Where was Connie?

Malachi smiled secretively. "Just think of the sudden blossoming of technology in our society—the rudimentary things we had before World War Two, and how, a very few years after, we're in a computer and technological age unimaginable just sixty years ago." As Derrick began to speak, Malachi dropped his voice to a whisper. "Fiber optics, integrated circuits, lasers,

even Saran Wrap—they all had to do with
Roswell."

Angie wanted to ask more, especially about
Saran Wrap, but the speaker was introduced to
some applause, and he immediately began his
lecture. Derrick stepped backstage instead of
joining the audience. Angie wondered if Connie was back there, too.

The speaker had a high, thin voice that rose
and fell as he spoke, making his words a bit hard
to follow. He showed slides of Mars and spoke of
how a replica of a human face had been built by
ancient aliens who used it to remind those who
ventured to Earth of their true home. The face
was on the Cydonia region of Mars. Space mis-
sions did their best to avoid that region because
the U.S. government thought it would cause
panic and religious chaos if people saw buildings on another planet.

In 1998, NASA photos showing the face to be
nothing but rock formations were proven false.
They were doctored photos of another part of
Mars, not the Cydonia region at all. It was more
lies from the government, the speaker said.

Angie wondered how, if no clear photos
existed, people knew the face on Mars had been
manufactured and was anything other than a
bunch of rock formations.

But the speaker never explained, and no one
ever asked. She was tempted to ask the question
herself, except that she was there to observe,
not to question. And anyway, after the speaker's

boring speech, she was having trouble simply staying awake. As soon as there was a break, she'd go backstage and look for Connie and Derrick herself.

Turning off the lights once again, the speaker showed more slides, droning on and on about the beings who built the face, how intelligent they were, and where they were now. No one knew the exact answer to the last issue, she discovered, but they knew the beings were near because they were constantly coming down to Earth and abducting people. She yawned, gave up the fight, and closed her eyes.

Before long, someone was shaking her arm. She hadn't realized her eyes were shut, but she opened them to find Derrick beside her. "It's over," he said.

She saw that people were putting on coats and leaving the hall. She rubbed her eyes. She must have been really tired to sleep so soundly. But then, maybe everyone had been lulled into quietly leaving. Like Malachi must have done. Derrick now sat in his chair.

She gathered her things. "I'm sorry. I didn't mean to fall asleep this way. How embarrassing!"

He jumped to his feet. "Nothing you do could possibly be an embarrassment, Angelina. In fact, I'm flattered you came to see me." He ran his fingers through his hair, rumpling it as he twisted this way and that looking over the rapidly emptying lecture hall. "Tell you what— why don't we go out for coffee after I close up the auditorium? Looks like you could use a cup. Then we could talk."

"That would be great." She glanced around. "Where's Connie?"

"Connie? I don't know. I haven't seen her. Let's go backstage." He grabbed her arm and started pulling her along with him. "It'll only take me about ten minutes to shut down the place, then we'll get out of here."

Angie walked onto the stage, and Derrick pushed the curtain aside, revealing an enormous backstage area. She'd forgotten that Tardis Hall had originally been built as a warehouse and was immense. Only a small portion of it—the entrance area, the auditorium, and the stage area—had been finished off and painted.

Backstage looked like a warren of rooms and hallways. Metal staircases led to upper and lower floors, and a side elevator had the wide-doored look of those that carry freight.

In all, backstage was a dark, unfriendly place.

Derrick led her to a chair to wait for him, then darted off. She pulled out her cell phone and punched in Connie's number.

"Hello," Connie answered.

"Hello?" Angie shrieked. "You sit there and say hello? What are you doing at home? Lyssa told me you'd be at Tardis Hall, so I'm here waiting for you!"

"Why are you doing that?" Connie asked. "I went to buy a new outfit first, but everything made me look fat. So I decided to starve for a couple of days before seeing Derrick again. No more tiramisu for me. So, what's up?"

Angie realized that now was not the time to discuss her concerns about Derrick. Besides, she might be overreacting. Sometimes she did that.

"I wasn't looking for you for any special reason," she said. "Paavo was busy tonight with those mutilation murder cases, and I didn't want to stay home. Oh, here comes Elvis. I'll talk to you tomorrow." She hung up.

Elvis, then Kronos, Phil, and finally Derrick joined her.

"We've just got to wait for Oliver to get back." Derrick paced back and forth like a caged tiger as he spoke to Angie and the others. "What's he up to, anyway? I didn't see him as I locked up."

"I didn't see him, either," Elvis said, sitting down, his hands primly folded on his lap.

"Shee-it!" Phil yelled, sprawled over a chair. "Don't tell me we've got another missing person. Man, I hate this spooky jive-ass stuff."

"Has Mosshad been heard from yet?" Elvis asked thoughtfully.

"Sir Oliver is not missing," Kronos said, holding a broom upright as if it were a shepherd's staff. "He is probably lying fast asleep somewhere. I should think the face-on-Mars controversy was not sufficiently stimulating to keep him awake. It has been going on since the early seventies of the twentieth century. I nearly fell asleep on the projector."

"I did fall asleep," Angie confessed. "Maybe Oliver went home?"

"Not without telling us. Let's call him to wake him up."

They all walked around yelling his name. The way "Oliver" reverberated through the former warehouse gave Angie chills.

"I'm getting nervous," she said to Derrick. "Do your friends often go missing this way?" She couldn't imagine anyone with Oliver's girth and odd looks not having his every move noticed by someone.

"They never have before." He rubbed his hair, making it even more askew. "I'm going to look around some more. He might be asleep—maybe hurt. I don't know why he didn't hear when we called him."

"I hope he wasn't abducted, too," Elvis said. He and Phil went in a different direction than Derrick.

"I had better lend my assistance as well," Kronos said, and walked away.

Oliver couldn't seriously have disappeared, Angie thought. He had been quite upset by the mutilation murders, though, so maybe he had gone home. She wished she had mentioned that to the others. *Well,* she thought, *they should be back soon. Maybe with Oliver, in fact.* If not, she'd tell them about it.

She poked around here and there herself. Considering how big the warehouse was, if Oliver had wandered off very far and either fell asleep or got hurt, it could take a long time to find him. She went to the open stairway. The stairs seemed to go up four floors and down one. The only lights were a few emergency lights around the stairs itself, to prevent accidents. She shuddered. The big building was empty and, according to Triana, would be destroyed soon to make way for redevelopment. The thought of wandering around in it looking for someone gave her a creepy feeling.

She hurried away from the stairs. Not sure what else to do, she opened a nearby door, turned on the lights, and looked inside.

It was an empty storeroom. She stepped out again and shut the door. She would ask Derrick if anyone had checked to see if Oliver's car was gone. If Oliver had a car, that is. When she looked around, she no longer saw Derrick or his friends. She was alone. She couldn't even hear their footsteps. No wonder, in a building that large.

She returned to the backstage area where they'd met earlier. She looked high overhead, where great coils of rope controlled the scenery and curtains. She looked into the dark corners, where more ropes and boxes lurked in the shadows.

It was certainly quiet in there. She wished someone would come back. They wouldn't have all gone home and left her there, would they? They weren't pranksters, she hoped. On the other hand, where were they?

The backstage lights were still on. They were still searching for Oliver, that was all. Nothing to get alarmed about.

Unless . . . like Mosshad . . . they had all been . . .

No! No one had been abducted by aliens! Not them, and certainly not Mosshad. Or Oliver. She was appalled that the thought had even crossed her mind. The bizarre beliefs of these people were more infectious than she had imagined.

Should she search for them? She walked over to the stage curtain and drew it back. The auditorium was a massive, pitch-black cavern.

She dropped the curtain and turned around. Still no one had returned. No footsteps. No voices.

To leave that area would be foolhardy. She didn't know her way around the hall. What if she got lost or hurt, stumbling around out there alone? The men would be back. They wouldn't leave her. She hoped.

She wandered around the backstage area, listening for their return.

Rest room doors, for men and women, were on one side of the area near the dressing rooms. Maybe she should quickly use the facilities while waiting for Derrick.

She went to the ladies' room and opened the door. The room was dark, but a light switch was right next to the entry. She flipped it up.

The light came on, showing an old bathroom with two stalls and a single sink with a mirror over it. The stall doors were slightly ajar, as if someone had pulled them shut, but not all the way.

A pool of red liquid lay in a puddle in the center of the bathroom floor. As she stepped closer, a smell, acrid but familiar, hit her. She stared at the liquid, a mounting horror stealing over her. A drop fell into the pool.

A drop of blood. Coming from . . .

Afraid, yet at the same time unable to stop herself, she raised her eyes to the ceiling.

A glass skylight was overhead. Splayed against it, his face pressed hard against the cracked glass as blood oozed from his mouth and nose, his eyes open and unfocused with the look of death, was Oliver Hardy.

15

"God, that was awful!" Paavo said, dropping into his desk chair.

"Hey, pal," Yosh said. "You look beat. What happened?"

"Angie has to be out of her mind to like going downtown to shop. I just grabbed a sandwich for dinner and thought I'd run into Nordstrom's to pick up a Christmas present for her. It was packed, so I went to Macy's. That was worse."

"Just some sweet little lady shoppers," Yosh said before he broke into a heartfelt rendition of "Silver Bells."

"I was pushed, shoved, and stepped on. Even kicked. The only clerks who'd pay attention to me were the ones who wanted to spray me with perfume." Frowning, Paavo lifted his lapel, sniffed it, then swore as he took off the jacket and hung it on the back of the chair.

"Where's your Christmas spirit?" Yosh said with a chuckle.

"Hah! I've got a whole new respect for the Grinch."

Yosh got up and poured them both a cup of black coffee from the bureau's pot. "What did you want to buy?" He put Paavo's cup on his desk.

"Thanks." Paavo took a sip. He couldn't remember the last time he'd been so miserable. "Nothing. I still don't know what to get her."

Yosh nodded with great commiseration. "I see your problem."

Just then the telephone rang. No one else was in Homicide that night besides the two of them, working on the mutilation murders. Yosh answered the phone, then, hand over the mouthpiece, he glanced at his partner. "Speak of the devil."

Paavo had scarcely gotten out a hello when Angie's words tumbled over the wire, loud and excited. "Paavo, come quick. There's a dead body. And I found him. I thought they'd send you to investigate, but instead they sent some bossy blonde and some spooky guy who stands on the sidelines and twitches! They're dreadful! We need you here."

He jumped to his feet, gripping the phone tighter. Angie with a dead body? Her words made little sense—except for her description of homicide inspectors Rebecca Mayfield and Bill Never-Take-a-Chance Sutter, that night's on-call homicide team. "Where are you?"

"Tardis Hall—foot of Brannan."

"I don't believe it!" He spun around and nearly pulled the cord out of the phone. "You went there again? At this time of night?"

"I . . . Connie . . . well, I came to another lecture." Her voice was small. "Afterward, Oliver Hardy disappeared. That's not his real name, but I can't remember what his real name is. Everyone else went to look for him, except me. I went to the bathroom. And there he was! You need to come find out what's going on here."

"Slow down. You found a body." He glanced up to see that Yosh was now also standing, a concerned expression on his face. "Did it look like an accident? Or, I should say, was there anything that made you think it might not have been a natural death?"

"You could say that. He was lying on a skylight. Outside the building, on a skylight. And he'd hit with enough force to crack it."

"Damn! Angie, listen to me. You keep away from everyone there but Inspector Mayfield. Understand? Inspector Rebecca Mayfield. She knows what she's doing."

"Seems to me she's doing a terrible job."

"Angie!" He stopped himself, sucking in his breath as he ran his free hand through his hair. In a moment he was a little calmer. "Just do what I say. Stick to Mayfield. I'll be there as fast as I can."

He hung up the phone and grabbed his jacket, struggling to shove his arm through the sleeve while he talked to Yosh. "Angie's with some UFO nuts in a converted warehouse down on Brannan. Near the waterfront. One of them was found flattened on the roof—on a skylight. I've got to make sure she's all right."

"She does know how to get in the thick of things, doesn't she?" Yosh said, putting down his report and twisting the cap onto his pen.

"No need for you to come along." Paavo flipped his jacket collar down, checked his gun, and patted his pockets for his ID and keys. "Mayfield and Sutter are already at the scene. These mutilation murders need all your attention. Checking on Angie will be the extent of my involvement."

"I'll believe that when I see it," Yosh said. Then he chuckled. "Landed on a skylight, you said? Sounds like the guy might have been tossed out of a spaceship."

Paavo stopped his old Austin Healey in the tow-away zone, got out, and headed for Tardis Hall. There wasn't anything for him to feel so frantic about. No reason to think Angie could be in danger—in one of the highest-crime areas of the city, possibly with a murderer in the building or lurking nearby.

He shoved the doors open, flashed his badge at the patrol officer guarding it, and sighed with relief when he saw Angie running toward him, arms waving. Behind her, open doors led to a large auditorium. All the lights were on.

"Paavo, thank God you're here!" she cried as she ran into his embrace. "You can't imagine how dreadful this has been! There was so much blood. And his eyes!"

He held her tight until her babbling and trembling stopped, then put her at arm's length to see if she'd been hurt in any way. "Are you all right?" he asked. She nodded, but wore a pinched, fearful look. He wrapped her in his arms again.

Rebecca Mayfield, the only woman in Homicide, walked up to them. She was tall and graceful, with thick, shoulder-length blond hair. "What took you so long?" she asked Paavo. She wore a dark brown pants suit and now stood with one hand on her hip.

"You knew I was coming?"

Mayfield gave Angie a glance, then sniffed. "I had no doubt about it, Inspector, since you know one of our prime suspects."

All the blood drained from Angie's face. She spun toward Mayfield. "Your what?" Her words were strangled.

"She's joking, Angie," Paavo said, shooting Mayfield an icy glare.

Mayfield folded her arms. "The person who finds the body is always a prime suspect," she said matter-of-factly. "That's one of the first lessons in homicide investigation. You know that, Paavo."

Before he had a chance to respond, Angie blurted out, "That is the most blatantly foolish—"

He took her arm and drew her away, furious with Mayfield's antics. "Let's go."

Mayfield smirked.

Paavo hurried Angie into the auditorium. The stage lights were lit, the curtains open, and the scenery drops lifted. In the backstage area, several patrol officers stood guard and crime scene tape had been hung. A patrolman directed Paavo to the side room where a group had gathered.

Instead of taking Angie into the room with the others, he stopped at one of the seats in the auditorium. "Wait here. I want to talk to Mayfield and Sutter to find out what we're dealing with."

She nodded.

As soon as she was seated, he left her to get a feel for Tardis Hall, for the area not cordoned off by yellow tape. The building was huge. Apart from the part that had been turned into a lecture hall, the rest of it was a warehouse with open space in the center and little storage rooms on the sides. The crime scene technicians had just arrived and were laying out their equipment.

"Paavo!" The assistant coroner, Evelyn Ramirez, walked up to him. Even at this time of night, every hair was in place, her makeup flawless. "At least tonight I'm able to work indoors, not like the last two cases you called me out on."

"This isn't my case, Doc," he said. "I just decided to drop in."

She drew a deep breath. "It's not another one, is it?"

Paavo was surprised to see the tough lady coroner squeamish about the thought of facing another mutilated body. "It isn't. From what I've been told, this one was only splattered all over a skylight in the bathroom," he added with heavy sarcasm.

"And me without a ladder." She shook her head as she followed the patrolman toward the body.

Paavo watched them go. He really shouldn't follow, since it wasn't his case and he knew how furious he got when other inspectors trampled through his crime scene out of curiosity. Not being able to see the crime galled nonetheless. He turned and studied the four men seated in the side room. All of them, whether they knew it or not, were suspects. One by one, each would give Mayfield and Sutter the particulars about who they were, where they lived and worked, and why they were there.

Four people.

Paavo walked closer to them. One looked like a thirty-something college professor, lacking only suede patches on the elbows of his corduroy sports jacket. One had long, stringy blond hair pulled back in a ponytail; his clothes looked even dirtier than his hair. Another either had done drugs and free love in his youth or was making up for lost time with his frizzy gray hair, love beads, and sandals. The last could have been a choirboy—white shirt, light gray slacks, and solid blue tie.

The college professor type stood up and called out to him. "You seem to be a friend of Angelina's."

"Yes," Paavo said cautiously. Was that line an attempt on a suspect's part to ingratiate himself, or what?

The man approached, rubbing his hands nervously. "With the police, are you?"

Paavo flipped open his badge, watching the man's every move. "Smith, Homicide."

The man read it over. "I'm Derrick Holton, president of the club that put on the lecture tonight," he said, holding out his hand. Paavo shook it. "Angelina's a great woman." Holton spoke quickly, his eyes nervously darting from side to side. "We're old friends, you know."

"Is that so?" Paavo said.

"Ah yes! Good friends." Holton smiled again and looked back at Inspector Mayfield, who was talking to the grubby blond fellow. His smile disappeared as quickly as it showed up when he again faced Paavo. "That's why she came here tonight. To see me." He was growing breathless. "She's interested in UFOs, you know."

Paavo's expression grew shuttered. "I didn't know that."

Derrick gave a high-pitched chuckle. "That was why she called me. Because of my background in the field." He leaned forward. "So, since we're all friends of Angelina's, maybe you can get them to cut us some slack, you know? It's not as if any one of us would hurt Oliver. They're saying they might keep us here for hours. This . . . this isn't a great place to be this late at night. Can you do anything to speed things up? Even though I'm president, I would have left early. It's not as if I cared to listen to a lecture about the face on Mars! I stayed to keep Angelina company."

Paavo took out his notebook, not trusting himself to speak right then, and made an annotation. He put it back into his pocket. "So you know Miss Amalfi pretty well, do you?"

Holton's smile broadened even more. He slid his hands in his front pockets and teetered back on his heels. "You could say that. We were close. Nearly got married."

Paavo's jaw grew so tight he could barely pry his lips apart to speak. "Really?"

"Yes." Holton nodded, his thoughts turning inward and a secret smile forming on his lips. Paavo resisted the urge to ram his fist in the man's face. "She was too young, though," Holton finally announced. "She had things to do. She went off and lived in Paris for a while, traveled. I've never been far away, though. I promised to wait for her, and I did. Never really met anyone else quite like Angelina. Now I just need to convince her the time is right for our wedding. Why wait?"

"Why indeed?"

"I can always call her old man and enlist his

support now that Angelina and I are seeing each other again."

A chill raced through Paavo's veins. "Her father approves of you?" He didn't need to ask. He was being masochistic—he could tell from Holton's words what the answer would be. Sal Amalfi had always made it clear he thought a cop wasn't good enough for his daughter.

"Her father and I"—Holton pressed two fingers close together—"are just like that."

"You live and work in the city, I take it?"

"I'm on sabbatical right now. Say, can't we talk tomorrow? Can't you tell them to release us?"

"You're on sabbatical—are you a teacher?"

Holton frowned impatiently. "Not exactly. An astrophysicist. I was with NASA." He gave a smile probably meant to look self-deprecating. In fact, it looked anything but. "I guess I should have introduced myself more properly as Dr. Derrick Holton. I have a Ph.D."

"Right." He coughed. "And now that Miss Amalfi's interested in UFOs, she called you."

"That's right—for her new job."

Christ! What else hadn't she told him? "Her new job?" He struggled to keep his tone light and casual.

Holton smiled and shook his head. "Sorry. I was beating myself up over there when I first saw you and Angelina together. I assumed there might be something between you two. I see I was wrong." He looked up. "Thank you, Lord. Angelina has a job catering dinner parties for rich clients. It's fun and she enjoys it. I would have thought she would have told more people about it, but I guess she's only telling those she's close to."

"Like you?"

"Yeah. Me. Connie. Earl at the restaurant."

"You've been to Wings of an Angel?"

"Sure. It's one of Angelina's favorite spots."

"So I've heard." Paavo took a long, hard look at the man in front of him. "That's all very interesting, Mr. Holton."

"Yes, I thought you'd agree."

"I do. But it doesn't have anything to do with the reason we're here tonight, does it?"

Holton's eyes widened. "Not directly, but I wanted to explain my character, my friends, my—"

"Your whereabouts, Dr. Holton? I'm interested in your whereabouts this evening, specifically from the time Oliver Hardy was last seen alive up until Miss Amalfi found his body."

Holton stiffened. "Surely you aren't implying that I . . ." He didn't continue.

Paavo's voice was cold. "I'm not implying anything, Holton. Inspector Mayfield will be questioning you soon."

Holton's mouth dropped open and he visibly shuddered.

Paavo turned away and went to Angie.

She stood up, alarmed at his frown. "Paavo, what's wrong?"

"Put your coat on. We're leaving."

Mayfield came running over to him. "Did I hear you say you're leaving? You can't take my witness until I say so."

"Have you gotten her statement?"

"A preliminary one, yes," Rebecca said.

"Then you know where to find her if you want more information later. And check out Holton real close. I don't like his attitude."

He grabbed Angie's arm and nearly lifted her from her shoes as he rushed her out the door.

Paavo followed Angie to her house, she in her Testarossa, he in his ancient Austin Healey. It was lucky that in San Francisco air-conditioning and powerful heaters weren't absolutely essential in cars, because his had never had air and his heater was so weak as to be almost useless. The cost to upgrade was at least double what the car was worth.

He followed her to the tenants' parking garage and took the spot that would have belonged to her neighbor, Stan, if Stan had a car.

They rode up in the elevator in silence. Paavo was too angry to talk, despite Angie's attempts at pleasantries.

She unlocked the door to her apartment. As soon as they stepped inside, she faced him.

"Why are you so upset with me?" she asked innocently.

"What the hell's going on, Angie?"

"With Oliver Hardy's death?" she asked.

"With you," he bellowed.

She took off her coat and opened the closet door to hang it up. "I have no idea what you're talking about."

"Your old fiancé tells me he's seeing you again and wants to marry you—with your father's blessing—and you ask me what I'm talking about?"

She paled, her coat in one hand, a hanger in the other. "Derrick said that?"

"That's not all he said." Paavo strode toward her, one hand against the wall next to the closet. She backed up and bumped into a row of coats and jackets.

"He said you've gotten a new business, that he's met Earl and eaten at Wings of an Angel, that you're seeing him."

She spun around and hung up her coat. "It's not the way he made it sound." Her words were so soft he had to lean closer to hear her.

"If I thought it was, I wouldn't be here." He wanted to touch her, to hold her and have her say everything was fine, but he couldn't allow himself that easy way out. "Why didn't you tell me about any of this? Your business . . . UFOs . . . Holton."

He was too close. She put her hand against his shoulder so she could pass by him and go to the center of the room, where she could breathe. He stepped aside, willingly giving way to her.

She stood with her back to him, her hands clasped at her waist. "I was afraid you'd laugh at me."

A long time passed. When he spoke, his voice was a whisper. "When have I ever laughed at you, Angie?"

His words cut through her. Tears stung her eyes and she looked down at her hands until she was able to speak again. "I came up with an idea for a fun business. I would arrange dinner parties based on a theme. Fantasy Dinners, I called it. Unfortunately, I only received one offer. Well, one legitimate offer, I should say. The very first offer I got, I threw away and forgot about. Some guy called and asked if the fantasy could involve fishnet stockings and Frederick's of Hollywood."

Paavo took her arm and turned her so that she faced him. His lips were tightly pursed.

"The only real response I received," she continued, "was from a wealthy society woman named Triana Crisswell. I wanted to be sure the business made sense before I told you or my family about it. There was just one problem. I had to learn about UFOs to develop the fantasy."

He nodded.

"That was why I called Derrick. That's all there was to it. Now, suddenly, Algernon's small dinner party has grown to three hundred people, one man's disappeared, another is dead, Derrick sees aliens, and you're mad at me." She couldn't hold back any longer. She started to cry.

He could endure almost anything—seeing dead bodies, the day-to-day tedium of paperwork, the emptiness of his home—but he could never endure Angie's tears. "Don't cry," he said, placing his hands on her shoulders.

Her tears made her even angrier—at herself for crying and at him for causing her to. "Do you think I care so little about you I'm calling up old boyfriends to see if they're any better the second time around? I could have been married ten times over. But I never met anyone I wanted to spend my life with until—" Her tear-streaked face lifted. "Until recently."

"Angie, stop."

"I want you to be proud of me, damn it! But no matter what I do, I screw it up. I thought, this time I won't tell you about it unless it's a success. If so, I'd spring it on you. If not, you'd never hear a word about it." She tried to turn away, but he stopped her.

"I am proud of you," he said. "Proud of the warm, generous, loving person you are. I don't give a damn about your business success or lack of it, Angie. Some of the most successful businessmen and women around are the worst assholes you could imagine." He put his hand on her chin and lifted it. "I don't care how successful you are, or aren't. I want to be with you." He wiped a tear from her cheeks with his thumb and lightly kissed her. "Don't hide what you're up to from me. Not ever."

He handed her his handkerchief to wipe her tears. She put her head against his shoulder, then looked up at him. "You smell like a

woman's perfume factory. Am I questioning you
about it? No, I trust you."

"I trust you, too, Angie. You know that." He
stroked her cheek. "It's Holton I don't trust.
And the perfume was thanks to a few overzeal-
ous salesclerks."

She perked up. "Oh? Were you in some
department stores or something like that? Was it
for work . . . or some other reason?"

"It's nearly Christmas, after all."

She tried to hide her excitement at the
thought of him walking around department
stores looking for presents. She had to be one of
the ones he was shopping for. Maybe the only
one he was shopping for. He and his buddies
weren't exactly the exchange-presents types. But
she was. The thought of her big, scowling detective stomping around a department store trying
to come up with something to buy her brought
a smile to her lips and warmth to her heart. "Yes,
it is nearly Christmas. We'll have our own celebration here Christmas Eve, okay?"

"Okay," he said, "if you promise me one
thing."

Her smile disappeared. "What's that?"

"Promise that you'll never keep secrets from
me. Promise that you'll never believe I'd laugh
at you about anything."

The intensity of his words, the realization of
how she had hurt him, nearly made her cry again.
"I can do that," she whispered. "I promise."

16

"How's the investigation going, Rebecca?" Paavo asked as he took the chair beside Inspector Mayfield's desk.

She looked over at him and smiled. "Well, hello." The other inspectors loved to point out to him that the only time Mayfield let down her I'm-as-tough-a-cop-as-any-man stance was when she was around him. "I don't think there's anything here that warrants much more looking into. Seems fairly cut-and-dried, actually."

"How so?" he asked.

"Well, like we concluded last night, Harding—that's his real name, John Oliver Harding—was depressed about his mother's death. The two had been close, and her death devastated him. He had no other relatives, no friends to speak of, and was weird, clumsy, and overweight. He apparently was unhappy about the lecture, and felt the world was going to end very soon. He was not only into the UFO side of the millennium change, but a fanatic about the coming Armageddon. He wasn't religious, though, and that fact might have made it even worse for him. He thought the world, and life, was meaningless. You're born, you suffer, you die. In other words, a prime candidate for sitting on a window ledge and just letting go."

"Nice psychology, Rebecca. Now let's hear it by the book."

She waved her arms helplessly. "There are no police procedures for this. He died from the fall—that's what the autopsy concluded. We'll wait for the toxicology reports. Maybe he was high or drunk. Apparently he was no stranger to Mary Jane, and even a little crack now and then. He might have gone up there to toke up."

"You would have found evidence."

"We might still."

"If you keep looking, yes."

She clamped her mouth shut, then breathed deeply. "All right, you've made your point. We will keep looking."

Paavo nodded. "One other thing. What have you learned about Derrick Holton? He claims to have been a scientist with NASA. Is that true?"

"Not only is it true, he was one of the brightest they had. Then something happened with a girlfriend—no one knew exactly—and he asked for a temporary transfer just to get away for a while. They sent him off to a facility in Nevada and he came back changed. He quit NASA and became president of a UFO group."

Paavo guessed the breakup with Angie had driven Holton away. But what could have happened in Nevada to change him so much he turned away from his profession?

"Did you ask him why he quit NASA?"

"I tried, but I couldn't get any answers that made sense."

"What were his answers?"

"He kept repeating that he could no longer be a part of a lie, not when he had seen the truth."

Paavo shook his head, not knowing what Holton meant. Mayfield left and Paavo went back to his desk.

"What's up, partner?" Yosh asked, lifting his head from the report he was writing on Felix Rolfe. "I can see the wheels turning full speed in that brain of yours."

"It's nothing," he said.

"Oh? You could have fooled me. Everything okay with Angie?"

"Angie? What makes you ask?"

"I guess women are on my mind." He turned back to his report. "It's nothing."

"Women?" Paavo asked. "Why is that?"

"Nothing."

Paavo sat down at his desk, swiveled his chair toward Yosh, and leaned back. He remembered Yosh's odd reaction to one of Calderon's comments about relationships, and Yosh's volunteering to cover on Christmas Day. "We've been partners too long, Yosh," he said after a while.

"We both say it's nothing when it's something. Want to tell me what's going on?"

Yosh snapped his head toward Paavo, surprise etched on his face. "You trying to tell me you can see behind my mysterious-East facade? And everyone in the bureau says you're the most inscrutable SOB they've ever met. What does this mean? We learning how to read each other?"

Paavo grinned. "Looks like."

Yosh tossed aside his pen and leaned back in his chair. "The thing is, I should be feeling really good about Nancy. She's developed an interest in calligraphy—writing stylized Chinese characters."

"She's studying Chinese?"

"It's a kind of art. We call them *kanji* in Japanese. An entire painting might consist of just one character—say, the one for *love*, or *trust*, or *tree*. The painter tries to make the kanji somehow evoke the feeling of the word. There's a lot of skill, too, that goes into the brush strokes used. The artist can't let his hand shake or use more than one brush stroke to make each line of the kanji. Each line must be perfect."

"It sounds pretty difficult."

"It is. She's apparently very good at it. She goes to class all the time. Her teacher—her *sensei*, as she calls him—encourages her."

"I don't get it," Paavo said. "What's the problem?"

Yosh took a deep breath before he continued.

"Lately, she's been working on the word *center*. Sounds simple, right? While she works, she has to think about the deep meaning of the word. About what's at her center. What's at the center of our marriage. Of me!" He stopped speaking, his expression pained.

"There's plenty at your center," Paavo said. "Your ethics, for starters, and your heart, and your empathy despite the world you deal with. Nancy knows all that."

"Not well enough," he said quietly.

"She needs to hang around the people we have to face every day. Talk about people with no center," Paavo said quietly as his thoughts turned to Angie, how she centered him and seemed to be the heart of everything he thought of, dreamed of, even believed in. He glanced up at Yosh. "Nancy should look at the people involved with all these millennium cults. For all their so-called searching, most have no idea what to believe, or where the truth is. They find truth in nothing, and as a result, they believe anything. Where is their center?"

"Nancy compared me and my center with her *sensei*," Yosh said. "I came up short. Actually, I came up tall. He's a squirrelly little guy—small, refined, like upper-class Japanese. Me, I'm big. Northern Japanese peasant stock. Not very exciting stuff."

"I can't believe it," Paavo said. "Nancy's crazy about you."

"She used to be. Now she's turning back to

other things Japanese. Calligraphy. The tea ceremony with all its stylized gentleness. This *sensei* encourages her in that, too. She's even taking Japanese lessons! Being third-generation, like I am, she never learned to speak the old language, just a word here and there. But with all this diversity stuff being so big here in the city, she's thinking that if everyone else in the country sees her as Japanese first and American second, she may as well study what it's all about."

"That has nothing to do with your relationship."

"I don't know. What's more Japanese, an artistic teacher or a cop who studies dead bodies?" Yosh studied the floor. "A man who looks for a mutilation murderer isn't the sort my wife finds thrilling these days."

Paavo's shoulders slumped. "I know what you mean," he said wearily. "Angie's got an old boyfriend hanging around her. She says she's not interested in him, and I believe her, but that's not the case on the guy's part. He's still plenty interested. And told me so."

Yosh's head lifted. "You're kidding."

"He told me her father approves of him."

"Shit."

"And he's got a Ph.D."

Yosh smacked his fist on the desktop. "Hell, does he walk on water, too?"

"He believes in UFOs."

Yosh's mouth dropped open, then he began to chuckle. "Now you're talking."

Paavo stared out the window. "It's easy to focus on that one quirk and overlook what makes the guy good for a woman like Angie."

"*You're* good for a woman like Angie, pal." Yosh was exuberant, sounding like his upbeat self again. "She knows it and so do I. I wouldn't throw you over for some scientific geek."

Paavo grinned. "That's encouraging. Well, if I were Nancy, I wouldn't throw you over for some scrawny painter."

Yosh laughed. "Why don't women have the good sense we do?"

"Damned if I understand them. Hell, I can't even figure out what to buy one for Christmas."

Yosh sighed. "I might get Nancy a vacuum cleaner she's been talking about."

Paavo shook his head, his eyes mischievous. "You do that, Yosh, and you're going to make that painter look better than ever."

Angie felt like a zombie when she walked into Wings of an Angel just before noon. Earl hurried her to a table. "What can I get you to drink, Miss Angie? You ain't lookin' so hot today."

"Gee, thanks, Earl. I really needed to hear that." She put her head in her hands. "Just some coffee."

"You wanna sangwitch? Some spaghetti?"

"I'll have something light—how about a frittata?"

"I don' t'ink Butch has much fancy stuff to put in one—no aspary-gus or any a dat kinda stuff."

"Diced onions, diced peppers, and a little cheese, ham, or Italian sausage is all I need."

"Oh. I t'ink he can do dat." Earl's eyebrows scrunched with worry. "So, how's da inspector dese days?"

She glanced up at him. "I'm not sure," she admitted. He'd been hurt and angry with her, and she couldn't blame him. She felt miserable about it. She should have told him what she was up to. It was wrong to have hidden it. But something more was troubling him, something he hadn't talked about yet.

Earl's gaze held hers a moment, his eyes sad, then he gave a small nod and walked back toward the kitchen. Angie slumped back in her chair. The previous night seemed like a bad dream. She'd fallen asleep watching a lecture, and from that time on, everything that had happened seemed fuzzy and slightly out of focus.

About six A.M. she had awakened to stare at the ceiling. Her mind kept replaying the horrible scene of the previous night at the lecture hall. Why would anyone kill Oliver Hardy? Personally, she had found him creepy, but the others didn't seem bothered by him. Phil, Kronos, to a lesser extent Elvis, and—she was sorry to say—even Derrick himself were all peculiar people. No wonder Oliver didn't bother them.

She'd tried to turn her thoughts to the fantasy dinner, tried to plan some menus, but images of Tardis Hall and Paavo's disappointment in her got in the way. That was why she had decided to come here to eat, and see her friends.

Earl came back with a tall, steaming cup of coffee and placed it before her. "Butch'll make you a real good frittata, Miss Angie," he said. "His cookin'll make you feel a lot better."

"Thanks, Earl."

Just then the door to the restaurant opened, and two of Earl's favorite customers, Rosie and Lena, entered. Earl slicked back his hair, straightened his spine, and strutted over to welcome them. He was obviously sweet on them both.

At the same time, Vinnie came through the kitchen doors, marched straight to Angie's table, pulled out a chair, and sat down. Vinnie, like Earl, was somewhere in his sixties, but where Earl was short and round and solid, Vinnie was short and round and soft—probably because his chief form of work was to order Butch or Earl to do something. Angie was surprised to see him, though. He rarely ventured out of his downstairs office.

"I heard that you're actin' real down," he said. All three of the guys had similar old-time San Francisco accents, which were an offshoot of the accents of the Brooklynites and Irish who had settled in the city over a century earlier.

"I started a new business," she began.

With a hangdog look, he slowly nodded. "That'll make a person miserable real fast."

"I've got to cater a big meal for a strange group of people, and I've got to do it in less than a week's time. I've been calling around for caterers, and they all act like I'm crazy. I think I'm going to have to prepare all the food myself."

"Oh yeah? How many people you talkin' about?"

"I don't know."

"What're you gonna serve 'em?"

"I haven't decided."

"You got a problem awright. Maybe you oughta serve 'em chips an' dip."

"Maybe I should just give up."

He leaned forward. "You ain't no quitter, Miss Angie. An' if this is so important to you, me an' the boys'll help you."

She glanced up at him. "You will?"

"Sure. You gotta remember, we don' do nothin' fancy. But we can get people fed."

"Thanks, Vinnie. I appreciate it."

He sat back, relaxed, his wrinkled face curving into a smile. "Hey, you helped us get this restaurant goin'. We couldn' a done it without you. It's payback time, that's all."

"I don't need any payback. But I'm glad of your offer."

"An' anyway, we gotta keep an eye on you an' see that you don' get no more sad or mixed up about stuff than you are."

As Angie looked at him in amazement, he got up, pushed in the chair, and went back into the nether regions of the restaurant to do whatever it was he usually did. Which, she suspected, wasn't much.

* * *

"Damn it to hell," Yosh bellowed. "We've got to get that bastard. I mean now. Right now!" Thick fog swirled around him like smoke from a fire. The little party that stood at the top of Twin Peaks seemed to be the only people left on earth.

Paavo pulled his jacket tighter to ward off the damp cold. Another mutilation murder, every bit as horrible as the last two, had been committed. The body was that of an African-American male, probably in his mid- to late fifties, although guessing the age of someone who had been exsanguinated wasn't easy. The skin tended to turn as dry and flaky as that of a ninety-year-old. Like the other two victims, he was naked, bloodless, and his orifices had been cored out. Like the other two, he had a number carved in his chest. This time, the number was 4. Only one thing was different. Wrapped around the victim's wrist was a piece of cable.

The man had been left in the middle of Twin Peaks Boulevard. The first patrolmen on the scene had already rung the doorbells of all the nearby homes and asked if the people living there had any idea what had happened. The neighbors stated that the fog had been so heavy on the peaks all night that they couldn't see the street, let alone anyone lying out there on it. Judging from the abrasions on the body, the victim had most likely been pushed out of a car and left exactly as he landed. It was only, in fact, when another car nearly ran over him, and the driver got out to see what was wrong with the man, that the police were called.

The driver was being held until the homicide inspectors could talk to him.

"The body's in full rigor," Paavo said, trying without success to wriggle a toe. "He's probably been dead some twenty-four hours."

"Felix Rolfe was freshly killed when we found him five days ago," Yosh said. "That means there were only four-plus days between the murders this time. We've got a real psycho on our hands. He doesn't seem to get physically tired or emotionally drained from these killings."

"And why is there a four carved on his chest? Seven, five, four," Paavo said.

"We need a break!" Yosh shouted. "Some prints on this vic, something. The doer's got to make a mistake. These killings are too bloody for there not to be any evidence!"

"Maybe three's the charm." Paavo scanned the eerie crime scene of another horrible, senseless murder. Through the fog, the holiday decorations on the homes were blurs of red, green, and white. When all was still, he heard in the distance the soft sounds of a Christmas carol:

> *Angels we have heard on high,*
> *Sweetly singing o'er the plain . . .*

He tried not to listen. The houses nearby held prospective witnesses who had to be interviewed. Again, he and Yosh would follow the routine for identifying yet another mutilated corpse. Again, he'd have to postpone seeing Angie, finding her a Christmas present, and trying to come up with a modicum of holiday spirit. He drew in a deep breath. "Let's get started."

The strains of the carol floated over the city streets.

It was morning before they were able to leave the crime scene and head back to Homicide. Soon after their return, a call came in from the Park station. "Smith here," Paavo answered.

"Sergeant Cooper, Inspector. Some of my men were up on the Peaks with you tonight. A call came in I thought you might want to hear about. A woman looking for her husband. He didn't come home tonight and she was calling to find out if there'd been any accidents. The husband fits the description of the corpse."

"Damn," Paavo muttered. It was bad enough talking to cold or heartless people such as Bertram Lambert's sister or Felix Rolfe's mother about a loved one who had been killed. To talk to a victim's wife was the worst part of his job. "What's her name and address? We'll check it out."

Paavo and Yosh went to a walk-up flat on Broderick near Waller. "Mrs. Cole?" Paavo asked when a tall middle-aged woman opened the door.

She was in her bathrobe and slippers. One

look at the men in front of her and she stiffened, her face etched with worry and fright. "That's me. It's not about Leon, is it? He's not hurt, is he?" Her voice held the soft cadence of Louisiana.

"We're checking on your call that he's missing, Mrs. Cole," Yosh said gently. "I'm Inspector Yoshiwara and this is Inspector Smith."

"Inspectors?" she asked, her dark brown eyes growing wider, clearly wondering why her call had attracted such high-level attention.

"That's right," Yosh continued. "Do you have any pictures of your husband? That would help us."

That rattled her even more. "A picture," she said, backing away from the door. "Come in," she murmured as she went into the living room. A gallery of photographs—young boys, smiling girls, toothless babies, all ages and sizes—lined the mantel over what had once been a fireplace but now had a gas heater in it. Pinecones and branches were interwoven among the pictures. In front of the window was a Christmas tree, and under it lay a number of colorfully wrapped presents.

"These are my kids and grandkids," she said proudly. "Our kids are all grown up. It's just me and Leon at home now." She picked up a photo of a military man wearing an Air Force uniform. Paavo and Yosh immediately recognized him as the man they had found on the street. "This photo is a few years old—his retirement from the

Air Force after twenty-five years of service. He was a captain. He hasn't changed too much, though. Still a handsome rascal. Does this help?"

Paavo and Yosh glanced at each other, then asked her to sit down. She would have to, eventually, go down to the morgue with them. But not right now.

17

At eight o'clock the next evening, Angie went into her living room, turned on the TV, kicked off her black Ferragamos with the four-inch heels, and flopped onto the sofa, exhausted. The night before, she'd had another troubled sleep. She had been quite sure Paavo would stop by to talk. He always had in the past when things were strained between them. This time, he hadn't. Even after she went to bed, she kept watching the clock and listening for his knock. When morning came, she'd got up, tired and discouraged.

She'd gone to her parents' house to have lunch with her mother, but Serefina zeroed in on her unhappiness and asked too many questions. Angie soon left.

Now she had just settled down to watch *Cooking for Fun and Profit* when the buzzer sounded on her door.

She spun around and faced it with surprise. Paavo never used the doorbell. He always knocked. So did Stan. She put her shoes back on, went to the peephole, and peered out.

Then she smoothed her dress and swung open the door. "Derrick! This is a surprise."

"Angie." He stood in the doorway, his eyes shifting and fearful. "I wanted to be sure everything was all right with you. Everyone is so upset about Oliver, I scarcely know what to do."

"I can imagine. Please come in."

"Thank you. I didn't want to impose. . . ." He glanced over his shoulder toward the elevator, then hurriedly stepped into her living room and shut the door behind him. He drew in a deep breath as he looked around. "This apartment is even more beautiful than I remember." He headed toward the windows and peeked behind an open drape. Angie watched him with growing discomfort. "Your father owns a gold mine with this building," he said. "Top of Russian Hill. Views. He hasn't given it to you, has he?"

What is with him? Angie wondered. "I don't think my four sisters would like it if he did." She gestured toward the sofa. "Won't you sit down? How about some brandy, or scotch, perhaps?"

"Brandy would be great. It's chilly out. The fog is thick again tonight. The airports are closed. Traffic is scarcely moving."

"Yes. I was out earlier." She poured him a snifter of brandy. He took off his jacket and sat. She sat on the antique yellow Hepplewhite chair.

"So . . ." Where could she start that didn't sound trite? "How are you holding up with all this going on?"

"It's hard." His gaze dropped a moment. "More than anything, I'm numb right now. First Mosshad, now Oliver. Not that Mosshad is dead—heaven forbid! But he's still missing. I'm afraid something's happened to him. I'm scared, Angie. I'm not too much of a man to admit it."

"Derrick"—she wasn't quite sure how to bring this up—"tell me the truth. Wasn't Mosshad's disappearance a publicity stunt? I mean, none of you sounded in the least bit upset about him."

As he held the snifter, he slowly turned it, his thumb running along the side of the glass as he did. "You're right. It started out as a publicity stunt. We had things rigged to look like an abduction. Some of us felt we needed the publicity. Others, like Kronos—the blond guy with the ponytail—disagreed. He and I argued about it quite a bit. I wish now that I'd listened to him. But NAUTS is a barely viable organization, I'm sorry to say. It seems we aren't far-out enough. If we had one-hundredth of the money that charlatan Algernon is raking in, we'd be fine. But we don't."

"You called Algernon a charlatan, but you faked the abduction."

"It was just a little joke to get some attention. Believe me, it's not all fake. Some of it is very, very real."

"I don't understand how you did it. I was there. I saw the lights. I lost time. Everyone did."

"It was just a trick, Angie. We had the chairs in the audience rigged up to make electromagnetic charges in the armrests. When we hit a switch, the charges were released and the batteries in your watches stopped dead. The big clocks in the hall weren't affected because they're all electric. Also, they're all tied into a master clock. Using the master clock, we moved them ahead ten minutes. The result was simple. People assumed they'd lost ten minutes in real time—a common phenomenon in abductions. By the time they left the hall and saw clocks with the real time, since their own watches had stopped, ten minutes more or less meant nothing."

"That's remarkable," Angie said, surprised NAUTS would have gone to such trouble to set up the stunt.

"It really wasn't difficult at all. We're scientists and engineers. We have access to all kinds of things not on the retail market, and the know-how to use them. So I announced Mosshad had been abducted. It made the newspapers. A few days later we were going to hold a press conference with Mosshad telling what had happened to him during the time he was with the extraterrestrials. Then we'd say that anyone who wanted more information should go to his lecture the next night."

"What a scam!" she cried.

"It's mild as most scams go, believe me," Derrick said with a shrug. "There was just one problem. Mosshad didn't call me the next day like he was supposed to do. I've called many times, but he never answers. No one has seen him. He's still missing."

"Are you sure he isn't simply hiding somewhere, letting the suspense build?"

"That's what I thought at first. When we talked about our press conference and the way to hold one to get maximum coverage, we decided that he needed to reappear before the public forgot the story—a couple of days at max. This isn't a case of an absentminded professor. Something has happened to him."

"Did you go to the police?" Angie asked.

"And say what? We told a guy to get lost for a few days and he hasn't come back yet?"

"Exactly."

"How much attention will they give us when they find out we're all with NAUTS?"

Angie sighed. "You've got a point."

"As I said, Angie, I'm scared. We were wrong to pretend he was abducted. I, of all people, should know better than to play around with that. Now, if someone, or something, is after NAUTS, I'm the president of the group!" Embarrassed at his outburst, he turned his head away and began rubbing his temples. His voice, when he spoke, sounded dejected. "I hate the thought of going back to my apartment, of being alone."

She knew what he was asking, but there was no way she was about to invite him to stay at her place. "Maybe you could stay with someone from NAUTS?"

He didn't reply. Instead, he drained his glass, then stood. "I don't think so. I'll figure something out. I shouldn't have bothered you."

"Wait." She stood as well. "Before you leave, we should call Paavo. Maybe he can suggest something as far as trying to find Mosshad. He can tell us, too, if Oliver's death was an accident or a suicide. Perhaps you don't need to be fearful about any of this."

"I'll find out in due course, Angie. For now, I need to decide what to do. It's not your problem." As he studied her, his hazel eyes seemed wary and strained in a way that didn't fit her old friend at all. Then, to her horror, his face started to crumble and she thought he was going to burst into tears. He swallowed hard a few times, looking like an inflatable doll that had just had a pin stuck into it. "It's so hard." He gazed at her. "You're the only person left in this whole world that I trust."

"Me? What about your friends?"

He drew in a deep breath. "What if one of them is behind this? What if one of them has . . . has hurt Mosshad, or was behind Oliver's death?"

"You're leaping to all sorts of conclusions, Derrick."

"What if those conclusions are true?" His

voice rose and he seemed near hysteria. "Do I have to be the next one killed before anyone believes me?"

She sat on the sofa and took his hand, pulling him down beside her. "Tell me the whole truth. Is there some reason you believe you can't trust your friends, your partners? If I'm going to help you, I need to know."

His hand tightened painfully on hers. "Angie, don't ask. Please. I wouldn't do anything that might cause you danger."

"Does this have to do with the Prometheus Group and NAUTS?" she asked.

"They hate me, but I swear to you, Angie, I was only trying to do the right thing."

"Who hates you?"

"All of them. A couple of years ago—after we broke up—I went to Area Fifty-one in Nevada, where the founder of the Prometheus Group had worked until he was killed in a laboratory accident."

"What's Area Fifty-one?"

"It's a secret base on the Nevada Test Site. Lots of black-budget experiments go on there. The military denies anything special happens in the complex. I know better. While there, I learned about Neumann and his work. I learned that Algernon had perverted it. For that reason, when I couldn't get Algernon to change, I started NAUTS."

"The split was pretty ugly, I take it."

"Phil thought he should lead NAUTS because

he'd once led a commune and he felt we should be similarly organized. He's too flaky. No one would listen to him. Mosshad thought he should lead it because he used to know Neumann. He's too old and too weak-willed. Kronos defected to NAUTS, and it cost him his marriage. Only Elvis came over in an untroubled way. He simply believed in the cause. My cause, and the original Promethean cause, not Algernon's stupid message."

"What was the original cause?"

"It was to let the world know that aliens do exist, that they landed on Earth at Roswell, and that the government—despite its denials—not only knows they exist but has taken alien DNA and added it to a human embryo. That a man walked among us, a brilliant man, who was in fact part alien."

Oh lordy, Angie thought, *here we go again.* She was almost afraid to ask her next question. "Who was that man?"

"The founder of the Prometheus Group." His eyes were wide, almost scary. "Igor Mikhailovich Neumann."

"Give me strength!" she cried, unable to take any more of this. "Igor Mikhailovich? You're saying he was a Russian space alien?"

"Some Russian defectors and ex-Nazi German scientists worked along with Americans for years after the Roswell crash on this project. Finally, sometime in the fifties, they succeeded. They named him. He went by his initials:

I. M. In other words, I. M. Neumann."

"Ah, but of course." She should have known. *I am new man.* It sounded like the sort of schmaltz Hollywood would come up with.

"He was brilliant, beyond human comprehension," Derrick continued. "From the time he was old enough to understand why he was so different from other children, he dedicated his life to learning all he could about science, both biophysics and astrophysics. He wanted to know everything; he wanted to do everything he could about the sad state of denial the world was in."

"Denial?"

"About extraterrestrials. That they exist. He wanted to prove it. Throughout his life he was watched and studied by the government, and as an adult he worked at Area Fifty-one, where he studied the alien technology from the Roswell crash. He was able to do more with it, to make better progress understanding it, than anyone else. He began the Prometheus Group in the early eighties. It grew in leaps and bounds in popularity. Then, about ten years ago, he was killed. His entire laboratory was destroyed in an explosion that burned so hot only cinders remained. Some people in the group prefer to think that he isn't dead but has returned to the mother ship."

"Derrick," Angie said, feeling heartsick. "What am I going to do with you?"

"It's true, Angie," he said. He stood and walked over to the windows. "Please believe me.

At Area Fifty-one, I not only learned Neumann's beliefs, I saw the scientific basis for them. I learned, to my horror, how true it all is. When I returned to the Bay Area and saw that Algernon had turned Neumann's work on alien life into touchy-feely, pyramid-loving nonsense, I was disgusted. Algernon has hated me ever since. Now there have been deaths. Horrible deaths. Oliver's. Maybe Mosshad's. Others."

"Others?" she asked, surprised.

"There might be." His eyes were hollow. "The mutilation murders. There was another, a third one, and it confirmed—" He clamped his mouth shut, his Adam's apple working as he seemed to swallow over and over. "The newspapers don't really tell what was done to the murder victims. From what I've read about these murders and about cattle mutilations, the patterns are the same. I think your detective friend won't be able to find who killed those men. He won't know where to look. He'll be looking for regular clues, normal methods. But these killers . . . these killers are not of this world!"

"I'll help you, Derrick," she said softly, cautiously. "I'll find a place for you to stay, somewhere you will feel safe. You've been under a strain. I hadn't realized how much of a strain. . . ."

He folded his arms tightly against himself as a shiver rippled through his body. "I shouldn't have troubled you with this."

"What are friends for?" She jumped up. "I'll

talk to my neighbor across the hall. I'm sure he'll be able to help you."

Stan opened the hide-away bed in his living room. He didn't have a big apartment like Angie's, but only a small living room and an even smaller bedroom. Only because of its small size—and years of rent control—could he afford it. He didn't mind Angie's friend staying with him a day or two. He might even have to call his workplace, say he had to stay home a few days to take care of a sick friend. That sounded downright noble of him.

"What are those?" Derrick asked, pointing at the two pieces of aluminum foil on top of the television set.

"Nothing." Stan snatched them and crumbled them up. "I was just twirling some aluminum foil while watching TV."

"Oh. For a moment there, they looked like something I've seen people do to protect themselves from strange waves in the air."

Halfway to the kitchen to throw the aluminum foil in the trash, Stan stopped. "I heard your interview on the radio when you talked about that. Angie made me think it was all a put-on."

"Would I joke about radio waves, sonic beams, or lasers?"

"I, uh, guess not. Do they all cause headaches?"

"Much worse than that. They can make your brain begin to deteriorate—cause the electrical charges to go haywire. Sort of like a short in a wire, if you know what I mean."

Stan gulped hard. "And those, uh, those people you know who use aluminum foil . . . does it help?"

"Of course. Otherwise, why would they do it? I suggest not wearing it in public, however. Most people don't understand."

Stan nodded slowly. "Angie did say you're a NASA space scientist, right?"

"Yes, until I took a, um, permanent sabbatical, shall we say? They didn't like my involvement with NAUTS. Who knows—someday, I might try to go back. That job is looking a lot better at the moment than it used to."

"I see." Stan slowly backed out of the living room toward his bedroom. "Well, sleep tight. Let me know if there's anything I can do for you."

"I'll be fine. I really appreciate this."

Stan rushed into his bedroom, took the aluminum foil pieces he'd crumpled, and began reshaping them into cylinders as best he could. He stuck them in his ears. Thoughts of shorted-out brains spurred him on. If NASA said wearing aluminum foil in the ears was a smart thing to do, that was good enough for him.

18

"This is for you," Paavo said, handing a colorfully wrapped present to Micky Kowalski, "but you can't open it until Christmas."

"Thank you, Uncle Paavo!" The towheaded child gave Paavo a hug, then carried the box, which was almost as big as he, across the living room to the Christmas tree. He gave it a couple of hard shakes before carefully laying it under the tree.

Paavo and the boy's mother, Katie, shared a smile. "That was very thoughtful of you," she said as she poured some coffee for him. He sat on the sofa; she, on a rocking chair beside it. "I've appreciated the way you've kept tabs on Micky. All the inspectors have, but you especially."

"I've enjoyed it." Paavo looked at the boy. "Matt would be proud of him." The sense of loss that hit Paavo whenever his thoughts turned to his old partner struck again. He and Matt had gone through the police academy together, served as rookies, and then ended up in Homicide just months apart. They were partners and best friends. Then one night, while on duty, Matt was killed.

As if Katie sensed where Paavo's thoughts had turned, she made a fuss about cutting him a piece of mince pie. "Eat up. I know it's one of your favorites."

"You still remember," he said with a smile. Katie was of medium build and a little overweight. She had a gruff exterior but a heart that was even bigger than Matt Kowalski's—and he was one of the biggest-hearted men Paavo had ever known.

"Of course I still remember," she said. She took a big bite of the pie. "So tell me, have you gotten all your Christmas shopping done?"

"There's not much to do—Micky, Aulis, and Angie. I've taken care of the first two."

"But not Angie?" Katie laughed. She had a deep-throated, raspy laugh. Matt used to say it held the promise of good times and good sex. He contended it was what had made him fall head over heels in love.

"Angie's a tough one to shop for," Paavo said. "She's got everything money can buy. If you have any suggestions for what I should get her, I'd sure appreciate it."

Katie gave him one of her long, hard, serious stares, the kind that Matt had sworn kept him toeing the line. Then her eyes softened. When she spoke, her voice was husky. "I'll tell you one thing, Paavo Smith. You just make damn sure you make it home to her, safe and sound, every night. Don't you go doing what Matt did. That's the best present you can give her. And me and Micky will stay happy that way, too."

Paavo was stunned; then, without letting himself think twice about it, he stood up and gave her a hug. "I love you, Katie."

"Sit down, you big lug, before you get me crying. Eat your pie!"

"Angie! This is for you." Stan and Derrick stood at her door the next morning, each holding one end of a seven-foot Douglas fir Christmas tree.

"Oh my God!" she cried.

"I knew you wanted one, Angie," Stan said. "We couldn't see you lugging it up in the elevator."

"You're quite right. Thank you." She had planned to ask Paavo to help, but the way his schedule was going, it'd be Easter before he found the time. "Bring it in."

She hurried to the living room and moved aside a chair. "Place it in front of that wall. No, more to the right. Now back. Great." After Stan and Derrick helped her rearrange the furniture and shift the tree a few more times, it was right where she wanted it.

"We'll even help you trim it," Stan said. "Of course, that would put us past lunchtime, and we haven't even had breakfast yet, but . . ."

Angie's eyes lit up. "It's a deal. You trim, I'll cook." She ran to the closet to get lights and ornaments.

"I hate to mention this, Angie," Stan said, "but your hands have a greenish tint. You weren't slimed by an alien, were you?"

"It's food coloring," Angie said, distinctly unamused by his joke. "It's ruined my French manicure and I'm in no mood to discuss it."

"Ah, sounds like you're baking!" Stan sidled past her and headed for the kitchen.

"Is Stan right?" Derrick asked as he followed Stan.

"He is. I'm making little green space monster cookies."

She picked up the rolling pin and used it to shoo Stan away from the cookie dough. He liked to eat it raw. A monster-shaped cookie cutter sat on the counter.

"I'll finish these up before making you a nice brunch."

"No hurry, Angie," Stan said. "We've got all day."

The doorbell rang.

"Now who?" She wiped her hands and went to answer.

"Hi!" Connie stood in the doorway with a big bag from Athena's. "You've been feeding me lately, so I thought I'd return the favor. Dolmas, moussaka, and fides pilaf."

"Sounds wonderful. Come on in. Join the party."

"What party? Oh! Look at that tree! It's enormous!" Connie said as she headed for the kitchen with the food. "How did you ever get it in—"

She stopped talking as she saw Derrick Holton standing by the sink. "Derrick! What a surprise! What are you doing here?" As soon as she asked the question, she realized the answer could be potentially embarrassing. She turned around and glanced at Angie with one of those what-in-the-hell-is-going-on-and-why-didn't-you-tell-me-about-it-before-this looks. Angie shook her head.

"I'm staying with Stan," Derrick said.

Connie hadn't noticed Stan standing by the counter eating green cookie dough. She gawked, her gaze bouncing from him to Derrick, as if she couldn't imagine a more unlikely pair.

"I'm getting ready for Algernon's party," Angie said.

"Who's that?" Stan said, a little garbled because the cookie dough stuck to his teeth.

"Algernon?" Derrick turned pale. "Are you still working on a party for that fraud?"

"Why wouldn't she be?" Connie said, helping her put the cut cookies onto a tray. "Why is Cookie Monster green, Angie?"

"These aren't Cookie Monsters," Angie said. "They're supposed to be Martians. Fat Martians. I'm also going to make some round gray cookies that will be, of course, flying saucers."

"It sounds really hokey, Angie," Stan said.

"Oh? You think you could do better?" His eye caught her rolling pin and he backed away.

"You don't think anyone will be insulted by these cookies, do you, Derrick?" she asked.

"It's a charming idea, Angelina. The kind that is very typical of you," he said. Connie rolled her eyes. "Of course, I think I've mentioned to you that aliens are gray, not green."

"How does anyone know?" Connie asked.

"Don't ask," Angie said, finishing rolling out the last bit of dough. Stan took the bowl and used his finger to get out the few remaining crumbs. Angie faced Derrick. "Do you have any suggestions for what I should serve that would be in keeping with a UFO theme?"

He thought a moment. "No one has ever seen aliens eat. That's the problem. They're interested in cattle, but not as food."

"Interested in cattle? It sounds kinky." Stan laughed.

Connie took over the cookie making so Angie could whip up some brunch for the men.

"Actually, it is kind of kinky," Derrick admitted. "Lots of farmers have found cattle out on the open range, drained of all blood and strangely mutilated. No one has ever had a good explanation. The vets officially report that wolves or mountain lions did it, but everyone knows their reports are false."

"How do you know that?" Stan asked.

"Do you really want to ask?" By now, Angie had learned that everything in UFO lore seemed to be grotesque, scary, or sexual. She pulled more ingredients for the brunch from her refrigerator. Her warning had come too late.

"The aliens, or whoever," Derrick began, "take a cow or bull and remove its lips, nose, ears, udder, and, er, other body, er, openings."

"Why do anything so horrible?" Connie asked.

"Probably to study them—like we study lab animals. Aliens don't have all the body parts animals do, and they're curious. That's why humans get so scared when we're abducted."

"You're frightening me, Derrick," Connie said, her eyes round as marbles.

"You should be frightened. ETs have no human emotions, no feelings. As far as they're concerned, we're little better than cattle. They might well have already done things as bad, or worse, to humans. Look at all the people who turn up missing each year. Look at all the horrible murders committed by people we've said had to be less than human. Well—"

"Enough, Derrick," Angie cried as she prepared mock hollandaise sauce while the eggs cooked and the English muffins toasted. Normally she made real hollandaise, but not for people who showed up at the last minute and told her horrible stories. Even if they came bearing Christmas trees.

She had just set out brunch for Stan and Derrick, and the Greek food for herself and Connie, when she heard a loud knock on her door. She

knew that sound. Homicide Inspector Paavo
Smith had come to call. Her first reaction was joy,
but then she looked at the two men seated at her
dining room table, eating their eggs Benedict
with fresh strawberries on the side.

She pulled open the door, holding it in such
a way that he could see into her living room but
not the dining area.

"Hello, Angie," Paavo said. She saw by his
clothes—jeans, oxford shirt, no tie, and black
leather jacket, the collar turned up against the
chilly fog—that he was off work that day. Her
pulse quickened. He looked much more edible
than the food Connie had brought. This would
have been the perfect time for them to spend
hours together, if only she were alone.

"Hello," she whispered. "I'm so glad to see
you."

"Something smells good," he said. When she
didn't step aside for him to enter, his brow
creased. "I see you've got a tree already. A big
one. Would you like me to leave, Angie?"

"Of course not!" With a baleful glance over
her shoulder at the motley crew, she stepped
back from the door. "Come in. I have company."

He walked into the apartment. The three
people at the dining room table gave awkward
little waves. He glanced at Angie but didn't say a
word.

She tried to smile. "Derrick is staying with
Stan for a few days," she said, lightly resting her
hand on Paavo's arm. "Want to join us? We've

got plenty of Greek food. Connie brought it."

Paavo's gaze leaped from her to them. He strode into the dining room. "Sure." Angie's place setting was at one end of the table. Derrick sat at the other and Stan and Connie on each side. Paavo took an extra chair from the side of the buffet and placed it beside Connie. He hung his jacket on the back of it. Three pairs of eyes widened at the sight of his shoulder holster and gun.

He sat down. Connie smiled. Stan squawked a hello. Derrick nodded. Angie dashed into the kitchen to grab a plate, napkin, and fork, and a glass for iced tea. She spread them before Paavo and he took a little food.

Conversation at the table had ended. Everyone gave full attention to eating.

After a while, Paavo said, "Holton, I hear you're staying with Bonnette."

"Yes," Derrick said, nodding. He seemed a little confused by the harsh glare Paavo was giving him.

"Why is that?"

Derrick cleared his throat nervously. "Well . . . things are happening. Strange things. I'm a bit nervous, I guess."

"Have you heard from Mosshad yet?"

Derrick looked at Angie for help. She concentrated on her moussaka. "No. I tried calling. There's still no answer."

"Did you go to his house?"

"No. He lives in an apartment."

"Do you know his address?"

"Yes. I went there once."

"But not since he's been missing?"

"I phoned. He's not there."

Paavo wiped his lips with his napkin and placed it beside his dish. "We should check his place out, Holton."

"Oh . . . but . . ." Derrick turned to Angie again.

She shrugged.

Paavo stood and put on his jacket. "Thanks for the meal, Connie." He eyed Holton. "Are you ready?"

Derrick shoveled the last of the eggs Benedict into his mouth and nodded as he stood. Then he gulped down his coffee.

Paavo walked to the front door and opened it. "Let's go, Holton. We want to be sure the man isn't lying there ill, don't we?"

Angie stood, not leaving the table, but waiting for Paavo to make some sign, some gesture, that he wanted to speak with her.

"Yes, I, er . . ." Derrick glanced woefully at Angie. "Glad you like the tree, Angelina. I'll call you."

"Bye," she called.

Paavo lifted one eyebrow slightly as he glanced back at her, then followed Derrick out the door.

Angie stood frozen, looking at the shut door, then sank into her chair. She didn't even notice as Connie patted her on the shoulder.

* * *

Holton sat scrunched against the passenger door of Paavo's small Austin Healey.

"Which way?" Paavo asked, starting up the car.

"Head for Alemany. He's just off it, on Ocean Avenue."

They rode in silence. Holton hugged his jacket tight against him. "It's freezing out. Looks like a cold December."

"It's about fifty out there," Paavo said.

"Yes, but it's a damp fifty. That makes it colder."

Paavo glanced at him and said nothing. The temperature inside the car seemed to drop even further.

"How much chance is there Mosshad has gone off on his own and is all right?" Paavo asked after a while.

"I never paid much attention to his comings and goings before this. He'd simply show up now and then."

"Who came up with the fake abduction idea?"

Holton blew on his hands. "Can you turn on the heater?"

"It is on." Paavo waited for a reply.

"The abduction was just for fun," Holton said. "It's the kind of thing that goes on in ufology."

"Hoaxes?"

"I prefer to think of them as stunts."

Paavo stopped asking questions as he watched the traffic zigzag its way across Market

Street. Between never-ending construction and the way the streets met at odd angles, it was always an adventure.

Holton cleared his throat. "Um, may I ask—aren't you investigating those bizarre murders where the bodies were mutilated?"

"Yes."

"There are three?"

"Why?"

"Just curious about the numbers on the bodies. A seven, a five, and a four. Have you come up with what they mean?"

"No. Have you?"

"Me?" Holton's voice screeched. "No. No, not at all. I'm a scientist. We play with numbers. That's all. They intrigue me. Any connection between the three men, by the way?"

"None that we know of. Why?"

"No reason. Idle conversation. Forget I asked."

Paavo watched Holton turn his head and stare out the passenger window while he nervously rubbed the fingers on one hand with those of the other. Why would Holton, with all that was going on with NAUTS, be paying attention to the mutilation murders?

As they neared the Ingleside district, Paavo asked, "How close are you and Mosshad?"

"Not close at all. He's friends with Phil. They both knew the original leader of our group—a man named Neumann, Igor Mikhailovich Neumann. Maybe you should call Phil—or go with him. Let me go back to Stan's. But don't tell them where I am, okay?"

"Why would Phil suddenly care about Mosshad? None of you seemed to give Mosshad a second thought earlier."

Holton glanced at Paavo, then stared straight ahead a long time before answering. "Because of Oliver Hardy," he said finally. "If Hardy's death was an accident, why was he hanging out an upper-floor window of an empty warehouse in the first place? If it was a suicide, what drove him to it? If, however, it wasn't a suicide or an accident, then what about Mosshad? What about all of us? And which of us is behind it?"

"That's why you're staying with Stan, isn't it?" Paavo asked.

Holton looked miserable. "You guessed it."

Paavo continued on to Mosshad's apartment. When no one answered Mosshad's door, they contacted the apartment manager. She entered and left the door open wide enough that Paavo could see into the studio.

There was no sign of any disturbance in it. In the lobby, they found Mosshad's mailbox stuffed with letters. They thanked the landlady and left.

Paavo drove Holton to the Hall of Justice and escorted him to Missing Persons to file a report. Paavo needed to forget about Mosshad and Oliver Hardy and all the other nut cases Angie seemed to have a knack for involving herself with, and get back to work on the mutilation murder cases—to stop the killer before he killed again.

He pressed the elevator button to the fourth floor as Holton's questions played in his mind. Seven, five, four. What could those numbers mean to Holton? To a mathematician? Seven times five times four? One hundred forty? What else?

"A watch!" Luis Calderon announced loudly.

Jarred from his thoughts, Paavo discovered he was already in the Homicide Bureau and halfway to his desk.

Had Calderon spoken to him? He glanced at the inspector. "Get her a watch," Calderon said, looking at him. "For Christmas. A nice expensive watch. One that costs one, two hundred dollars. She'll go ape over it."

"A watch isn't romantic," Bill Sutter said. Paavo spun around. Even Sutter had an opinion on this? The man never said anything at all. To anyone.

"A sexy negligee. That's what women love," Sutter continued.

"I don't know if women love them," Rebecca Mayfield said. "I think that's a present men give to women that's more for themselves. I think a weekend away—just the two of you, in some romantic setting—would be wonderful. It doesn't have to be far. Carmel, maybe. Or Mendocino." Her gaze met Paavo's. "That's the kind of present I'd love to receive anytime at all."

"Nah!" Calderon cried. "A woman like Angie

wants something tangible. Something she can show her friends. Like a watch."

Rebecca sauntered over to Calderon's desk. "What do you know about women like her? She's probably got an armful of watches."

"I'll bet she hasn't bought herself a really sexy negligee." Bill Sutter's eyes glazed. "Baby dolls. Sheer lace. The neckline plunging, and skimpy little panties with—"

Paavo walked out. He didn't want to hear it. Since Yosh wasn't one of Santa's little helpers, Paavo thought he must be out tracking down a killer. Paavo needed to be doing the same.

Holton's question about a connection between the victims caused his thoughts to travel along a new path. Because the three men had been so outwardly different, he and Yosh had been working on the assumption that the killings were random.

What if they weren't? What if there was some connection between them despite their surface differences?

He sat in his car. The day had started out as a day off, but he'd already shot that concept to hell. Why stop now?

He took out his notebook and flipped through it. In his jottings on Felix Rolfe, he noticed that some of the panhandlers around the ballpark had said Felix Rolfe spent a lot of time at Harvey's Liquors on Third Street. That was as good a lead as any.

An old man named Tom ran Harvey's. He

remembered Felix Rolfe. Ran him out of there
at least once a week, whenever Rolfe came by
without money. The rest of the time, Rolfe
could pay for the cheap whiskey he liked. Like
mother, like son, Paavo thought.

Tom's rheumy eyes went teary when he heard
of Rolfe's death, though whether it was out of
sadness at the loss of the man or the loss of a
customer, Paavo couldn't tell. The old man
directed Paavo to another friend of Rolfe's,
Cheryl Martin, who lived down on Gilman in
public housing with her three kids.

Paavo reached Yosh and had Yosh join him as
they went into the public housing building. Not
too many years ago, it would have been a lot more
dangerous to go into public housing than it was to
walk down a street in the city. Then city hall began
to listen to the tenants instead of the lawyers of
the gang members who terrorized those tenants,
and put enough of the gang members in jail that
things settled down and became safer. A little, at
least. It still wasn't a place for a cop to enter alone
unless absolutely necessary.

Paavo and Yosh kept their hands under their
suit jackets, on the handles of their guns, as they
walked down the littered, graffiti-covered halls
to Martin's apartment. They did their best to
look forward, backward, and sideways as they
passed doorway after doorway.

Cheryl Martin shed no tears when she spoke
of Rolfe, and readily told them what little she
did know: the street people Rolfe had known,

liquor stores he'd visited, places he'd panhandled and anything else she could think of. They wrote it all down.

"Can you tell us when you last saw him?" Paavo asked.

"Last week or so. I didn't pay too much attention."

"Did he talk about doing anything different than usual, seeing any new people, or anything at all new or special?"

She thought a moment, then smiled. "Come to think of it, he sure did. I didn't believe him, though. Glad I didn't or I jis woulda been disappointed. Now I'm not. I expected something would happen when he tol' me, I jis didn't expect it'd be this bad."

"What did he tell you?"

"He said he'd joined some group with some fellas he met when he was in the army—and they had a drawing, and that he'd won. He said he was goin' to collect him one hundred dollars, and after he got it, he was goin' to take me out to have a fine dinner. I knew better'en to believe 'im. I knew better. Heck, if he'd a won, he'd a drunk it before I got that dinner anyways."

"Who was the group that had the drawing?"

"I don' know."

"Do you know where he was going to meet them?"

"No. He didn' tell me."

"Do you know anything at all about this group?"

"No. Oh, wait, there's one thing." She began to rummage through a big stack of old newspapers and magazines and mail that covered the coffee table in front of the TV. "Here it is. He said they give him this paper."

Paavo took the brochure from her hand.

Roswell: The True Story.

19

Angie rearranged the yellow day lilies on the dining room table and straightened the pillows on her sofa one more time, then paced back and forth. Her company was late. Maybe they had changed their minds. That would make things a lot easier for her.

She heard a knock on her door and hurried to open it. Triana Crisswell and Algernon stood in front of her. As they entered, Algernon gazed deeply into her eyes and handed her a box of See's chocolates.

She hoped he didn't notice that she turned slightly green. Ever since an unfortunate episode during which she had decided to become a chocolatier and had spent too much time cooking and testing the little dollops, she had trouble looking at a box of chocolates without feeling a bit woozy. "Thank you," she said weakly, then took Triana's coat.

The two guests sat in the living room and Angie brought out a tray with prosciutto-wrapped melon balls, sliced kiwi, an assortment of petits fours, and strong Italian-roast coffee from North Beach.

"The view from this apartment is incredible," Algernon said, turning toward the window that faced the northern portion of the city from the Golden Gate Bridge to the Bay Bridge.

"Your things are lovely, too," Triana said, running her hand over the arm of the sofa. "Are these real antiques or reproductions?"

Angie was taken aback by the question. "Real."

"I never could tell myself." Triana plopped an entire petit four into her mouth. "Um, scrumptious!"

Algernon picked up a piece of kiwi and, catching Angie's gaze with his, curved his mouth around it and bit down. He didn't let go of her eyes as he chewed. Angie cleared her throat and concentrated on her coffee cup.

"Well," Triana said. "About your plans for the dinner. You've kept me in suspense long enough. Do tell us everything."

It was show time. Angie took a deep breath. "I'd like to use the theme of Roswell," she said. Triana's lips turned downward at the name.

Angie hurried on. "Everyone seems to know the story," she said, "and it would be easy to build a fantasy about it. Women could dress up in nineteen-forties outfits—high heels with ankle straps, tight slinky skirts, short fitted jackets, their hair done up in poufs on top, then pulled back and smoothed to a roll or a cascade of curls at the nape of the neck—a very Joan Crawford or Betty Grable look. Men could wear old army uniforms—those very starched and polished khaki ones, like Eisenhower or Patton. Or people could dress up like an alien if they wished."

Triana thought a moment. "It has possibilities." She turned to Algernon for his reaction. Busy eating a prosciutto-wrapped melon ball, he simply nodded.

"I like it!" Triana said immediately, with a big smile. "We can even work up an act, if we can find a third person to join us, and do a sort of Andrews Sisters routine, like that song about the boogie-woogie bugle boy of company B."

"Let's not get carried away," Angie said with a laugh, delighted at Triana's reaction to her idea. "And Roswell was after the war, not during."

"From my perspective, that long ago is all ancient history," Triana said, blatantly lying.

"We can watch some old TV shows—Jack Benny, Milton Berle," Angie mused. "I guess they were from that period."

"I've got it, sweetie! *War of the Worlds!*" Triana cried. At Angie's confused expression, she explained. "Orson Welles put on a radio show sometime back then. Such a panic it caused! Listeners thought it was real. It's about alien invaders."

"Was that during World War Two?"

"I don't know, but it's close enough for government work, and that's what this UFO stuff is all about—the government keeping it from the citizens. So with some people dressed like government workers and others like aliens, that would be perfect. Don't you think so, Algernon?" Both Triana and Angie turned to him.

"I believe your original concept is one of humor—to let people come to the event and be joyful," he said grandly.

"Absolutely!" Angie said. "People usually go places to have a good time."

"But in this case, we need to be serious," he explained. "This is not a good-time issue. While I agree with the theme of Roswell, we must handle it seriously. With dignity."

"I agree wholeheartedly," Triana announced. "I really didn't care for that bugle boy song, Angie."

Angie's heart sank. "What about the costumes?"

"I don't think they would contribute to the seriousness of the affair," Algernon said.

Why in the world had they hired her, then? She kept her voice even. "The whole idea of a fantasy dinner is to allow people to take part in the fantasy of the event," she said. "I think it would only enhance the reality of Roswell if we allowed the attendees to come in the dress of the period. They would know, and feel, what it meant to be in Roswell on that historic day over fifty years ago when the spaceship crashed. You could then build on an event that will seem far more real to the participants because they will be living it."

"Hmmm." Algernon put his hand to his chin and pondered this. "You may have a point."

"Also, I'd like to set up a pictorial display of Roswell and newspapers at the time. We'll use reproductions—old *Life* magazines and so on. It would be a nice touch. And just think how interested the press would be in something like that. They could pick up the whole story there."

"Yes. To prove that there is something to this," Algernon said. "I'll even have the Prometheans build a replica of a flying saucer. I like it. Some fun, plus seriousness, side by side."

"My thinking exactly!" Triana cried, girlishly clapping her hands.

"Afterward, we will become serious," he said. "I will talk to the people in attendance, to let them know about me and the Prometheus Group. I expect that some of the press will be there—that is so, isn't it, Triana?—and we will need to give them information that they can write up in their newspapers and magazines. This is for publicity, as you know."

"Of course," Triana cried. "We'll get you a world of publicity for this event. I'm working very hard on it."

"I'll be sure to set up a fantasy exactly the way you want it," Angie added.

Algernon gave her a long, smoldering gaze. "That is precisely what I had in mind."

* * *

"This is a silicon chip." Ray Faldo, black lacquer chopstick in hand, pointed to the small square as he spoke to Paavo and Yosh. They sat in the crime lab, the chip lying on a clean white cloth. "It's old, from the fifties. As far as I can tell, it's a prototype of an integrated circuit chip—the chip that led to personal computers and all the microcomputer technology we have today."

"Where could anyone get something like that?" Paavo asked.

"Defense research and development is one spot. Possibly R and D at some of the big private labs like Bell," Faldo answered before continuing. "It's an interesting object. The chips have changed remarkably since these early, crude attempts."

"This chip is from the fifties?" Yosh asked.

"That's right."

"Same as the night goggles we found on the earlier vic," Paavo said as much to himself as to the others.

"Now this," Faldo said, holding up the cable, "is even more interesting. It's a bulky prototype of a fiber-optic cable."

"That's interesting?" Yosh asked dubiously.

"It is to me. It isn't like any fiber-optic cable we have now. The earliest attempts at fiber optics that are documented are from the early sixties. This is older. It's fifties technology—and undocumented. It's incredible."

"That is strange." Yosh agreed.

"You guys are getting all this stuff from the

mutilation murderer, right?" Faldo asked.

"He left one of them beside each body," Paavo answered.

"Well, then, you should start looking at some scientists, or maybe engineers. Or sons and daughters of men who worked on defense R-and-D contracts in the fifties. This stuff all led to the creation of the high-tech life we have today. I'd love to meet the guy who owned it all. Too bad he's a crazy murderer. He must be an interesting man."

"Do the numbers seven, five, four mean anything to you?" Paavo asked.

"As in seven hundred fifty-four, or seven-six-five-four and the six is missing?"

"I don't know. Any way at all. And we don't know if the number is complete, or if there are more numbers to come."

Faldo wrote the numbers down and studied them a moment. "Right now they don't mean a thing. I'll play around with them."

As Paavo and Yosh headed for the door, Paavo stopped and looked back at Faldo. "Is there any connection between all this stuff and—" He hesitated to even say it. "And UFOs?"

Faldo's lips slowly curved into a smile. "You nearly got me with that one! And they say death cops have no sense of humor!"

"What was that about?" Yosh asked as he stepped onto the Hall of Justice elevator and hit the button for the fourth floor.

"I'm not sure yet," Paavo said. The elevator doors slid shut. "All the materials left with the victims are early prototypes of high-tech equipment—equipment that has changed our way of life. The guy who disappeared at Tardis Hall was a scientist. The group he was a part of calls itself the National Association of Ufological Technology Scientists. They may be UFO nuts, but they're scientists nonetheless. Now one of them is dead and another is asking me about seven-five-four. And two of the three victims had Roswell brochures."

"There might be a connection, Paav," Yosh said, watching the floor lights come on and off as they neared four. "With the millennium change, though, San Francisco has become a haven for people interested in UFOs and weird science. You know that. I don't think you've got enough to hang your hat on."

"There's one way we can narrow the odds either for there being a connection between the mutilation murders and NAUTS, or against it," Paavo said. The elevator doors slid open. Neither man got off.

"I got you. Let's go." Yosh hit the button for the first floor.

"Sorry to bother you, Mrs. Cole," Paavo said as he stood in the doorway and spoke to the wife of the third mutilation victim, Leon Cole. "We were wondering if Captain Cole ever said any-

thing to you about UFOs. Did he have any interest in them?"

"You mean those space things? Like all those
science fiction movies coming out now trying to
scare poor God-fearing people?"

"Yes," Paavo said. "More or less."

"Leon didn't care none about that trash. He
was a good man. Even when he was stationed at
Nellis AFB in Nevada, near that Area Fifty-one,
he tried to stay clear of it."

"What do you mean?"

"Area Fifty-one is where Dreamland is located,
out at Groom Lake. It's a research center and
secret air base. They're supposed to have dead
aliens and UFO spacecraft and Lord only knows
what out there.

"Leon went out there a few times, got a little
too close to all that nonsense to suit me. It's the
work of the devil as far as I'm concerned. Then
something happened. He never said what it was,
but he stopped having anything to do with all
that." Her confused gaze met Paavo's. "Until
recently."

"What happened recently?" Paavo asked.

"There was a drawing. Some UFO group held
it. My, yes. He was so excited about that. He won
a hundred dollars because of that Roswell."

"You're saying Leon won?"

"That's right. In fact, the day he died, he was
going to collect. I don't know if he got the
money or not. Now, I wonder if somebody

robbed my husband? If he was killed for a lousy hundred dollars!" She pulled out a handkerchief and quickly wiped her eyes.

"Do you know anything about the group, Mrs. Cole?"

"Not much. All I've seen is a brochure about Roswell—the true story, or something—that he brought home. It's on his bureau with a bunch of other stuff. I just haven't had the heart to clean it up yet. I'll go get it for you."

As she walked away, Paavo caught Yosh's eye. "Bingo!" Yosh said.

20

Angie was shocked when she heard the knock on her door. It was only five o'clock. Paavo almost never left work this early. She'd been reading about the HAARP project in Alaska that controlled the weather—another government conspiracy. There were times she wished the government were half as clever as the conspiracy theorists believed it was, and other times she was glad it wasn't. She put down the magazine article and ran to open the door. Cops had a way of knocking in a no-nonsense manner: open up or else. She figured they must learn it at the police academy.

"Paavo." She gave him a hello kiss. "I'm sorry about Derrick and Stan and Connie here yesterday. If I'd known you were free—"

"Don't be sorry. They're your friends." They walked into the living room. "I'm not crazy about a couple of them, but that's my problem, not yours."

"I can't believe you're already off work. This is wonderful. Do you want to go out to dinner, or can I cook up something here? We can enjoy the tree, Christmas carols . . . each other."

"That's tempting, Angie." He stood in front of the Christmas tree filled with colorfully painted porcelain and old-fashioned wooden ornaments in all kinds of shapes—Santas, elves, reindeer, and toys among them. Below the tree was a hand-painted antique English creche with the three Wise Men bearing gifts. It was homey and warm, yet elegant. Like Angie. "But I'm still working. I'm here on a case."

"A case?" She sat on the sofa.

He removed his jacket and put it on a chair, then took off his shoulder holster. He joined her on the sofa.

"Is this about those horrible murders?" she asked, her posture stiff.

He nodded. Seeing the way she tensed up, he knew it was impossible for him to question her as if she were some stranger with information. "Come here." He held out his arm and she slid next to him. "For some reason, your friend Holton was asking me about the numbers on the murder victims' chests—seven, five, four. Do they mean anything to you?"

"Not a thing. Heaven only knows what he's thinking. I'm worried about him, Paavo. He's on edge—maybe over the edge. The other day he came here convinced aliens are killing the mutilated men you're investigating. He said the men are being mutilated the same way extraterrestrials do to cattle."

"He believes that?" Paavo sounded worried about Derrick's sanity.

"It's part of the lore. I understand a lot of people—sane people—believe it. Anyway, Stan will let Derrick stay with him until Derrick starts to feel better."

"Or until Stan drives him completely bonkers."

"Be nice, Paavo."

"I'm as nice to Bonnette as he is to me. Back to your little alien-loving buddies. One thing we've just learned, and which we'll keep out of the newspapers, is that all the victims had a similar brochure about Roswell."

Her mouth dropped open. "Wait a minute." With that she rushed into the den. When she came back, she handed him one that read *Roswell: The True Story.* "Is this it?"

"This is it." He looked over the brochure. It was exactly the same as the others. "Where did you get it?"

"From Oliver Hardy." She sat beside him again. "I only spoke to him a couple of times, as I told Inspector Mayfield. In fact, the last conversation I had with him was about you."

"Me?"

She took a deep breath. "He asked if I was seeing Derrick, and I said no, I was seeing a homicide inspector. He said you should have been there with me, and I told him you were busy trying to find the mutilation murderer. But that's not the strange part. When I mentioned Bertram Lambert, Oliver turned ghostly pale."

"You think he knew Lambert?"

"I asked him that. He said he didn't. Now that I'm talking about it again, I can't help but wonder if he was telling the truth."

"Did you tell Inspector Mayfield this?" he asked.

Angie's mouth tightened. "Not all of it. She cut me off, so I never did get a chance to mention Lambert to her."

Paavo shuddered at the image of Mayfield trying to interrogate Angie. He was glad he'd missed it. "All three men who were mutilated had these flyers about Roswell. Now Oliver Hardy is dead and Mosshad has disappeared. It's a strange coincidence."

And coincidences, Angie knew, were something Paavo didn't believe in.

"The people I've met at NAUTS are strange, but I hate to think any of them are killers."

"We have to find out why these murders are happening. Then the killer—whoever he or she is—will become evident."

"I just hope Derrick has nothing to do with it."

She felt him stiffen. "Why? You still care about him?"

"No. Because Connie does. And I was the one who got the two of them together. If I ever think about matchmaking again, Paavo, will you tell me to keep my nose out of it?"

"Sure I will. And I'm sure you'll listen and do exactly as I say."

"Don't I always?" she asked.

He wasn't about to open that can of worms. "I'd like to talk to Holton. You said he's at Bonnette's?"

"Yes. Let me phone." She dialed Stan's number and the two had a short conversation. "Derrick isn't there, and he won't be back until late," she said to Paavo. "NAUTS is having a meeting at eight tonight at Tardis Hall to talk about Oliver's death."

"Why don't we go pay Holton a visit before the meeting?" Paavo suggested.

"Good idea."

As Paavo fell into a thoughtful silence, Angie shut off all the lights except those on the Christmas tree, put on a CD of Leonard Bernstein conducting Christmas music, and sat beside him. She put her arms around him and watched his blue eyes widen in surprise. "We have a couple of hours. If you're not hungry, we could stay here, as I suggested earlier. Enjoy the tree, Christmas music . . ."

He drew her closer. "Did I ever tell you how much I love listening to carols?"

Almost immediately after they entered the hall, Paavo found Holton. Paavo excused himself from Angie and went off to talk to Derrick alone. It was clear to her that Paavo didn't think she should listen in on the questioning.

Well, she just might do some questioning of her own. Later, when she and Paavo compared notes, it would be interesting to see which one had picked up the truly "inside" information.

Angie spotted Kronos setting up his projector. After a few words of greeting and condolences about Oliver, she steered the conversation toward Algernon and Kronos's ex-wife. "I'm surprised she liked Algernon enough to stay with the Prometheans," Angie said. "The man seems to be such a playboy."

Kronos frowned. For a moment, Angie thought he'd refuse to answer. "She doth believe she is the reincarnation of a goddess of yore, and that the knave is her god."

How many Promethean women believed such a thing? "Not Isis?" Angie said.

Surprise, then pain, then resignation flickered over Kronos's features. "You have met my lady? Or ex-lady?"

"Yes. Once. She and Algernon are married or living together now, I take it."

He yanked the old film off the projector and put a new reel on. "Hell, no. He's too ambitious." Angie noticed that he dropped his phony accent as soon as he had anything emotional to say. "He wouldn't tie himself down with some cheap-ass divorcee. He doesn't care how jealous she is, or how many fits she throws. What he wants is a rich broad who'll help him get to the top of his line. He wants to be the Oprah of the UFO movement. He was having a fling with Triana

Crisswell until her old man found out she'd donated something like eighty thousand dollars to him."

"What!"

"It's true. For old man Crisswell, it was chump change, but he put Triana on a tight leash after that. Makes her life hell. Algernon's probably looking elsewhere now. Judging from your clothes and jewelry, I wouldn't be surprised if he didn't show up at your place one of these days."

"He already has. Triana was with him."

"Instead of killing Oliver and Mosshad—if they were murdered—and people like those poor guys who got themselves all carved up, someone should do in Algernon. Unless, of course, he will be killed. Maybe the others are just to throw the cops off the real victim. You never know."

Angie was shocked. "This NAUTS/Prometheus Group feud isn't bad enough to lead to murder, is it?"

"There's a lot of money in UFOs these days. Prime pickings for charlatans like Algernon, uh, methinks. It wouldn't bother me a bit if whoever killed the others would finish the job and get rid of him."

"Who do you think is behind these murders?" Angie asked.

He got close to her and whispered in her ear. "The government."

Angie marched away. Was there no talking to these people without hitting right up against their government conspiracy theories? In the distance, she saw the only sane one in the group. "Hi, Elvis," she said when she reached him. "How are you doing? The news about Oliver must have been a horrible shock. I know you liked him."

"Not really. In fact, I didn't like him at all," Elvis said. "Stuffing his brochures in people's faces. No wonder somebody killed him."

"We don't know that for sure. He might have committed suicide."

"So they say. It might have been a clever murderer."

"Who would want to murder Oliver?"

"Isn't it obvious?"

"Not to me."

"Derrick Holton." He smiled.

"Derrick?" Maybe Elvis was as crazy as the rest of them. "You can't mean that."

"But I do. Oliver was a spy for Algernon, and Derrick found out."

"Even if that were true, Derrick couldn't kill anyone. He's as gentle as they come."

"Not where NAUTS is concerned. Oliver would get the names of interested people at NAUTS events by giving them brochures and telling them they might make a hundred dollars in a drawing. Then he'd pass the names to Algernon, who got them to join the Prometheans."

"Derrick wouldn't kill for a reason like that!" Angie cried.

"Wouldn't he?" Elvis asked. "Odd. I would."

Chills ran through her. She excused herself and walked around looking for Paavo. He and Derrick still hadn't returned.

Phil walked by. Even though it was December, he wore sandals with no socks. His toes were blue.

"Phil, wait," Angie said. "I was just talking to Elvis and I'm really troubled."

"Be cool, sister. You're looking real stressed-out. Elvis is just a kid. You shouldn't let him get to you that way."

"You're right. And it probably means nothing."

"What did he say?"

"That Oliver was a spy for Algernon, and when Derrick found out he . . . he was really upset."

"That could be. Oliver knew I. M. Neumann. He followed the great man himself. But I think Oliver truly despised what Algernon did to the Prometheus Group. Neumann never cared about pyramids and all that garbage. He was a scientist. I once heard Oliver say Algernon deserved to die for what he did to the group." Phil smoothed his mustache. "Of course, Elvis might feel that way, too."

Angie couldn't believe these people. "Elvis? He has no anger about any of this."

"He keeps it well hidden. He grew up on the streets. In a gang in L.A.—a white supremacist gang to combat all the ethnic gangs around the town. He was badly knifed—nearly died. When he got healthy, he insisted he'd had a near-death experience. He left his body, saw the light, the whole nine yards. That told him there was more to life than we think we know. He began to search and ended up with NAUTS. He can't stand phonies."

"The near-death experience makes him sound more like someone who'd join the Prometheus Group than NAUTS," Angie said.

"Maybe he's your spy. Not Oliver. Excuse me, I've got to go sign up some new members now that Oliver's no longer around to do it."

She couldn't imagine there being any new members. Especially since Phil didn't walk to the entrance to the building where new members might be, but headed backstage.

Just then, Paavo and Derrick emerged from the same area. The doors opened, a signal that the meeting would begin.

Paavo took Angie's arm and they left.

21

"I think Angie is right. These mutilations are related to UFOs and aliens," Paavo said to Yosh as he sat reading Internet reports on alleged animal mutilations by aliens.

"I hate to tell you this, Paav," Yosh replied with a shake of his head, "but not even the San Francisco PD will let you get away with that one. Nut cults, Satanists? Yeah, sure. But little killers from space? No way."

"I'm learning quite a bit about these so-called aliens. I need someone with a science background to look at it, though. I think I'll ask a favor of Ray Faldo again."

"Partner, unless you want Lieutenant Hollins to put you on stress leave, just keep this stuff under your hat. Faldo's a good guy, but what if he opens his mouth where he shouldn't? Make this sound like some wacked-out millennium stuff and there's no way you'll convince a DA to take it to court."

"Take what to court?" Rebecca Mayfield asked as she put her purse under her desk and her jacket on the back of her chair. "You two haven't figured out who the mutilation murderer is, have you?"

"You're just the person we need to talk to," Paavo said. "We have a lead that might give some motive. Even a suspect."

"That's great," she said. "How can I help?"

"Tell us how the Oliver Hardy case is coming."

"Accidental death. We'll be filing the paperwork soon."

"I've heard he distributed brochures about Roswell. Do you know anything about that?"

"He had so much stuff about Roswell it was almost spooky. The guy was buggy on the subject. He not only had thousands of brochures, but also a card catalogue of names of prospective members of his group. They held drawings and gave away hundred-dollar bills to some new members. It was unreal."

Paavo caught Yosh's gaze. "Could that be how the vics were contacted?"

"Could that be what?" Rebecca asked, looking from one to the other. "I didn't follow."

"We're on to something, but we need proof," Paavo told her. "Do you have a problem if Yosh and I go over to Oliver's house and take a look?"

"Like I said, I'm ready to file a report that his

death was an accident. If you can find something to stop me from being wrong, be my guest."

As the two men stood to put their jackets on, Mayfield propped her chin on her hand and said, "If you're just poking around for some kind of clues or what have you, you might want to check out his mother's house."

"His mother's? I thought she was dead."

"She is, but apparently he was still taking care of her home."

"Thanks for the tip."

Rebecca leaned back in her chair and regarded the two inspectors. "If you guys come up with anything big based on what looks like a crummy little accidental death, I'll never forgive you. Or myself."

Paavo's hunch only grew stronger as he went through John Oliver Harding's tiny apartment. The man was definitely three cans short of a six-pack. There were boxes of unopened Roswell brochures piled in every corner. Harding also had a stack of completed forms for the hundred-dollar drawing. Among them Paavo found the names Bertram Lambert, Felix Rolfe, Leon Cole . . . and Angie's neighbor, Stanfield Bonnette. Stan was lucky that he wasn't a winner.

The one thing that was missing was any kind of evidence to link Harding with the deaths of the three men. The strong possibility existed as well that Harding was himself another victim. Could

he have fallen to his death trying to get away from
the murderer? If so, that could mean the murderer was one of the four men in the hall with
Angie when she called him. Each of the four—
former NASA scientist Holton, grubby Kronos,
love-beaded Phil, and choirboy Elvis—was, at
minimum, eccentric and obsessive. Murderers
came in all shapes, sizes, and disorders. Sometimes they even seemed absurdly normal. He
wasn't about to discount any of them.

In the apartment, he and Yosh found papers
with Harding's mother's address. "Hey, look at
this!" Yosh said, holding up a key from a kitchen
drawer filled with junk. The key had a chain
with a label on it—and on the label was the
same address.

They locked up Harding's apartment and
drove south of the city along the peninsula. Even
though they were crossing into another jurisdic-
tion, since they were looking at the property of a
man who had mysteriously died in their jurisdic-
tion, they could do so as long as they weren't
about to take any action. The address was located
on a narrow road at the top of a hill in San Mateo.
The front lawn was overgrown and weed-infested,
and the house looked as if it hadn't been cared
for in years. They knocked, announced themselves, then unlocked the door. The house was
quite small, just four rooms, although the lot it sat
on was nearly an acre. Dirty pots and dishes filled
the sink. In the refrigerator, the milk had gone
sour, and much of the food was moldy.

"Looks like your fridge, pal," Yosh said with a laugh.

"Everyone's a critic."

Nothing in the house gave any hint of Harding's obsession with Roswell. Paavo opened the back door. "Good God, look at that!"

Yosh joined him. In a far corner of the property stood a small octagonal building. Jutting from the top of it, clear of the trees, was the tip of a telescope.

"I wonder if he was communicating with the mother planet," Yosh said as the two of them trooped across the weeds and dirt of the yard to the building.

They opened the door and walked inside. It took a moment for their eyes to adjust from the bright sunlight outside to the dark gloom within. Even after they were able to see again, it took another moment for their brains to register what they were seeing.

"God!" Yosh cried. He couldn't stop himself from gagging, and he spun around, ready to bolt outdoors if need be.

In front of them, lined up on a table against the wall, were glass jars in many sizes, filled with what smelled like formaldehyde. Floating in the jars were the body parts that had been removed from the three dead men.

"Christ, he was one sick bastard," Paavo said.

"I guess we've got the proof we needed," Yosh said when he was able to talk again.

"What's that smell, Yosh?"

"The formaldehyde?"

"No. Something else. Something rank." Paavo walked toward a ladder that went up to the loft on which the telescope stood.

"Up there?" Yosh said. He was still spooked by the find in the glass jars.

Paavo nodded. He tested the ladder to see if it was strong enough to hold his weight, although if the rather obese Harding had used it, he didn't think there would be any problem. He went up. Yosh pulled out his gun as he waited. Something about the strange little building with its grisly contents was making him very nervous.

From the circular opening in the ceiling, sun shone onto the telescope and the floor of the loft around it, but the walls past the telescope were obscured in shadow. Paavo couldn't make out what was there, but the stench was much, much stronger.

He removed his gun from the shoulder holster and with his left hand switched on his penlight. At first, all he could discern were a bunch of blankets. Then a black, nearly lifeless eye opened and looked straight at him.

"Dr. Mosshad?" he whispered.

22

"You mean all this fighting is over the Great Pyramid?" Connie asked. She, Angie, Derrick, and Stan were walking through the farmer's market helping Angie make a list of foods to serve at the fantasy dinner. Since she had come up with the Roswell theme, she thought a 1947 all-American buffet would be a nice touch. But when she tried to find out what that was, she learned it wasn't much. During the war, food had been limited and had stayed that way for several years thereafter. At least she didn't have to serve the wartime standard, chipped beef on toast.

She finally settled on traditional baked ham, southern fried chicken, and potato and macaroni salads as the cornerstone of the buffet, plus Jell-O molds—very big in the forties. She'd have lots of Jell-O molds—green aliens, red planets, yellow suns, and blue spaceships.

Now, armed with a notepad, she and her

friends walked through the market to come up with interesting foods as side dishes that wouldn't require cooking, since she couldn't find a chef and she wasn't masochistic enough to attempt to cook for between two hundred and three hundred people. Washing and chopping fruits and vegetables would be quite enough work.

"The Great Pyramid is just one part of it," Derrick said in answer to Connie's question. "The Prometheans have some wild theory that the pyramids were built by people who came here from the star Sirius."

"They can't really think extraterrestrials built the pyramids," Connie said.

"The proof is based on people called the Dogon in West Africa," Derrick explained. "They have ancient rock paintings that show aliens from Sirius. The aliens told the Dogon that two stars not visible to the naked eye orbit Sirius. In the mid-nineteenth century, one such star was actually discovered!"

"Well, doggone!" Stan cried.

The others booed.

"Here we go, Angie," Connie cried, pointing to the fruit stands. "You need to serve pomegranates, mangos, and papayas."

"Add figs and mandarin oranges," Stan said.

"Over there are artichoke hearts," Derrick said. "Though why I should be helping you choose food for a party to give my competitor more publicity is a mystery to me."

"It's because you're such a good friend," Angie

said, madly writing the suggestions into her notepad as they were called out. "Artichoke hearts are good. We'll have a garden salad section, but only with imaginative vegetables—no celery or carrots—and with them a big selection of dressings."

"Ah, over there." Connie dashed ahead, shouting to Angie, "Braised fennel, avocado, yogurt with cucumber. This is great fun!"

Angie stopped, stared, then turned and faced Derrick and Stan, drawing them close. "Don't look now," she said, "but I just saw the same strange man I've seen a couple of other places lately. He's standing by the flowers watching us."

"There are lots of people by the flowers," Stan said. "Is he the guy near the carnations or the sunflowers? Or near the gladioli?"

"I don't know!" Angie cried. "And I don't want to turn around to see what flowers he's standing by, for Pete's sake! He's the creepy-looking man with the black suit and sunglasses. How many of them can there be?"

"Look at all the nuts!" Connie cried, farther away now. "How about pistachios, cashews, and honeyed almonds?"

"Don't tell me." Derrick leaned closer to Angie, his back to the flowers. "Is his face white and pasty, his mouth tiny and completely expressionless, and when he takes off his glasses his eyes are almost white?"

Angie looked at him as if he were crazy. "I've never seen him with his glasses off," she said slowly. "But the rest is true. How do you know this?"

"He's one of the men in black," Derrick said, his voice a raspy whisper. "You heard the lecture about them. They're sent from up there, or by the government—we aren't exactly sure which—to stop anyone who has had experience with extraterrestrials from going to the press about it."

"They must be from the government, then," Stan said, hands on his skinny hips. "Because they've done a piss-poor job. Stuff about UFOs is all over TV and radio."

"But with no proof," Derrick said. "They're watching you, Angie, for some reason. Be careful."

"That's too creepy," Stan said. "The guy you've described is gone, anyway. Let's get back to the food."

"Come on, you guys!" Connie returned to them. "What's the holdup? I was already down at the breads. They've got warm Indian fry bread, plus black rye, baguettes, sourdough, croissants— are they bread?—brioche, and something called flan-filled pretzels, which I've never heard of."

"They're from Spain," Angie said.

"Don't forget to serve bruschetta," Stan said.

"Come over here," Derrick called. "There are more cheeses than you can shake a stick at." He pointed at the Brie, Gorgonzola, Gouda, Pont L'Evêque, chèvre, Serpa, feta, Morbier, and on and on.

Angie stared at the cheeses. Her list was already longer than she could handle. She could use three or four at most.

"I think it's time to sample the desserts," Connie said. "I'll grab that table in the corner, and you guys can get one of everything. We don't want Angie to make the wrong choices, now do we?"

"I like the way that woman thinks," Stan said. "Are you sure you don't want to marry me, Connie?"

"Get lost, Stanfield."

Angie was already checking over the glass display cabinets filled with all kinds of pastries and other desserts—charlotte russe, pine nut and honey cakes, a variety of fruit tarts, hazelnut torte, lemon squares, chocolate blancmange, savarin chantilly, puff pastry cakes with almond cream, rum babas, marzipan-chocolate torte, and Russian wedding cookies.

"I'll get us all some coffee," Derrick said.

"Lattès for me and Connie," Angie said. "Stan likes regular."

Angie ordered a selection of the desserts—so much for Connie's plans to diet—and took them to the table where the others sat. Derrick was talking. "I wish it were that easy. I've got to learn to deal with it."

"Deal with what?" Angie asked as she placed the tray of pastries on the table.

No one paid attention. "What is it you're afraid of?" Connie gave Derrick a soulful look.

He rested his arms on the tabletop and hung his head. "It's so hard to talk about."

"What is?" Angie asked as she carefully cut each pastry into four equal pieces.

"You can trust me," Connie said, lightly touching his wrist.

Derrick placed his hand on hers and smiled. Angie and Stan glanced at each other. Stan waggled his eyebrows. "It's because of them," Derrick said, gazing soulfully into Connie's eyes.

"Them?" she asked.

"Them," he answered, glancing upward.

Uh-oh, Angie thought. She handed out forks and napkins.

"I think they're here, Connie." Derrick gripped both her hands in his. "I think they walk among us, trying to learn about us. Trying to take us over, make us part of their lives—part of them."

Just then a waitress came over with two lattès, a regular coffee, and one espresso.

Connie never took her eyes from Derrick. "If you're talking about aliens, I don't believe in all that, and you shouldn't either, Derrick."

"Believe it. I know it's true. I *know.*"

Angie doled out some pastries, careful not to miss a word Derrick said.

"How do you know?" Connie asked, then put a piece of savarin into her mouth.

He waited a long while, gazing into her eyes as she chewed and swallowed, and when she didn't pull back, didn't look away, he lowered his voice and said, "Eighteen months ago I was abducted."

Stan, already on his third sampling of pastry, dropped his fork. "Wow."

Angie froze. To think she'd been worried that he was going to say something simple, like the end of the world was at hand.

"Impossible," Connie said.

"I wouldn't lie about such a thing, Connie. Not to you or Angie." His gaze met Angie's, then he turned back to Connie. In that moment Angie knew he was telling the truth—his truth, perhaps, but he believed it. "It was the most devastating experience of my life," he continued. "I had no way to protect myself. I was completely at their mercy."

Connie's eyes, when they met Angie's, were troubled. "Where did this happen to you?" Connie asked.

"I was home in bed, asleep, when they came. They came into my room. Little men. Six of them. They were small, like eight-year-old boys, and they surrounded my bed, looking at me with those big black eyes of theirs—frightening, cold black eyes." He shut his own eyes and drew in a deep, quivering breath. His face had gone pale and beads of perspiration appeared on his forehead. "They were all dressed alike, in a filmy gray skinlike suit. Their faces were flat, with pointed chins. Some have said they have the face of a praying mantis, and those people are right. It's what they're like. Like . . . like insects."

His voice was growing loud and shrill. Connie murmured words of comfort as she patted his arm, then lightly touched his face, brushed his hair back. "You don't have to talk about it. It's over. You're all right."

He clutched her wrist. "They reached out for me. I tried to run, but I couldn't. Their hands were like little suction cups, taking hold of me, then lifting. I screamed as I was lifted off the bed, upward toward the ceiling. I don't know if I fainted or what, because the next thing I knew, I was no longer in my apartment, but outdoors, being lifted into a spaceship."

"You were drunk, man." Stan rolled his eyes. "I went to a party once and was given some bad drugs and—"

"Be quiet, Stan!" Connie slid her chair closer to Derrick's and placed her hand on his shoulder. "You poor darling."

"So, did you see the inside of the spaceship?" Stan asked.

"Oh, I saw it. One part of it, anyway. They took me inside a big room with lights shining on me. They tied me down and poked needles and tubes into my brain, eyes, and scrotum, draining fluids from me. I was terrified that they might do something that would be fatal or cause blindness or sterility. I couldn't stop them. I was afraid to try, afraid to move, no matter how painful or how invasive it was."

"Jesus," Stan said with a shudder. "What a story."

"It's not a story. They're here. They tried to take me again, three more times. The most recent was just last week. I've managed to escape so far.

I've hidden from them, but I don't know how long I can keep it up. That's why I'm afraid to be alone."

He looked down at his clasped hands. Connie touched them. "My God, Derrick, your hands are like ice."

"I don't feel well. It's the memories. I can't get rid of them. Then, when they came after me again, it scared me so much." His teeth began to chatter.

"Let's get him home," Angie said, standing.

"What will I do with him?" Stan cried.

As Derrick stood, Connie put her arm around his waist and drew his arm over her shoulders. "I've got my car. I'll take him to my house, give him some hot soup, and let him relax. When he's himself again, I'll bring him to your place, Stan."

Derrick's hand tightened on her shoulder. His face seemed to soften, to lose its strained, rigid expression. "You're a very kind woman," he said.

She blushed and her eyes sparkled. "You're very brave."

Without a word to the others, they left the marketplace.

Stan and Angie sat down again, side by side, and watched them go.

"Sheesh," Stan said, reaching for some marzipan-chocolate torte. "I thought being concerned about laser beams and radio waves was far out. That guy takes the cake."

"Cake I can deal with," Angie said, looking at

the uneaten cakes and pastries in front of them. "It's Connie that I'm worried about."

"Congratulations!" Angie cried when Paavo opened the front door to his home that night.

She watched a smile cross his mouth, then brighten his eyes, even though they were dark-ringed and heavy with weariness. "Angie," he said, her name sounding like a sigh of welcome. "What's this?" He took the large square Tupperware container she held and stepped back as she entered the living room.

"It's your reward for solving the mutilation murder case and saving Dr. Mosshad. It's all over the news. You and Yosh are heroes. I guessed that you might be a hungry hero, so here's some home cooking." She took off her coat and tossed it over a large easy chair. One sleeve flopped onto the seat and hit Hercules on the head. As the cat woke up and scolded her, Angie petted him, begged forgiveness, and then marched into the kitchen.

Paavo's kitchen was large and old-fashioned, with all-white appliances that were freestanding instead of built-in. It reminded her of the kitchen her grandmother used to have.

"I haven't turned on the TV or radio," Paavo said, setting the casserole on the kitchen table. "What are they saying?"

"That Oliver Hardy, or Harding, was crazy. That after killing three men, he killed himself out of remorse."

She had brought a beef enchilada casserole—enough for three meals. She spooned a third of it onto a plate and covered it with plastic wrap. While she put it in the microwave, Paavo refrigerated what was left.

"Did the press tell where he killed the men, or how, or explain the numbers on their chests?" he asked.

She faced him. "Did you give them answers to all that?"

"No. I'm still trying to figure it out. Not having facts hasn't always stopped the media in the past, though."

"Did Mosshad have any explanation for Oliver's kidnapping him?" She sat at the round wooden table. She liked sitting there, especially when the oven was on and the room warm and filled with the cooking smells of roasts or casseroles or pies. It reminded her of when she was a kid, sitting in her mother's kitchen in the old house, before her father got rich from his shoe stores and they moved to a monster-sized place in Hillsborough. The new house was beautiful, but there were times she missed the small Marina-district home where she and her four sisters shared two bedrooms and the kitchen was the main spot where the family gathered. As busy as her mother was helping her father with his growing business, she always had time to talk to Angie in that kitchen.

The microwave dinged. Paavo grabbed a pot holder. "Mosshad wasn't able to talk. He was traumatized, and he's an old man. The doctors expect him to make it, but it'll take time. We'll ask him those questions when we're able, plus a few others. Like why did Oliver do any of this? Also, he was short and heavy with no muscles to speak of—how did he carry the bodies? Did he have help? If so, who? And why would such a cold-blooded killer commit suicide? It just doesn't fit."

"Eat," Angie said. "Worry about it later."

The beatific look on Paavo's face when he removed the food from the microwave told her he was every bit as ready to eat a home-cooked meal as she had expected he would be. "I hope he's the only nut case this millennium change brings my way," Paavo said as he grabbed a fork, a napkin, and a bottle of Anchor Steam beer. "I thought the end-of-the-world crowd would wreak havoc, not the ufologists. There seems to be some overlap between the two. Would you like a beer, Angie?"

"I'd rather have coffee. I'll take care of it." As he sat and ate, she filled his Mr. Coffee with water, then took the French roast from the freezer, where she had convinced him to store it so it would stay fresh. "There's a small amount of overlap, but not much. In a way, that's a really unfortunate part of this whole thing. That the UFO crowd is going to get such a slap in the face. The press will have a field day with these murders."

"That's a problem?"

"I've learned a lot about things in this world

that are strange, and are interesting, and that I believe are really taking place. The UFO people aren't completely mad. The only part I'm not convinced of is that aliens have landed on Earth. Of their existence, though, out there somewhere in the entire universe, well . . ."

She guessed she'd gone too far, judging from the look on his face.

"Maybe you've been associating with these people too long, Angie."

"You could be right. The fantasy dinner at Tardis Hall is in two nights. After that, I don't have to see them any longer. I swear, I'll be glad when it's over. Triana Crisswell's fantasy has become my nightmare! Because of all the catered parties going on at workplaces, private organizations, and public events, I can't even find reliable help to hire. I'm going to have to do everything myself, with the help of some friends."

"Connie?"

"Plus Earl, Butch, and Vinnie." She opened the refrigerator to look for milk or half-and-half for the coffee and shuddered. Mustard, mayonnaise, and wilted lettuce were on the top shelf. A few smaller things were pushed far back and probably long forgotten. She had some throwing away to do; several of the leftovers were surely lethal by now.

"Do you think you might have any success getting your friend Derrick and some others from NAUTS there as well?" he asked thoughtfully.

Angie popped her head up from the refrigerator. Something about his tone hit her squarely in the pit of her stomach. "Why would I want to do such a thing to my party?"

"The press, and my boss, think this case has been tied up with a neat little bow. They may be right. I've got questions, though, with no answers yet. I'd like to get some. That party might be the way."

She shut the refrigerator door. "You found the remains of the dead men on Oliver's property. You found Mosshad there. What more could you possibly need? The case is solved, Paavo."

His gaze was hooded. "I wish I believed that."

23

"You two are the luckiest SOBs alive!" Rebecca said as she walked into Homicide the next morning.

"Not luck, woman. It was skill, pure skill. Are we hot, or are we are hot!" Yosh bellowed. "I even brought home a bottle of champagne last night to celebrate." He glanced at Paavo and lowered his voice. "Turns out Nancy isn't nearly as crazy about her calligraphy teacher as I thought she was. She just likes calligraphy. Can you beat that?" He laughed.

"So that's why you're so jolly this morning," Paavo said.

"Yessirree. I still got it. Don Juan Yoshiwara—that's me. Say, I was a little too hasty taking the Christmas on-call duty. Nancy wants me home. If someone else wouldn't mind taking it . . ."

"Give it to me," Paavo said.

"Doesn't Angie expect you to go with her to

her parents' house?" Concern crossed Yosh's
brow at Paavo's willingness to take the duty.
"What if you get a stiff to check out?"

"Don't worry about it," Paavo said. "It's more
important for you to be with Nancy and your
kids."

"I surely appreciate it, pal," Yosh said. "And
I'll ask around some more. If someone else has
no plans, I'll have him or her handle it for you."

"No problem." Paavo turned back to the files
he had pulled that morning, old cases that hadn't
been resolved, still open because there was no
statute of limitations on murder. Since his current
cases were either cleared up or taken as far as they
could go, the practice was to take a look at
another inspector's open log. Fresh eyes might
see something that had been overlooked by the
inspector too close to the case. The trouble was,
most of the open ones were Never-Take-a-Chance
Sutter's. The soon-to-be-retired cop tended to let
a lot of things slide. Paavo was reading through
the cases to see if anything looked worth pursuing.

"Your celebration didn't seem to do you as
much good as Yosh's. Or didn't you have one?"
Rebecca said, coming over to his desk.

"I'm glad we found Mosshad. And the evidence," he said, turning a page on the old report.

"You don't sound very glad," she said.

"Paavo thinks it was too easy," Yosh said. "He's
bothered by the killer's already being dead. Justice denied, and all that."

"The killer's dead. How much more justice can you get?" Rebecca asked.

Bo Benson stumbled into the bureau. He took out a handkerchief and wiped his forehead.

Rebecca jumped up. "What's wrong?"

"Claudette was lying in wait for me on the elevator. She wants me to spend Christmas Day with her. So does Bambi."

"Bambi?" Yosh asked.

"Probably Monica, too."

"No comment." Yosh glanced at Paavo.

"Anybody want to give me Christmas duty?" Bo asked. "No way I can see all three of them in one day. That's too much even for me."

"Sold!" Paavo said.

"Let's go get a cup of coffee, Paavo," Rebecca said. "I can't take listening to any more of Benson's so-called problems. I should have it half so bad. Anyway, you should be feeling good, not bad, today."

"No thanks," he said. "I just had a cup."

She shrugged and sauntered out of the bureau.

Yosh bent forward in his chair. "You still having troubles with Angie, pal?" he asked.

"She's fine. I found out what was bothering her. She understands she was worrying about something she didn't need to worry about. It's okay now."

"And?" Yosh asked.

Paavo lifted his head from Sutter's sloppily documented report. "And what?"

"Did you two talk about the stuff that's still bothering you?"

Paavo jotted a note on a Post-it and stuck it on the report he was reading. "Nothing is bothering me. Nothing at all."

"Angie, I'm so glad you're home," Connie cried as soon as Angie pulled open the door to her apartment. "I was awake half the night. I couldn't sleep. I have to talk to you, and what I need to say is best said face-to-face."

"Come in," Angie said, leading her into the kitchen. "I'm making a Saint Honoré cake to take to my sister Maria's house. It's her birthday. The week before Christmas, poor kid. She never gets to celebrate properly."

Connie's hair looked as if a cat had walked through it, she wore no makeup, and she had on a pink blouse with a neon yellow skirt. "Can I get you some coffee?" Angie asked, wondering what could be so wrong that Connie would leave the house looking that way. "If you didn't sleep, you must be awfully tired."

"That's true. I have a headache, too. But I'm not here for coffee." Angie went ahead and poured them each a cup anyway.

"We've got to talk. Seriously talk," Connie said.

"All right." Angie picked up her pastry sack. She was filling eighteen miniature cream puffs with rum custard, and then she would place them around the top edge of the cake. It was a beautiful sight. "First, let me say I'm sorry about Derrick. You were great with him, but I know he's too strange to be believed. I should never have gotten you involved in any of this."

Connie sat at the little table. Her face flushed slightly and a dreamy look filled her eyes. "Derrick is wonderful."

"He is?"

"Yes. That's why I'm here." She hesitated a moment, then the words gushed out. "Angie, I think I'm in love."

Angie stared at her, her brain trying to make sense out of what she'd just heard. "With Derrick?"

"Of course with Derrick!"

"You've only known him a few days."

"Yesterday, at my house, I gave him split pea soup, then had him lie down on the sofa to relax. Before I knew it, I was lying down beside him. He stayed with me all night and we spent a lot of that time talking. Not all of it, but some. He's so cerebral, so masterful."

"Derrick?" The custard overflowed the little cream puff and oozed onto her hand and the counter.

"The thing that I'm concerned about is . . . Angie, does it bother you that I'm in love with your old boyfriend?"

Angie's eyebrows nearly reached the top of her forehead. She put down the pastry sack and began to clean up the mess.

"Now, I know you wanted the two of us to meet,"

Connie continued. "I appreciate that. But women are strange that way. It happened to me once. I told a girlfriend about my ex-husband. She was unattached and interested, so I introduced them after warning her about all his faults. I never dreamed she'd see anything at all in the big dork. But she liked him! And the two of them dated for about six months. Now, I know I introduced them. I know it was my idea that they meet, but at the same time he was my ex-husband, and the thought of her with him, of her getting to know him in the same way as I had . . . well, I didn't like it one bit. It ruined our relationship. I don't want that to happen to us. Your friendship is important to me. I'll admit that I'd like to get to know Derrick a whole lot better, but I don't know what to do about you. So I came here to talk about it."

"I don't care if you date Derrick," Angie cried, tossing the sponge into the sink.

"That's easy to say, but think about it from deep, deep down, Angie. How would you feel in your gut about us seeing each other?"

Angie dropped into a chair. Trying to decorate a cake while giving advice to the lovelorn was impossible. "As long as you're not seeing Paavo, I don't care. That's from deep down, high up, wherever you want it. I'm not talking to you in platitudes, Connie. If you like Derrick— although I don't see why, considering that he's a nervous breakdown about to happen—go for it! You've got my blessing."

Connie squealed, flung herself toward Angie, and planted a big kiss on Angie's cheek while nearly squeezing her friend to death. "You're a doll, Ang!" She perched on the edge of her chair. "Now you've got to help me. I just don't know where to start. What can I do to become a part of his life?"

"Listen—are you really sure you want to be? He thinks aliens abducted him. I mean, he really believes aliens abducted him. I'd worry about that if I were you, Connie."

"What if he's right?" Connie suggested.

Angie rubbed her ear to make sure her hearing hadn't gone haywire. "Right? Of course he isn't right! He had some sort of trauma, I guess. He didn't believe in them when I dated him, although now that I think about it, he was always a bit fanatical. But it was a measured fanaticism, or at least one grounded in traditional science. I don't know what happened."

"It's simple, to me," Connie said. At Angie's questioning look, she continued. "He followed his science until it couldn't answer all his questions. That was when he started looking for other ways to find answers, and ended up with aliens. My ex was the same, but instead of aliens, he found drugs. I prefer aliens. Maybe we can help Derrick."

"I don't think so."

"Angie, please! What if some other woman came along and straightened him out, and then she ended up with him? I need to try. I want to be the one to make him a normal, healthy, happy man, and then keep him all to myself."

"You care that much about him?"

"Absolutely. He's important to me. What can we do to help him?"

Suddenly, Paavo's suggestion that she get some NAUTS members to go to her fantasy dinner came to mind. Why not kill two birds with one stone and make both Paavo and Connie happy with one selfless gesture?

"Well, from what I've seen, both the NAUTS members and the Prometheans would be better off if they were friends again. Someone has to take the first step. I think having Derrick and his close friends show up for Algernon's book launch—at my fantasy dinner—would be a goodwill gesture. You and I could see that they treat each other respectfully. By the end of the evening, they might even be friends again."

"You may be right. If he stops feeling so bad about the Prometheus Group, he might stop being so paranoid."

"Exactly—if we can get him there."

"Angie, you're such a good friend," Connie cried. "Your idea may very well help me with my life!"

Angie just smiled. "Sometimes, I surprise even me."

Angie handed Paavo's stepfather, Aulis Kokkonen, a large freshly baked loaf of Finnish Christmas bread. She'd put it in a basket and covered it with towels to keep it warm. A red bow adorned the basket's handle.

Paavo stood by, beaming, as Aulis's eyes lit up. Aulis wasn't really his stepfather, wasn't really related to him in any way, except that he'd taken in Paavo when he was only four, after his mother abandoned him and his older sister. Aulis was just a neighbor, but he had kept the two children in his apartment while waiting for their mother to return. When it became evident she wasn't going to, he kept them because he'd grown to love them, and they loved him in return.

When Paavo's sister died, Aulis was all he had left.

As Aulis folded back the towels, the scent of the rye bread flavored with molasses, currants, and anise filled his small apartment. "It smells just the way my mother's bread did. She used to make little loaves of it and gave almost all of it away, to the unhappiness of me and my brother and sister." He smiled as he remembered those times. His hair was white now, his skin crisscrossed with age, but his eyes were sharp and clear. "Thank you, Angie, for something so special."

"If it tastes half as good as your mother's, I'll be happy," she said.

"Let's find out." Aulis led them to the table. "Sit down, both of you. I've made some coffee already." He put a cube of butter on the table and poured the coffee.

"We called this bread *joululimppu*," he said. "It's been such a long time since I thought of that word, I can scarcely believe it." He put the bread on a cutting board and sliced a few pieces, giving the first one to Paavo. "It's still warm."

"As soon as Angie took it out of the oven, we made a mad dash across town," Paavo said. "We thought it'd be especially good this way."

It was. Slathered with butter, the bread was moist, rich, and delicious.

"Paavo tells me you usually spend Christmas Day with some close friends," Angie said. "But if you'd like, we'd love to have you come to my parents' house with Paavo and me."

"Thank you, but no," Aulis said. "My friends are family to me. It would be wrong not to be with them."

"You don't mind that I'll be stealing Paavo that day?" she asked, strangely guilty that she and Paavo couldn't be in two places at once.

Aulis glanced at Paavo a moment, then back to Angie. "He'll be where he belongs."

Relief filled her. "Thank you," she said softly.

Just before it was time to leave, Angie went off to the bathroom to freshen up. Paavo stared after her and shook his head.

"What's the matter?" Aulis asked.

"I'm going crazy trying to figure out what to do about Christmas, Pa. I don't know what to get her—or what I can afford to get her. I don't want to give her anything cheap, but even when

I look at expensive things, there's nothing she wants—she's got everything! I don't know what to do."

Aulis chuckled. "No, no, no, my boy! You're going about this all wrong. You're lucky there's no special thing she wants or needs. This way, she won't be disappointed if you guess wrong. Whatever you give her, make it come from your heart. Something you like. Something you want to see her wear, perhaps. Whatever you choose, she'll like because it comes from you."

"You think so?" Paavo asked.

"I've had a few lady friends in my day." Aulis nodded knowingly. "Trust me on this."

24

"Paavo, you need to listen to your partner about this. Yosh is right," Ray Faldo said the next morning. He and Paavo sat at a high worktable in the crime laboratory. The criminologist gathered the papers Paavo had printed off the Internet and fastened them together with a butterfly clip. "Take these materials and burn them."

"But they explain the implements found on the victims," Paavo argued. "The night goggles, the integrated circuit chip, even the fiber optics."

Faldo handed the documents back to him. "The killer—Oliver Hardy, or whatever his name is—is dead. Forget it."

Paavo reached for his paper coffee cup and finished the last dregs. The coffee had grown cold. "The part that bothers me, Ray, is that from what little we've learned of John Oliver Harding's background, he had no scientific training. His father died when he was a young boy, and he lived quietly with his mother. He enjoyed astronomy, but as an amateur. He grew up in the town of Tonopah, Nevada, and in his twenties moved to an even smaller town called Rachel. About ten years ago he moved to San Francisco and got a job at the main library. He was a clerk. It makes me wonder if we've got the right man."

Faldo got up off the high stool he'd been sitting on and rubbed his back. He was perpetually round-shouldered, even when standing. Paavo guessed it was from spending too many hours hunched over a microscope in the lab. "Let me get this straight, Paavo. The defense R-and-D boys studied the materials found at Roswell and were able to determine what a few of them did. Then they funneled some of them to the private sector, where labs were conducting similar research—places like Bell, IBM, Monsanto, Dow, Hughes, and so on. The military gave those labs the materials and told them to reverse-engineer them, right?"

"Right," Paavo said. "That's the ufologist explanation of how so many enormous technological advances happened within a very short time. Alien technology from a crash site was seeded into U.S. companies by the military."

"The ultimate military-industrial complex conspiracy." Faldo clucked his tongue. "And this is what you want to use to toss out the case against Harding as the mutilation murderer? That he wasn't scientific enough?"

Paavo didn't know what to think. "Whoever killed those men apparently believes we are using alien technology, and the killer had pieces of that early technology to prove he knows what he's talking about."

"You know, the murderer brings up an issue that isn't half bad," Faldo said, stroking his chin. "If the technology didn't come from some extraterrestrial source, how did we develop so much so quickly?"

After leaving Faldo's lab, Paavo went back to his desk and called up a map of Nevada on the Internet. He looked up Tonopah, and then Rachel. "Unbelievable," he whispered.

He got in his car and drove to Bertram Lambert's house. In the bedroom he went through the box of photos Lambert had squirreled away in his closet. The first time he had flipped through them, he hadn't been looking for anything in particular. He remembered one of them, though, and he wanted to check it out. It might be nothing at all.

He quickly found the one he'd been thinking of. It showed a twenty-something Lambert squatting down on a dirt road next to three signs:

WARNING
Military Installation

WARNING
RESTRICTED AREA

WARNING
U.S. AIR FORCE INSTALLATION

He turned over the picture and saw a small
notation: GROOM LAKE, NV, 1985. "Unbelievable,"
he repeated.

Groom Lake was the location of Area 51, on
the Nevada Test Site. The town of Rachel, where
John Oliver Harding had lived, was the closest
civilian town. The third victim, Leon Cole, had
been stationed at nearby Nellis AFB. Felix
Rolfe's social worker had said that Rolfe had
once been in the army and had traveled
throughout the Southwest. And now he had
proof that Bertram Lambert had been there as
well.

Area 51—Dreamland—was where UFOs were
said to have been brought and studied. That
had to be the connection between the victims. It
seemed farfetched, yet Derrick Holton had
asked about the numbers on the victims' chests.
Seven, five, four. Those numbers must have
something to do with UFOs. Now, if only he
could figure out what . . .

Holton had clammed up when asked, but
there might be a lot more talkative group at
Angie's fantasy dinner.

He'd find someone who'd say. Or, if nothing
else, someone willing to speculate.

* * *

Angie and her sisters were sitting in Maria's living room to celebrate Maria's birthday.

"So, Angie." Her eldest sister, Bianca, turned and solemnly faced her. Bianca was always serious. "Do you think Paavo will give you an engagement ring for Christmas?"

"Oh yes!" Francesca, the next to youngest, squealed. Frannie had recently had her first child and was disgustingly bubbly. "I can't imagine you haven't caught him yet. Your boyfriends were always wanting to get married. I was afraid you'd marry before I did. That would have been very rude of you."

"Maybe she's losing her touch." Caterina, the second oldest, sniffed.

"Don't say that," said Maria, the pious middle sister, who took on the role of peacemaker in the family. "You know Paavo is crazy about Angie. He's just not crazy about marriage."

"She might be better off if he doesn't pick out a ring," Bianca said. "If she goes with him, she can get exactly what she wants. It's not like he can go out and buy her some huge rock to show off. Cops don't make much money."

"You couldn't pay me to do that job." Cat caught her reflection in the silver tea service and fluffed her hair.

"I think it's neat that Paavo's a cop," Frannie said. "He's so much more interesting than another lawyer in the family."

"My husband's a lawyer," Cat said.

"See what I mean?" Frannie was smug.

"We don't have any scientists in the family," Maria said, "and I understand from Mamma that Derrick Holton's back in your life, Angie."

"Papà liked Derrick Holton," Frannie said. "Derrick wanted to get married bad. Do you remember that, Angie?"

"Of course she remembers," Bianca said. "Just because she's the youngest doesn't mean she doesn't have brains."

"If she had brains, she'd have married Derrick." Cat smoothed an eyebrow.

"She told me Connie was interested in Derrick. Didn't you say that, Angie?" Bianca asked.

"You mean she's letting her best friend steal a rich, famous scientist out from under her nose?" Cat shook her head and sighed. "Angie, how could you allow such a thing to happen?"

"She doesn't like Derrick anymore," Bianca explained. "If she liked him, she would have married him a long time ago."

"I hope Papà never hears about this." Frannie shook her head sorrowfully. "He'll be so disappointed."

"So, Angie, why don't you answer?" Bianca asked. "Is Paavo giving you a ring for Christmas?"

Angie waited a moment to be sure they'd finished dissecting her love life, then she simply said, "No."

"We're going to have a wonderful dinner party tomorrow night," Angie said to Paavo as she led him into Tardis Hall. She had spent the morning, before going to Maria's, running around making sure the food would be delivered, and taking care of details. Her plans seemed to be coming together beautifully. She wanted to make one last stop at the hall to be sure everything was right for the party before she and Paavo went out to dinner.

She led him into the auditorium. Round tables and chairs had been set up. A sound system was in one corner, and at one end of the room was a flying saucer.

A sign over the back of it read Roswell, July 5, 1947.

He glanced at the sign again. Something nagged at him about it. Roswell. What was bothering him?

"The Prometheus Group—that's Algernon's group—built the flying saucer. Isn't it cute? Around it we'll be displaying photos from Roswell, the site of the crash; the newspaper headline based on the press release the army issued after the spaceship crashed; and pictures of Jesse Marcel and Roy Danzer, who were big names at the time. I simply love it."

"They did a good job," he said. "Quite realistic . . . if such a thing can be realistic."

"It certainly can." A deep voice sounded behind them.

"Algernon!" Angie cried. "I didn't expect to see you here today. Let me introduce you to my friend, Inspector Paavo Smith. Paavo, this is

Algernon, head of the Prometheus Group, and guest of honor at tomorrow's dinner."

The two men shook hands. Algernon turned to Angie, clasped her hand in both of his, and held it as they spoke. "I thought I'd stop by to see how it was shaping up. It looks like everything's under control."

"It is. I have several friends to help. Vinnie will pour drinks and handle the music—CD's with nineteen-forties songs, big-band tunes, all that. Butch will oversee the food. Connie, Earl, and I will serve and make sure everything runs smoothly."

"So, Angie, did you ever find out what aliens eat?" he asked with a rakish smile.

"No. But I came up with a better idea. Who would want to eat what aliens eat, anyway?"

"Good point." Still holding Angie's hand, he looked at Paavo. "Tell me, Inspector Smith, are you a believer?"

"I'm afraid not." His pointed gaze rested on Algernon and Angie's clasped hands, then lifted to Algernon. "Just an observer."

"As long as you have an open mind, you will come to believe."

"I don't think it's a matter of belief," Paavo said, "but of science. I'll wait for some scientific basis before I accept the existence of extraterrestrial life."

Algernon kissed the back of Angie's hand, then let it go, turning all his attention to Paavo. "Then you'll never accept it," he said dismissively. "Not because such proof doesn't exist, but because the scientists won't divulge it. They get their funding from the government. They'll say only what the government allows them to say. They don't want to lose their gravy train."

Paavo gave Angie a cold stare.

"Excuse us," Angie said. "We were just leaving. Oh, by the way," she called, "Derrick Holton will be coming to your party tomorrow. Isn't that wonderful?"

Algernon scowled fiercely.

She grabbed Paavo's arm as they hurried away. "Sorry about that." She didn't want him to hear any more of this. He might change his mind about coming with her to the party.

"Wait a second." He stopped to read the sign again. Roswell—July 5, 1947. He shook his head and followed her.

They got into his Austin Healy for the ride to the restaurant, Fior d'Italia. He pulled out his notebook. "What are you doing?" Angie asked.

"That Roswell sign. Something about it bothers me." He took out his notepad to jot it down. He wrote, ROSWELL—7/5/47.

"That's it!" he cried.

"What's it? What are you talking about?"

"The men who were killed by John Oliver Harding. On their chests were those same numbers—seven, five, four. July fifth, 1947. The killer was carving the date of the Roswell crash." His eyes narrowed. "I suspect Holton knew it all along."

"It makes sense," Angie said, "when you consider how fascinated with Roswell they all are. Oliver Hardy spent all his free time giving away brochures about the crash there. Maybe that's why, when he went over the edge, he took Roswell with him."

"All of them are interested in Roswell, and there's also some connection with Area Fifty-one," Paavo said.

"It's because that's where the Prometheus Group got its start," Angie explained.

"That's exactly what I've been thinking."

25

The next morning, Angie realized her new business venture was just about over. That night would be Algernon's event, and she hadn't received a single inquiry for a fantasy dinner since. Maybe it was time to pull the plug on her Web site.

Fantasydinner.com had become fantasydinner.turkey.

She read through the newspaper looking for any information about new restaurants opening up in the city. Even though she hadn't done any restaurant reviews in some time, she had always enjoyed doing them. They might be worth pursuing again. After her successful discovery of Wings of an Angel, she hadn't gone looking for any other new restaurants.

One particularly nice thing about San Francisco was the tremendous variety of restaurants and cuisines that could be found in the city. *Ah!*

A new Nepalese restaurant. She wondered what the food would be like. Probably a blend of Chinese and Indian. That would be interesting. Curried chow mein?

Just then the doorbell rang. She looked through the peephole and couldn't believe who was there.

She opened the door. "Algernon! What a surprise."

He held out a bouquet of carnations. "For you."

"Thank you. Won't you come in?"

He stopped in the middle of the living room and faced her. "I've been thinking about our party."

"Oh? Sit down, please. Can I offer you some coffee or anything?"

"Some white wine would be nice, if it's convenient," Algernon said.

"I'll be right back." She ran into the kitchen and put the flowers on the sink, then raked her fingers through her hair, smoothed her pullover sweater, and finally uncorked a chilled bottle of Mondavi chardonnay.

Since Algernon sat at the far end of the sofa, she sat on the opposite side and poured him a glass of wine. She had coffee. It wasn't even lunchtime yet.

He clinked his glass against her cup. "To our fantasy party," he said.

Angie sipped some coffee; Algernon nearly finished his wine.

"There's nothing to worry about regarding the dinner," she said. "It'll be fine."

"I know that." He poured more wine into his glass. "Sure you won't join me?" She shook her head. "The real reason I'm here is to see you," he admitted.

At her surprise, he hurried on. "Ever since I saw you at the Prometheus Group, I felt we needed to get to know one another better." He drank more wine.

"I don't think so," she said.

He chuckled and put down the glass. "That came out wrong, didn't it? What I meant is, I want to know you as a friend. Perhaps interest you in our group."

Angie took in his arrogance, the way he smugly leaned back against the sofa, drinking wine and all but propositioning her despite his denials. She knew a come-on when she saw it. But since he was there, and since the wine seemed to make him even more talkative than usual, she poured more into his glass. She had some questions she needed answered. "So tell me," she began, smiling sweetly, "about the Prometheus Group. When did you become head of it?"

"Years ago. I was young then. Our leader, I. M. Neumann, was killed in a horrible blast at Area Fifty-one. I had traveled there to see him, but I was too late. The Prometheans, who were meeting in Phoenix at the time—Neumann would travel to them, since outsiders aren't allowed in Area Fifty-one—were like sheep without a shepherd. I called them together and told them we would continue to meet. That we would do that in remembrance of Neumann, and I would lead them to a new world, a new order."

"And you led them to San Francisco?"

"Phoenix was awfully hot. The Bay Area is mentally, spiritually, and physically more in tune with my message. The Prometheans have grown tenfold since we've been here. With my book, it will grow even larger."

"Everything would be fine if it weren't for NAUTS," she suggested.

His face clouded over. "A cheap, sleazy bunch. You should have nothing to do with them. You need to ignore that horrible Derrick Holton as well. He isn't worthy of you. The people involved with NAUTS are insane, as the one they call Oliver Hardy proved to the world. I've always worried for my safety around them. There have been threats. Many threats. I suspected the source; now I know it."

Indignation on Derrick's behalf rose in her. "You can't blame everyone in NAUTS for Oliver's instability."

"They nurture it. They teach science without spirit. What do they expect when they attract people with no soul?"

"You need to meet with Derrick and discuss this. I think you'll find him changed. You both need to set aside your differences."

Algernon rubbed his hands. "Ah! If he's willing to talk, that means he's hurting. NAUTS is self-destructing. I should have realized this business with Hardy was the last straw for the group. Now Holton wants to grovel." His gaze met Angie's. "Don't let him use you this way. You're too good for him."

"He's not using me."

Algernon slid across the sofa to her side and took her hand in his, turning his dark eyes on her. The air seemed to shift. "At the book party, join my group. Let me announce that you've seen the light. That you are one of us."

She tried to pull her hand free. "I don't feel that way about the group. I'm sorry."

He grabbed her other hand and pressed them both against his chest. "We are destined for each other. It's in the stars."

She guessed she'd overdone it with the wine. She stood up, yanking both hands free. He nearly toppled off the sofa. "The stars say you've had too much wine too early in the day. You need to go home and sleep it off."

"I can sleep anywhere. Right here, in fact." He leaned toward her. "Why don't you join me?"

She stepped back and folded her arms. "Time to say good-bye, Algie baby."

"Good-bye?" He sounded shocked.

"You got it."

"But I'm Algernon. Everyone loves me. Perhaps after the party you'll be in a better mood. I know women sometimes get in moods. The stars and the moon play havoc with your bodies. Such a body." His gaze swept up and down her figure and he sighed deeply. "Until later."

She held the door open. "Try the next millennium."

"You don't know what you're missing."

After he left she clicked the deadbolt in place and leaned back against the door. This was not the most propitious start to her business's last hurrah.

26

News and publicity could make or break an event. Just as quickly as news of Frederick Mosshad's abduction had caused a flurry of excitement and interest in the UFO community and a concomitant surge in interest in Triana's party for Algernon, so the opposite could and did occur. When the story hit that the three men so horribly killed and mutilated were the victims of a follower of a UFO group, people in the city recoiled. An outcry rose from the public about the strange millennium cults taking over the city by the bay, and public opinion polls ran 70 percent in favor of cracking down on them. They ran 80 percent in favor of stringing up their leaders.

Angie didn't let the news deter her. She and her friends would present the fantasy dinner, as requested, for two hundred guests. Paavo even left work early to help.

They carried all the food in refrigerated containers to the backstage area, where they would arrange it on platters and chafing dishes and bring it into the auditorium a little at a time, as needed. The only thing Angie had planned that hadn't worked out were the green alien and gray flying saucer cookies. Stan had eaten a lot of them the day he and Derrick trimmed her tree, and took the rest home as a snack. Angie decided the Jell-O molds would more than make up for them.

"We're going to have a wonderful party, no matter how hard the *Chronicle* has tried to ruin the event," she said to Paavo as she carried a platter of fruit to the buffet table.

"It's hardly their fault that they reported the story about Harding, Mosshad, and the murders. If you think that, you might say it's my fault for having solved the case . . . or, I hope, solving it."

"You're right. It's solved and I'm grateful for that, no matter how adversely it affects the party." She sighed as she looked over the empty hall. Then she patted her hat to make sure it was still on straight. She wore a pinched-waist maroon suit with huge shoulder pads, a wide collar, and white trim. The skirt was very narrow and fell to midcalf with a kick pleat in the back. Her open-toe shoes were white with ankle straps and a leather flower on the vamp, and she'd even found dark nylons with a black seam down the back. On her head she wore a pointed maroon hat with a long white feather angled across the back of it. She had felt like a reincarnation of Carole Lombard or Myrna Loy from an old classic romantic comedy until Paavo came by to pick her up. The look he gave her made her feel more like Minnie Pearl.

"What is that on your head?" he had asked.

She explained that she had found it in a 1940s magazine on the Internet, and her mother's dressmaker had worked around the clock to sew it for her. "Isn't it cute?"

"Words can't describe what it is," he had muttered. He said a lot more than that, though, when she pointed to a khaki uniform, round army hat with black brim, aviator sunglasses, and corncob pipe and said, "That's yours."

"I'm going as General MacArthur?" he had asked.

"You've got it!" she cried.

"Thank God for the sunglasses," he said as he began to loosen his tie. Angie sat on the bed and watched him change clothes. He had a great body, and she enjoyed looking at it every chance she got.

Now, at Tardis Hall, they set out the food and waited for the party to begin. The hostess, Triana, and the guest of honor, Algernon, still hadn't arrived. Earl, Vinnie, and Butch all wore white shirts and slacks and white sailor's caps—they said that was military enough for them. Angie was afraid they had all spent more time in jailhouse blues than in military wear, but she didn't want to bring that up.

At a vintage dress shop, Connie had found a red polka-dot dress with padded shoulders, short sleeves, a narrow belted waist, and a full skirt. With it, she wore red shoes with high, chunky heels and had styled her blond hair so that the bangs were curly and the rest was pulled sleekly back into a polka-dot bow so large and stiff that it stood out from the sides of her head like wings. If Fred Astaire had danced by, he might have mistaken her for Ginger.

The buffet setup was going smoothly and quickly despite the fact that Derrick wasn't there to help. He hadn't shown up at Connie's apartment, and she didn't know where he was. So much for Angie's big NAUTS/Prometheus Group reconciliation plan.

Vinnie put on a CD of "Pennies from Heaven." Connie grabbed Butch and dragged him out to the dance floor with her. The big, chunky heels caused her to tower over him even more than usual, but he didn't care. He held her as if she were made out of glass, and smiled from ear to ear as he led her in a jaunty World War II–style two-step around the hall.

Angie laughed as they danced by, waving and grinning for all they were worth. Maybe this wouldn't be the big, classy party she had initially imagined it would be, but she was sure that anyone who showed up would have a good time. She checked her watch. Where were Triana and Algernon? They should have been there already.

Vinnie kept the music going, but Connie bailed out on Butch to go outside to catch her breath and wait for Derrick. As Angie and Paavo danced the swing to "Blue Skies," a man in black, the same one who had been watching her from time to time throughout the city, entered the hall and stood in a corner. "Oh dear," she murmured.

Paavo's gaze followed hers. "Do you know him? He looks like something out of a horror film."

Holding Paavo's hand tightly, Angie stepped closer to the strange man. "You're a little early," she called.

"I'll wait." He walked to a far corner and stood in it, his arms folded.

Angie glanced at Paavo. He turned her around and said, "Looks like it's time for me to put on my jacket and shoulder holster."

She peered back at the man. "Oh, I'm sure he's harmless. Let's get the rest of the food out before you put on that nice jacket. I'd hate to see it get greasy from the fried chicken or ham. MacArthur didn't become a general wearing buffet-splattered jackets, I'm sure."

He looked over the hall. "Let's get this done quickly, then."

Phil walked in, followed by Elvis and Kronos. "Hi, Angie," they said. They stiffened when they saw Paavo. They all remembered him from the night Oliver Hardy died.

"Thanks for coming." Angie shook hands

with them. "You're a little early. Just you guys
and the man in bla— Where did he go?"

"We came to help," Phil said. "Where's Derrick?"

"He's not here yet. Connie was waiting for
him out front."

"She was? I didn't see her," Elvis said.

"That's strange." Angie looked around. Connie
wasn't inside either, it seemed. "Oh, I know. She
and Derrick must have taken the side hall,
around the auditorium, and gone straight to the
backstage area. Connie probably thought I was
already back there setting out the ham and
chicken. I probably should be, as a matter of fact."

"I'll help," Paavo said.

"Me too, Miss Angie," Butch said, following
her.

The area was deserted. "How odd. I wonder
where Connie and Derrick went?" Angie said.
"Well, let's get started. They'll be here soon
enough."

Butch wandered off. "I'll look around for
them," he called back.

"It's all right. They'll show up." She glanced
at Paavo. "First, we'll put some of this chicken in
big metal pans that go over the burners out on
the buffet table. Do you know how to light the
burners?"

"I think I can manage," he said dryly.

"Here's something strange, Miss Angie."
Butch sounded farther away. Angie looked up
and saw that he was near the stairs.

"Don't worry about it, Butch," she called, then turned back to Paavo and the task at hand. She put two more pieces of chicken in the pan. "That's it for now. You bring it out to the buffet while I take care of the ham."

"Aye, aye, Cap'n." Paavo lifted the heavy pan and carried it into the auditorium.

"Miss Angie," Butch called, "I really think you gotta come see this."

She didn't have time to go see anything, but Butch wasn't one to bother about unimportant details. She put down the serving fork she'd been using. "See what?" she asked, walking toward him. To her surprise, he was standing at the bottom of the stairs. "What are you doing down there?"

"I noticed Miss Connie's hairpins. You'll see three of them at the top of the stairs and a couple on the stairs."

"Connie's hairpins? Whatever are you talking about?" She looked at her feet. Sure enough, three light-colored bobby pins were on the ground. She walked down the steps, searching each as she went. She saw another bobby pin on the middle step, another on the last one.

"When we was dancin' I noticed they kept fallin' off," Butch said. "An Miss Connie tol' me she put a bunch in her pocket so she'd be able to keep her short hair pinned back with the big bow."

"So she must have come down here for some reason," Angie said. The door at the bottom of the stairs was open. The night they had searched for Oliver Hardy it was locked. She walked through it. Hallways went off in three directions from the staircase. The basement floor seemed to be made up of a warren of hallways with small rooms off them—probably storage rooms. "I wonder what she's up to?" she said quietly.

"I don' know, but there's another hairpin down that hall."

They walked past it, and at the next four-way intersection of narrow halls, they spotted another hairpin deep inside one of them. "I don't like this," Angie said. She called out, "Connie! Connie, are you down here?"

They waited a moment, and when there was no answer, they turned down the hall with the bobby pin and continued to the next intersection of halls. "Connie! Are you all right?" Angie called, louder this time. "Connie! Answer me!"

Butch kept going, looking for more bobby pins. He spotted another one. They turned again. "Wait." Angie caught his arm, stopping him. "We need Paavo. Something's wrong here."

"Maybe she's just havin' a little whoop-de-do with her boyfriend," Butch suggested.

"But why leave the bobby pins?" she asked.

"To find their way back."

Angie thought about it. "You may be right, but it's not like Connie to disappear when I need her. Look, I can't move fast in these heels or with this tight skirt. Will you run up and get Paavo? I'll wait right here."

"Sure thing. I'll be right back. Don' you move a muscle."

"Don't worry, I won't."

As she watched Butch head down the hallway, she almost regretted not going with him. The basement was creepy. "Connie," she called again. But her voice was decidedly smaller this time.

She walked just a little way forward, to the next intersection of hallways, and called again. Up ahead, on the ground, she saw something that made her heart stop.

She ran toward it to make sure it was what she thought. It was. Connie's hair bow lay on the floor.

"Miss Angie wants to see you," Butch said to Paavo, who was still fiddling with the burners under the pan of chicken.

"This contraption doesn't make any sense," Paavo said. "I'll be right there."

"She went down to the basement and needs you to help her."

Paavo glanced up at the man. "Help her do what?"

"I don't know."

He straightened. "Well, lead the way."

Curious, Elvis, Phil, and Kronos followed Paavo and Butch across the auditorium toward the backstage area and the stairs. Only Vinnie and Earl were left behind.

"Ain't dis da place people get abducted from?" Earl asked Vinnie, his eyes round.

"Shuddup!" Vinnie ordered. "You're makin' me nervous."

As Paavo walked through the empty warehouse, he remembered Angie's description of searching the huge place when Oliver Hardy was missing.

When he reached the stairs, he first looked upward. The warehouse was four stories tall. Rebecca Mayfield had talked about how big, filthy, and empty the top floor was. The only sign of anything but rats being up there was the lack of dust on the window ledge Oliver Hardy had jumped from.

He followed Butch down the stairs to the basement. "Why did she come down here?" he asked.

"We were following Miss Connie's hairpins," Butch said, going down one hall and then turning down another.

"What?" Paavo said, stopping in his tracks.

"Me an' Miss Angie followed them. But we don' know why she went down there."

At Butch's words, a chill rippled down Paavo's back. "Where's Angie?" His voice had turned cold and hard.

"Down there just a little ways, Inspector," Butch said, suddenly nervous.

"Let's find her and get out of here," Paavo ordered.

"The basement is like catacombs," Kronos

said, coming up behind them. Elvis and Phil were with him. "The door at the bottom of the steps was usually kept locked. I guess the owner came by to make sure the place is empty, since the building will be demolished soon. Perhaps he didn't bother to lock up again."

Butch pointed to a bobby pin farther down a hall. Paavo was halfway to it when the lights flickered and then went out.

Oh Lord, Angie thought when the lights went out. She held her breath. *Come back on!* she prayed. They didn't.

The basement was darker than night. There were no windows, no light of any kind. She reached out her hands and walked slowly forward, searching for a wall to hug. It was bad enough being down there in the dark. Being in the dark without anything at all nearby to hang on to was intolerable. "Connie?" Her voice was barely a whisper. The thought struck her that maybe letting her whereabouts be known wasn't such a good idea. The wrong person might find her. Paavo should be nearby by now. She should head back toward him. She'd meet him even sooner that way.

She turned what she thought was 180 degrees, took two steps, and bumped into a wall again. Which way was back?

She pressed herself against the wall, afraid to move another step. In the distance, she saw a light. She turned toward it, then stopped and watched in fascination as a shadowy figure eased out of a room and quickly shut the door behind him. She listened as the footsteps walked away from her.

She couldn't see the figure well enough to know if she recognized him or not. His head, though, seemed to be very strangely shaped. And how could he see in the dark so easily? All the strange stories she'd heard about alien encounters came rushing back at her.

"Angie!" Paavo called. "Angie, can you hear me?"

No answer.

"How far away is she?" he asked Butch.

"I . . . I'm not sure. I know we turned a few times down different hallways. We just followed the hairpins."

"There's a good chance those lights didn't go out by accident," Paavo said. "Butch, you try to remember which way to find her. Elvis and Kronos, you two go upstairs and tell Earl and Vinnie to call the police. Then try to find the circuit breakers."

"Hey!" A shout came from the end of a hallway.

Paavo looked toward the flashlight. He couldn't tell who was holding it. "He's got them! Come on!" the male voice shouted.

The man turned and started down a hall.

"Let's go! Algernon's got them!" Kronos ran down the hall toward the man. Phil took off after him.

"Butch, stay here so we'll know how to get

back," Paavo ordered. "Elvis, call the cops now!" With that, swearing at himself for not wearing his gun, Paavo too ran after the man with the flashlight.

Phil stood in the pitch-black hallway. He had run after the man with the flashlight to search for Derrick, but he must have taken a wrong turn. Kronos was no longer with him. Neither was Paavo. And he could no longer see the flashlight. In fact, he couldn't see anything at all. He had tried to go back to the stairs, but after a couple of turns he didn't know which way was back. He guessed he could start shouting for help—or maybe start to blubber like a baby. In time, the lights should come back on. He could simply wait right there.

He decided he probably shouldn't have taken those uppers before coming down to the hall. He'd taken only a few—just enough to help him get through this so-called party. He hated the thought of seeing Algernon's success. He hated Algernon.

Everything would have been fine if Algernon hadn't taken over. If I. M. Neumann hadn't died.

Things had been fine when the great man was alive. He had respected Phil. He didn't see him as some poor junkie. He knew Phil was someone important. Someone special.

Where were the others? God, his head felt strange. He ran his hands along the wall. He needed to hurry and find his way out of there. It was too dark, too claustrophobic. He was feeling trapped, caged in. Like in 'Nam.

Something touched his neck. He clawed at it. A rope. He tried to scream for help, but his throat was being crushed. His legs went weak and he fell to his knees. As the last shards of consciousness drifted away, he twisted around to see who was doing this to him, what was happening, and why.

With a laugh, his attacker lit a match and held it near his face. He recognized it. Even though the face had aged and no longer had hair or eyebrows or lashes, he recognized it.

"Neumann," he whispered.

"You shouldn't have let them destroy the Prometheus Group—my Prometheus Group," Neumann said, speaking as if to a naughty child. "But then, you always were useless."

Neumann dropped the match, then yanked the rope tighter.

"I found a phone," Vinnie said.

"Da number is nine-one-one," Earl said.

"What's with you? You think I'm stupid? You think I ain't never called emergency before? But maybe we should just call PG and E."

"Call nine-one-one. Let da cops come see what's goin' on here. I don' like it."

"Uh-oh." He clicked the button on the phone a few times. "I don't hear no dial tone."

"Is dere anot'er phone around?"

"How the hell should I know? It's pitch black in here."

"Now I know why all dose guys on TV always carry aroun' a cell phone," Earl said with dejection.

"Quiet! I just heard a noise."

Footsteps grew louder, one by one, up the stairs.

Vinnie and Earl didn't move. The footsteps stopped, then at the top of the stairs they eased forward in a shuffling motion, like an old man.

Shoes swished against the concrete, closer and closer. Silently, Earl and Vinnie scooted toward each other, huddling close. Then Earl tugged on Vinnie's arm, and the two men knelt down.

A leg bumped into Earl and stumbled. A man's leg. Earl grabbed the foot and lifted. The man shouted as he went up in the air. He came down on top of Vinnie.

"I caught him!" Vinnie cried.

"I got him, too!" Earl said.

"Kick him! Gouge his eyes! Hit him in the nuts!" Vinnie yelled.

"Stop! It's me, Elvis. Paavo said we've got to call the cops, quick!"

"I t'ink we got some bad news for you."

Angie tried to ignore thoughts of aliens and UFOs that paraded through her head, and instead tried to think of more earthly things, like why there was light in the room the strange

figure she'd seen had been in, but nowhere else
in the basement. Could it mean that, instead of
a power outage, someone had purposely shut
off the basement lights?

The bobby pin trail had been heading in that
direction. Could that be where Connie was? Had
that man forced her into the room? Angie's
instincts told her yes. Nothing else about Connie's behavior made any sense. But who would do
such a thing to Connie? And why?

Holding her hand against the wall, she made
her way down the long hallway until she felt the
frame of a door—very likely the door she'd seen
the figure emerge from. "Connie?" she called.

She heard a thump.

"Connie? Is that you?"

Two thumps.

She tried the door. It was locked. Thumps
and muffled cries that she knew were being
made by Connie gradually moved closer and
closer to the door. An eternity seemed to pass
before she heard a noise against the lock. It
sounded as if Connie was trying to turn the
deadbolt. "Hurry, Connie!" she cried.

The deadbolt twisted again partway, but
clicked back into place. Finally, it twisted all the
way around.

Angie waited a moment, then reached out for
the doorknob and turned it. The latch clicked.
Holding her breath, she cautiously pushed the
door open.

The first thing that hit her was the smell—

metallic and acrid, horrible, yet strangely familiar. The room was lit in the garish fluorescent
lighting of a hospital. It was a laboratory with
shelves and counters lined with bottles of chemicals, beakers, a Bunsen burner, microscopes,
flasks, condensers, and a whole litany of other
laboratory implements.

She opened the door a little farther, and
there, kneeling on the floor, her hands and
ankles bound, her mouth taped, was Connie.
"Connie," she whispered, relief and fright filling
her.

As she stepped into the lab toward Connie,
her gaze swept over the far side of the room.

She gasped and squeezed her eyes shut.

27

"What the hell's going on here?"
Algernon stood on the sidewalk, flapping his
arms and looking up at the enormous dark
warehouse. Usually when an event was going on,
they lit the outside lights, opened the lobby
doors wide, and enlisted ticket takers; Oliver
Hardy would set up a stand to give away
brochures. He shuddered at that last thought.
Still, where was everyone? "Why are all the lights
off? Who wants to go to a party that's so dark
and dreary?"

"I don't know what's wrong." Triana stepped
to his side. They walked to the doors and tried
to open them. The doors were locked. "I guess
no one is here. I tried calling to say we were
going to be a little late, but the phones weren't
working."

"Did they cancel my event without telling me?"
Algernon was literally hopping mad. "What the

hell is wrong with all of you? Do I have to do everything myself?"

"Frankly, I don't see that it matters," Triana
said. "After the news broke about that murder-
ous lunatic Oliver Hardy, people were calling all
day long with one excuse after the other not to
attend."

"What do you mean, it doesn't matter? It matters to me—to my book, my career! What kind
of imbecile are you?"

"You don't have to get nasty! This is hardly my
fault," she cried.

"Not your fault? Whose is it, then? It's a disaster! A fiasco! It's all your fault. You and that stupid incompetent you hired, who didn't even
appreciate all I tried to do for her."

Triana arched an eyebrow. "Oh? And what
did you try to do for her?"

"I—" He snapped his mouth shut. "Nothing."

"I thought you were a little too interested in
her!" Triana yelled.

"Me?" he asked coyly.

"Don't play innocent! I've gone out on a limb
for you, you playboy. Not to mention what the
food for this nonexistent party will cost me. If
my husband finds out I've spent more money
on you, he'll be madder than ever. Now I learn
you're trying to mess around with the hired
help!"

"Miss Amalfi is hardly in the category of hired
help, Triana," he said, unable to stop a smile
from touching his lips as he thought of Angie.

"You old goat!" she ranted. "You're old enough to be her father. Those face-lifts haven't erased years, only wrinkles!" She turned and marched toward her car.

"Triana, you're being unreasonable." He followed her.

"The only thing unreasonable about me was paying attention to you in the first place. See how far you get without me—and my money! Good-bye."

She got into her big Mercedes and locked the doors.

"Triana, wait!" He clutched the door handle. "You aren't going to leave me out here in this neighborhood at night, are you?"

She gunned the engine and took off. He ran after her, waving his arms and shouting. But she didn't stop.

"Oh my God," Angie cried, running across the laboratory. "Is he still alive?"

In the center of the lab stood a large metal bathtub. Derrick Holton lay in it. He was unconscious; on his chest the numeral 7 had been carved. Blood from the wound covered his torso. Horrified, Angie's eyes took in the implements surrounding him: butcher knives, a meat cleaver, a hacksaw, power saws, plastic tarps, a meat hook. Suddenly it all came together. She understood what she was seeing. "God help us," she whispered. They were in the laboratory of the mutilation murderer. Oliver Hardy wasn't the killer after all. The mutilation murderer was still alive . . . and he was killing Derrick.

Her knees felt weak, her head light. Little black and purple dots flashed before her eyes. Gulping great quantities of air, she turned and faced Connie. She had to compose herself, untie Connie, and get them all out of there. It was up to her.

She took hold of the tape covering Connie's mouth and ripped it off.

"Thank God," Connie whispered, pressing her hands to her lips. "He wanted me to watch! He cut Derrick! It was so . . ." A sob broke. "Then he heard you calling me. That was why he stopped." She began to cry harder, unable to go on.

Angie grabbed a knife and cut through the ropes on Connie's hands and feet. She couldn't help Derrick yet. If she and Connie didn't get out of there, none of them would escape.

She had just cut Connie's ankles free when she heard a noise at the door. Then the door swung open.

Kronos tripped over something huge lying on the floor and went down in a heap. "By God's wounds! What is that?"

He reached back. It was hard, bony. An arm. His fingers traveled up the arm to the face, the long, frizzy hair. "Phil, is that you, knave?"

Phil's mouth was cold. He didn't seem to be breathing. "What's wrong with you?" Kronos said. He reached for his pulse. It was there, but faint.

Not knowing what else to do, Kronos applied mouth-to-mouth resuscitation. Amazingly, Phil's breathing grew stronger. "Wake up, man," Kronos said, slapping his face. "We've got to find a nice cave to hide in until all this is over. I think someone wants us all dead."

Paavo stood in the darkness, more frustrated than he'd ever been before. He'd gone after the man with the flashlight but had lost him. He didn't know if the guy had turned down a hall Paavo had missed, or shut off the light, or what. Was the man trying to be helpful or to make things worse for them? His instincts were failing him—because of his worry about Angie, or because he couldn't see or hear a damn thing, he didn't know. Maybe both.

By calling out to Butch and listening to his responses, he had gotten his bearings and found his way back. Now he and Butch were slowly making their way to the stairs. Once upstairs, he'd get a flashlight—there had to be several up there—and call for backup himself. He couldn't understand why the police were taking so long. They should already have been there. He swore at himself once again for having been taken in by the man with the flashlight, whoever he was.

The bigger worry was what had become of Angie and Connie. He couldn't believe that any-

one would have made a move against them at an
event like this. It didn't make sense.

Could it have been Derrick? If so, why? He'd
seen the women continuously, even while he was
in hiding. No, it wasn't Derrick.

That was it! Derrick had been in hiding. He
was the target. The one place the NAUTS people and the Prometheans knew he would be was
at Tardis Hall that evening. If Derrick was the
target, then Connie, on the lookout for him,
might have gotten involved simply due to bad
luck and bad timing.

Paavo's main hope was that Angie had not
succeeded in finding Connie. As long as she
didn't find her, she might be safe. Who was
behind this, though? Which of the NAUTS or
Prometheus Group people could it be? Algernon?
He still hadn't shown up, but Paavo couldn't
imagine him laying a trap for Holton. Algernon
was a con man. Con men rarely killed. If things
got bad, they simply moved on to the next con.

Who else could it be?

He found the door to the stairway to the
main floor. Someone had shut it. That was odd.
Elvis had gone upstairs—would he have shut the
door? Paavo slid his hands over the door until
he found the knob. He turned it. The door was
locked. He tried again, tugging and rattling it to
get a feel for how strong the lock and the door
were. They were solid.

He tried to find the keyhole. Where was it?
With one of Connie's bobby pins, he should be

able to pick it open. He'd gotten pretty good at that in his years in Homicide. He ran his hands over the edges of the door. There was no keyhole. That meant the door had been electronically locked.

That gave him pause. Whoever was behind this had the ability to electronically control a door. If he could do it to one door, he probably could do it to all of them. He most likely could lock and unlock them at will from a central place in the warehouse. Same for the lights. It was the mark of a scientist—a very capable scientist. The type that might be involved with UFOs and all the advanced electromagnetic technology that went along with them.

Paavo strained to see in the darkness, but it was impossible. A creeping dread came over him. If whoever was behind this could lock a door remotely, what else could he do?

"You just stepped on my hand," Vinnie yelled.

"I couldn' step on not'in' 'cause I'm crawlin' so I don' fall over," Earl yelled back.

"Well, you kneed my hand, then. Keep on your own side!"

"I t'ink I found da front door." Earl reached up, felt the doorknob, and stood. "I got it."

"Don't just stand there, open it!"

"I'm tryin'. Da doorknob don' toin."

"What do you mean, it don't turn? Maybe your hands are as weak as your head. Let me do it."

"Where's Elvis?" Earl said.

"I don't know. Hey! What is this? These doors won't open."

"Let's holler. Maybe dere's somebody outside."

"If there is, how're they gonna open a door that's locked?"

Earl's shoulders slumped. "I t'ink dat's a good point."

The door opened. Angie's hand tightened on the knife she had used to cut the ropes that held Connie. She hid it behind her back.

A man walked into the lab and removed the night vision goggles that covered his eyes. But even before he did that, even while still wearing the goggles, even though his wig and facial hair were gone, Angie recognized the black turtle-neck, the gaunt frame.

"Malachi!" she whispered.

"Why are you doing this to us?" Connie cried. "Who are you?"

"I'm no man," he said, then laughed.

At the bizarre words, a strange possibility struck Angie. *Could it be?* "No man," she asked, "or new man?"

He nodded. "Very good, Angie. Very good. I knew I liked you. Yes, they all thought I was dead. They tried to ruin everything I'd spent my life building. Splitting up the Prometheus Group was a big mistake. Their last mistake. Instead of teaching the world that they walk among us—or, I should say, that we walk among you—the idiots fight over trivia. They all deserve to die."

"All?" Angie whispered.

"In time, in time. Right now, I have more important things to do. I trust you've looked over my laboratory. Did you notice my laser? Not nearly as good as the one I used at Area Fifty-one, but then everything there is at least ten years or more ahead of what you civilians use. I enjoyed having Connie in the corner to watch it all. I'll enjoy having you watch even more, Angie."

Angie's voice was strangled. "What are you talking about?"

"The date wasn't finished. Seven-five-forty-seven. I don't have the last seven yet. That was reserved for Holton. He knew it, too. That was why he was scared—why he ran and hid. He couldn't stay hidden forever. I knew Tardis Hall would lure him back to me, and so it did. Too bad you girls got caught in my trap. Such is life. Or death."

"What about Algernon?"

"He's a fool. He's nothing. Once I finish here, I'll own Algernon and everything the Prometheus Group stands for. There won't be anything to connect me with this, you see. It's all very simple. I'll finish my work with Holton—I won't get to do such a fine job on him as the earlier three because I'm rushed. But it won't matter.

"I'll take him out to Treasure Island in the middle of San Francisco Bay. From there, I'm going to flash a hologram in the sky—that's a

three-dimensional picture using laser beams, in
case you aren't up on the very latest technology.
It'll be an enormous hologram of a flying
saucer. When the people of San Francisco see it
hovering overhead, they'll flock out to Treasure
Island. There they'll find Holton's body. That's
when seven-five-forty-seven will be complete.
Ufologists across the country will make the connection."

"They'll connect it with Roswell, you mean?"
Angie asked. As she spoke, she and Connie circled away from him. She was sure he had a gun,
but still, if she could get near the door, she
might be able to stab him and then run. Or
something more practical might come to mind
if she was lucky.

"They'll recognize the date," he continued,
"the most important date in all of mankind's
history. Christmas day, Mohammed's birth, the
discovery of America—they all pale against July
fifth, 1947. The day the Earth was given proof
that we are not alone. The day my father fell to
Earth." He smiled. "Everyone will be screaming
about Roswell as a result. Their interest will flow
to NAUTS and the Prometheus Group. And,
dare I say it, to me."

Angie continued to inch sideways, but he
stepped in front of her, his eyes red and intense
as he blocked her path to the door. "Next year,
on July fifth, I will let the world know that I am
still alive. They will beg me to take back the
Prometheus Group. And I will. Yes, I've planned

this a long, long time. It's perfect. The perfect crime. With all the publicity I want. I can hardly wait. Too bad you'll miss it all."

Angie and Connie glanced at each other. "You can let us go," Angie said. "We'll be able to tell the world how great you are."

Connie was too petrified to speak, but she nodded.

"No, because you'll also tell them I'm a murderer, Angie. I'm not stupid! Right now there's nothing to link me to the murders. I really quite prefer it this way."

"Except us," Angie whispered.

"Except you. But I'll give you a nice death, not a painful one. When I finish here, I'll simply put on a gas mask, and then light a very smoky fire—I have the chemicals and supplies in this lab to do it. You and your friends will die of smoke inhalation. Oh, I forgot to mention. Your friends are locked in the basement, too. A couple of inconsequential ones are upstairs. I might have to simply shoot them, I haven't decided yet."

Keep him talking, Angie told herself. *Delay*. "How do I know you're really Neumann? Everyone says he was killed. I believe them."

He laughed. "I escaped. Quite easily, I might add. I knew the government was trying to kill me because I had found out too much about their space programs and the important information they concealed from the people. I hid for a time, planning to rejoin the Prometheans.

But they changed. Holton changed them, dividing them, weakening them. I watched and waited."

"Why kill anyone? You could have gone to the public, told your story. You would have been safe."

"You're so naive, Angie. The public believes whatever the media tells it, and the media is a tool of government. My victims were people who had been in Area Fifty-one with me and had moved to San Francisco like the Prometheans did. It was interesting to learn how their little exposure to Area Fifty-one—to me—had stayed with them over all these years, and when given the slightest encouragement, they sought us out. They happily gave my friend Oliver their names and addresses."

"So Oliver worked with you?"

"Yes. He was the only one I trusted enough to tell I had returned. He thought he was recruiting old Area Fifty-one workers for me. It was too bad he got so upset when he learned he'd sent those men to their deaths that he took his own life. Before that, he believed everything I told him—he was quite the idiot."

"Poor Oliver," Angie said. "I knew he was no killer."

"But I am. Enough of this! I know what you're doing, Angie, but it won't work." He took hold of a rope and reached for her. "Turn around so I can tie you up. I don't want to hurt you."

"No!" She lunged at him with the knife.

* * *

Paavo remembered seeing a freight elevator on the wall past the stairs. He'd crawl up the shaft if he had to, but he was going to find Angie and get out of this damned basement.

As he tried to find the elevator, he saw the soft glow of a light in the distance. Quietly, he inched his way toward it.

Neumann grabbed Angie's arm, stopping her before she could jab it into him. She continued to yell, kicking and flailing, knocking over bottles and flasks, and generally trying to create as much noise and chaos as she could.

Connie picked up a meat cleaver and moved toward Neumann. He spun around and with one hand slapped her in the face, sending her sprawling as the meat clever fell from her hands.

A gunshot reverberated through the lab. The door sprang open and the man in black came into the room. His eyes scanned the room for Neumann. He raised his gun—

Too late.

Neumann fired first, and the man in black fell forward into the laboratory, his hands outstretched. In one was a gun, in the other, a flashlight.

Angie dived for the gun.

"You fool!" Neumann cried, running toward her.

The door to the hallway was wide open. She knew she couldn't pick up the gun, turn, and

shoot—that would be suicide. Instead, hoping
against hope that she was guessing right, she
reached toward the gun and shoved it hard,
causing it to skid across the concrete floor and
out into the hallway.

In one rolling movement, Paavo picked it up
and, as Neumann shot at him, returned fire.

Neumann was hit. He fell, unconscious.
Angie turned to Paavo in the doorway, but it was
empty. She screamed.

Two ambulances stood outside Tardis Hall.

The doors were open and the lights back on.
Derrick Holton and his friend Phil were
wheeled into one ambulance. Derrick had lost a
lot of blood and was unconscious from a severe
blow to the skull. Phil had a bruised neck.

Into the other went the man in black and
I. M. Neumann. The man in black had been
wearing a bulletproof vest and was only stunned
by the bullet that had hit him. He had refused
to give his name or say anything other than to
insist he was a special agent and had to go with
Neumann.

Neumann had been shot in the stomach and
was expected to survive.

The ambulance drove away, sirens screaming.

Angie and Connie huddled against Paavo, who
had one arm around each of them. Earl, Butch,
Vinnie, Elvis, and Kronos stood nearby, offering
whatever support they could. After stopping
Neumann with a bullet, Paavo had found the

controls in the lab to unlock the doors and turn the lights back on.

It looked as if Neumann had built himself a miniature Area 51 in the basement of the building he owned. He might have stayed hidden there a lot longer, simply playing at being Malachi, except that the city had decided to demolish the building as part of the urban renewal of the area. Not even a scientific genius like Neumann could fight city hall. He finally had to move on his plan to take revenge on those who had destroyed his life and his group, and then to retake the leadership of the Prometheans, who he expected—as a result of his plan—would become bigger and stronger than ever.

"Let's go home," Angie said, holding Paavo tightly. "This place reminds me of how scared I was when I looked at the doorway and you weren't there."

"It was all reflexes. We're taught to roll and keep going to get out of the way of a bullet. What was remarkable was your timing in knocking the gun to me in the hallway. How did you know I was out there?"

"I didn't. But I knew if you could be anywhere, that was the place—and I knew you didn't have your gun."

"Oh my," Connie murmured, still shaking. "I'm glad I fainted at the first gunshot and missed it all. I swear, if I never see or hear anything about UFOs and aliens again, I'll be happy."

As they all moved out of the building onto the sidewalk, they saw Algernon running down the street toward them, waving his arms.

"Here I am! I thought the event had been canceled," he cried, breathless but smiling. "I was trying to find a taxi, and then I saw a couple of ambulances go by. Sorry I'm late! I didn't miss anything much, did I?"

28

As Angie sat at her dining room table, Paavo brought her a dish of spumoni ice cream with a maraschino cherry on top.

It was Christmas Eve. He had cooked the entire meal while she sat in the living room, listened to carols on her CD player, and wasn't allowed to even peek in the kitchen. She only cringed a few times at a crash or flurry of very un-holiday-spirited oaths. He prepared steak, baked potatoes with sour cream and chives, and a salad with oil and vinegar dressing. He'd bought the spumoni dessert in honor of her Italian background. Simple, but to Angie's mind, absolutely delicious.

"How lovely," she said. "This was the best fantasy dinner I could imagine."

"You're the only fantasy I want in my life, Angie." Paavo poured them both some coffee.

She smiled as she waited for him to return

from the kitchen. It was rare for Paavo to express his feelings openly, and when he did, it always touched her deeply. "Well, I don't want any more fantasies in mine, either. UFOs and aliens have cured me of that."

"Don't remind me." He sat down. "I'm pissed off as hell about the way that man-in-black character and Neumann disappeared. FBI, NSA, DOD, CIA—no one will admit to knowing either of them, and the fingerprints we found of the two don't match with anything on file. Even their guns were untraceable."

"It was a clever plan, you have to admit, Paavo," Angie said, taking a spoon to her ice cream. "The switch to another ambulance at San Francisco General was inspired. It happens enough these days due to overcrowding that no one questioned it."

"I just hope Neumann pays the price for what he did."

"I'm sure whoever sent the man in black after him will see that he does."

"They'd better," he grumbled. He attacked his ice cream.

Angie thought it was time to change the subject. "At least Derrick is doing well—except for an ugly scar. He and Algernon might even learn to get along together."

"They can have each other," Paavo said. "At least this is one old boyfriend your father won't want to trade me in for."

She put down her spoon. "That really bothers you, doesn't it?"

"How could it not bother me? I know the kind of man your father expects for you. I also know I'm not it."

She placed her hand lightly on his arm. "Remember when you told me it didn't matter what I did, it was who I am that you loved?"

"Yes."

"Well, listen to your own words, Inspector. They were good ones. And if I ever, ever hear you belittling yourself again, I will leave you. For stupidity! You saved my friends' lives, Paavo. No one can ask more of you than that."

"I hope you're right," he said.

"I know I am."

She started to lift the ice cream bowls to take them into the kitchen. "Leave them," he said. He blew out the candles they'd dined by, took her hand, and led her into the living room.

They shut off all the lights except those on the tree, then sat on the floor, face-to-face, in front of it. "When I was a boy," Paavo said, "we always opened our presents on Christmas Eve."

"My family did, too." Angie reached for the present for Paavo that lay under the tree. "You first."

Without a word, he carefully peeled off the tape and unfolded the wrapping paper, giving her a glimpse of the serious, thrift-conscious child he must have been. He lifted the box to find an imported Bijan hand-stitched cashmere sports jacket and brown leather gloves. The material was soft and elegant. "They're great, Angie. I've never had a jacket or gloves so nice. I'll be afraid to wear them."

"You'd better not be. I expect to see them on you."

"Yes, ma'am," he said with a smile.

Then he got up and walked over to his coat. From the pocket, he pulled out a small square box. "I'm not very good at this kind of thing," he said, sitting on the floor again. "I'll have to explain it."

He had obviously wrapped it himself. The paper and Scotch tape were rather creatively applied. Smiling at his worried expression, she quickly tore off the ribbon and paper. Breathing deeply, she caught his gaze, then lifted the lid.

Inside was a small cameo brooch in a gold setting.

"It was my mother's," he said. "I want you to have it."

She was stunned. "Your mother's?" Paavo never spoke of his mother. Angie didn't know he owned anything that had belonged to her. She doubted he had much that was hers, yet he was giving her this piece of jewelry. She held it in her hands a long moment. "It's beautiful, Paavo, but I can't accept something that belonged to your mother. This is for you to keep."

He tried to shrug off her words, pretending the

gift was no big deal. She knew otherwise. "I've had it tucked away in a drawer for years. It's something that should be worn and enjoyed."

"But I can't—"

He clasped his hands over hers, the brooch held between them. His casual manner was gone now, his face stark, all pretense set aside. "When I was a little boy," he said, "other kids would talk about the presents they'd received and about giving gifts to their families. Aulis is a wonderful man, and I love him, but it wasn't the same. I was old enough to remember my mother. I missed her. I couldn't understand why she'd left me. Sometimes, I'd even pretend she was still there with me. But most of the time, I would take this brooch and hold it and look at it, and wish very hard that I wasn't alone anymore."

Her heart ached at his words.

His eyes met hers. "I finally got my wish."

Her eyes filled with tears. "Thank you." She wrapped her arms around him, holding him and the brooch tight. "Merry Christmas, Paavo."

"Merry Christmas, Angie."

From the kitchen of
Angelina Amalfi—

Angie's Favorite Tiramisu

The literal translation of *tiramisu* is "pull me up." Whether this derives from the caffeine content of the coffee and chocolate, or from the liqueur, is anybody's guess.

> *³/4 cup brewed espresso coffee (or triple-strength*
> *regular coffee), cooled*
> *1/4–1/2 cup liqueur (brandy is most often used, but*
> *Triple Sec or Chambord are excellent, and many*
> *people enjoy a berry-flavored liqueur)*
> *24 (or more) ladyfinger cookies—if you can find the*
> *hard kind rather than the soft ones, they'll be*
> *easier to work with*
> *4 eggs, separated*
> *1/4 cup granulated sugar*
> *1 pound mascarpone cheese (it's like cream cheese,*
> *but do not use cream cheese as a substitute)*
> *6 ounces (or more) semisweet chocolate, grated*

Combine the cooled coffee with the liqueur. Arrange half the ladyfingers in a slightly rectangular, flat-bottomed serving dish with high sides. The entire bottom of the dish should be covered (which is why you may need more than 24 lady-fingers). Sprinkle or soak the ladyfingers with half the liqueur/coffee mixture. You don't want the ladyfingers to be soaked completely soft, but you want to make sure they've absorbed the flavor.

Beat the egg whites in a bowl until stiff. Set them aside.

In another bowl, beat the egg yolks together with the sugar until the mixture thickens and lightens in color. Add the marscarpone to the egg yolk mixture and stir to combine thoroughly. Fold the egg whites into this mixture.

Spread half the mascarpone mixture over the ladyfingers in the serving dish. Sprinkle half the grated chocolate on top of the mascarpone mixture (be generous here—you might need more than the 6 ounces of chocolate called for, depending on the size of your serving dish; you can still see the mascarpone below, but make sure the mixture is definitely covered).

On a separate plate, soak the remaining ladyfingers with the remaining coffee/liqueur mixture, then make another layer of ladyfingers on top of the chopped chocolate. Layer it with the rest of the mascarpone, and then the rest of the grated chocolate.

Cover the tiramisu with plastic wrap and chill overnight, or for at least 5 hours. Serves 6–8.

From the kitchen of
Angelina Amalfi—

Angie's Chocolate-Dipped Coconut Macaroons

4 large egg whites
1 1/3 cups sugar
1/2 teaspoon salt
1 1/4 teaspoons vanilla extract
1/4 teaspoon almond extract (optional)
2 1/2 cups sweetened flaked coconut
1/4 cup plus 2 tablespoons flour
8 ounces fine-quality bittersweet chocolate

Preheat oven to 300 degrees.

In a heavy saucepan stir together the egg whites, sugar, salt, vanilla extract, almond extract (if using), and coconut. Sift in the flour, and stir the mixture until it is combined well.

Cook the mixture over moderate heat, stirring constantly, for 5 minutes. Increase the heat to moderately high, and cook the mixture, stirring constantly, for 3 to 5 minutes more, or until it is thickened and begins to pull away from the bottom and side of the pan.

Transfer the mixture to a bowl, let it cool

slightly, and then cover with plastic wrap until it is just cold. Drop heaping teaspoons of the dough 2 inches apart onto buttered baking sheets and bake the macaroons in batches in the middle of oven for 20 to 25 minutes, or until they are pale golden. Transfer the macaroons to a rack and let them cool for an hour or so.

In a double boiler (or a small metal bowl set over a pan of barely simmering water) melt the chocolate, stirring until it is smooth. Remove the bowl from the heat and dip the macaroons, one at a time, into the chocolate, coating them halfway and letting any excess drip off. Transfer the macaroons as they are dipped to a foil-lined tray and chill them for 30 minutes to 1 hour, or until the chocolate is set.

NOTE: The macaroons keep, chilled and separated by layers of waxed paper, in an airtight container for 3 days. (Let them stand at room temperature for at least 20 minutes before serving.)

Makes about 30 macaroons.

Tasty mysteries by
JOANNE PENCE
Featuring culinary queen Angie Amalfi

IF COOKS COULD KILL
0-06-054821-5/$6.99 US/$9.99 Can

BELL, COOK, AND CANDLE
0-06-103084-8/$6.99 US/$9.99 Can

TO CATCH A COOK
0-06-103085-6/$5.99 US/$7.99 Can

A COOK IN TIME
0-06-104454-7/$5.99 US/$7.99 Can

COOKS OVERBOARD
0-06-104453-9/$5.99 US/$7.99 Can

COOK'S NIGHT OUT
0-06-104396-6/$5.99 US/$7.99 Can

COOKING MOST DEADLY
0-06-104395-8/$6.50 US/$8.99 Can

COOKING UP TROUBLE
0-06-108200-7/$5.99 US/$7.99 Can

SOMETHING'S COOKING
0-06-108096-9/$6.50 US/$8.99 Can

TOO MANY COOKS
0-06-108199-X/$6.50 US/$8.99 Can